I0699767

WAY OF THE WIZARD

MICHAEL MICHEL

CHAINBREAKER BOOKS

For my mother, whose love showed me the way.

And for my father, who taught me how to pave it in stone.

CONTENTS

PROLOGUE

The Way

Secrets are life and death, the only currency that matters. Bread and water are but distractions for one who knows the Hand of Life spell. Gold and diamonds, mere chattel for one who has mastery over sky and earth. To those who duel with lightning and can summon a legion of titans at their whim, the sharpest blade may as well be a spoon.

I am a wizard.

I'm no longer proud of my story but the time has come to share it. The centuries have sifted truth to the surface, and in its presence, naught but dust fills my hands. There is no darker or lonelier place than godhood. Blood soaks these pages in equal measure to ink. I have grieved the loss of friends. I have stolen lives with a covetous and hateful heart. I have ascended the treacherous peak known as love, then descended into the abyss to betray it.

If I have learned one thing, it's that satisfaction earned follows sacrifices made. So be warned: this road is suffering. Pain will be your guidepost. Power, the sole discretionary force that drives you. Fate, the unraveling memory of passing deeds both thrilling and terrible.

If you have the courage and curiosity to do so, read on. The path has been made clear. You must only follow the steps.

First, you must be a Seeker and find others like you. These are your brethren. They will almost certainly try to kill you.

Second, you must claim a wizard's topknot. Be smart. Be quick. Never hesitate. They're the most dangerous creatures alive.

Third, you must find a wizard's tower. Trade them food for the secret location of the Spirit Gardens. Go there with haste so you might raise your own tower when the time comes.

Fourth, you must cast the wizard's topknot into the Occuli Rift at the center of the Seething Sea. You will gain a Tome of Callings, the compendium of knowledge possessed by the wizard you slew. But beware the savage creatures of the sea.

Fifth, you must raise your wizard's tower. This is the beginning and the end. Your birth and your death. A flicker of eternity in the chasm between worlds.

My story starts there.

CHAPTER ONE

THE END

The death of my mother was an insidious thing.

A sickness burned through her. What was, what is, and what could never be again passed from her listless gaze straight into my heart. That's when I knew she would soon be gone. Every rattling breath carved something from me, made me numb, a helpless child.

I sat there holding her hand, fingers nearly as wooden as hers. "Drink."

She refused, mouthing the word 'no' with lips that rustled against each other like autumn leaves. Her stomach poked from beneath her shift, bulging against her spine such that she'd lost the ability to walk. Whatever was killing her had started there. And the smell; I hated being repulsed by her during a time I'd never wanted to be closer.

"My child," she rasped, the words seeming to claim me in some final way. I touched her cheek, icy flesh stretched taut over bone despite the fever. Dread of the deepest kind assailed me at the idea of one day sharing her fate.

Her eyelids fluttered, battling to remain open. "My child..."

I was the last of our family. All of them had succumbed to pestilence or starvation. Except my eldest sister, Sahn. A drunk knight of the Stormseye Brotherhood had run her through. Their version of justice was the worst of the common day atrocities I lived with. Famine, disease, rampant crime—all were inevitabilities. But wanton murder dealt down to the weak from the height of the mighty was a fiendish wrong. The cruel reign of the Stormseye Brotherhood forced me to keep my defenses against grief well maintained.

With my mother bound for the grave, that armor dissolved. My last defense stripped to reveal a scared, naked child. Grief crashed through me. Sobs bubbled in my chest and at the back of my throat.

My mother brushed leathery fingertips over my smooth cheek. "It's okay."

I was so young. The Elder said only two thirds of Cannalis's citizens reached the age of sixteen. If he considered *me* lucky, then thinking about the misfortunes that needed to befall those who weren't unnerved me.

My mother seized up in frozen torment.

I gave a slow exhale as she moaned relief then relaxed.

"Please, El," she wheezed. "Tell me a story about Idrinnia."

My mother had raised me on tales of the Everlasting Maiden. For nearly a century, Idrinnia had ruled over the lands of Kelundar as the most powerful wizard in the world. Then, two hundred years ago, the Great Archon had risen up and deposed her. To speak her name now, much less teach stories of her to children, was a death sentence. Idrinnia was a scion of hope, and at the threshold of death, that was more nourishing to my mother than water.

"Okay, momma." Comfort is a simple thing, desperately needed and easily given. Even with the danger involved, how could I say no? I looked over a shoulder and spoke low. "After the Burning that stole history from the Overlords, a gorgeous woman wreathed in light arrived at—"

"Citizens of Cannalis!" A voice amplified by a horn boomed in the street outside. "The Stormlords call you to the plaza!"

I rose, glancing at my mother. Shallow breaths. Long intervals between. Swollen belly pumping out the reek of death. I looked back at the door. The clang of the knights' armor as they hurriedly swept homes was already close. "Momma," I said. "I must go."

I turned away but a skeletal hand held me fast. "Please." A tear squeezed from the flesh around her weathered eye. "A story about Idrinnia...please."

I hesitated.

The drape hanging in the entrance to our home whooshed aside. I jerked around just as a sword clashed against the entryway. Daub crumbled in flakes to the ground. "You heard the lictor! Out of the fucking hovel and on your way!"

My mother clutched at my wrist with impossible strength. "One story...please."

My heart thudded against my breastbone. I licked dry lips as I watched her. If I left, I might never see her again. "She's dying, Sir. I can't just leave her."

I heard the knight behind me step inside. "You're not listening." Threat edged his words.

My sister Sahn had died defying a knight of the Stormseye and I didn't wish to share her fate. A fast death or a slow one mattered little when it was assured. And yet, if I could survive one more day, I might take the first step on a path of my own making.

"I'm coming. Just let me say goodbye." I dropped to a knee at her side and gathered her frail hand in mine. "I'm sorry. I have to go."

The knight snorted. Bootfalls scuffed the dirt. His hand wrapped around the back of my neck and hauled me upright. "Little twat!"

My skin screamed, feeling like it might tear. I gritted my teeth, planted my feet, and shrugged against the pain. I heaved against the knight's grip to lean over my mother as he clamped his other hand around my elbow. Hoarse words, tumbling quickly. "I'll tell you a story when I return."

My lips hovered over my mother's forehead for a kiss that never touched.

The knight pivoted hard and hurled me toward the entryway. I stumbled, wrists slamming down in a swirl of dust. My hip went numb where the knight kicked me a moment later. I yelped and started to crawl.

"Pathetic." Another kick, less violent than the first, but it still sent arcing pain through my backside.

In the alley, I found my feet and ran for my life.

CHAPTER TWO

STORMLORDS

Every year, conditions worsened for those living along the city's outer ring, like a wave through time marching ever inward, leaving poverty, disease, and starvation in its wake. All the wealth and riches were situated around the central plaza. Around the Stormlords.

A womb gestating the greedy.

The Great Archon's ziggurat bubbled from the center of the city of Cannalis like a crone's boil. Banners bearing the swirling golden eye of the Brotherhood rippled above obsidian walls. Causeways angled fifty feet to the topmost story of the black marbled structure and a dozen stairways criss-crossed its girth. Knights in gleaming midnight armor ringed the masses, two thousand strong. They herded them down into a bowl of hollowed earth surrounding an altar, slapping heads or shoving backs with the hafts of their spears.

Guarding the altar were a hundred lictors. Except for amber amulets adorning their necks and golden capes snapping in the wind, these wore the same armor as their subordinates. These men carried out executions and the occasional 'cleansing' of supposed criminal groups, winning them the everlasting hatred of the entire citizenry. I could count on my fingers the number of times I'd seen the mass of bloodied rags and pale limbs towed through the city streets on handcarts with a lictor leading the way.

My balled fist ached. A woman to my left spat and cursed.

A blinding flash followed by a peal of thunder silenced the crowd. A hand of cold clenched my spine.

Stormlords. A dozen motionless figures were arrayed in a line across the top of the center-most causeway, scanning the gathered crowd. Silver tattoos wrapped around their heads like circlets, culminating in an empty oval on their brow. Saffron robes flowed around them, splashing my eyes with reflections of the midday sun. I shielded my gaze.

As one, the Stormlords opened their hands, palms upturned in supplication. Another detonation of light. Another whip's crack of thunder. The crowd gasped. The Stormlords had transported and now stood around the altar.

Murmurs swept the crowd. I stared in wonder at their power. If they could disappear and reappear elsewhere, what couldn't they do? Healing my mother—or any citizen of Cannalis for that matter—would be a paltry affair. If I knew what they knew, I could save her.

My shoulders sagged at the thought of her dying. I glanced back. The line of knights was sentinel-still, a wall of menacing steel. Was she already dead?

"Oof!" Someone bulled into my side. I rounded and found a familiar face. "Trin?"

Porcelain skin creased around a frown. Behind her, a Stormseye knight shot spit through a gap in his teeth and then strode off. She winced and touched her back where he'd shoved her.

I touched her shoulder. "Are you okay?"

She nodded then straightened, flaxen hair sweeping like a wave over one shoulder. "Definitely going to bruise." Blue eyes wrapped around my soul as she locked eyes with me.

She was tall, taller than me, but it never felt as though she looked down on anyone. She frowned. "What's wrong?"

I swallowed the rock in my throat and looked away.

"Your mother...is she..."

"Soon." I sniffled. "I—I didn't want to leave her. But I had to. I had to."

"I know. We all know what it's like." Trin slid her arms around my torso. Her warm cheek pressed against my temple. "I'm so sorry, El."

As much as I wanted to, I couldn't bring myself to do more than be held. My arms were limp, my will to move them nonexistent. Besides, the crush of the stinking masses was no place to show emotion. While there was a dizzying presence of fully armored knights, they did little to protect commoners like myself. Thieves and swindlers and worse preyed on the weakest of the herd. A hug was dangerous enough.

I disentangled myself as an ethereal voice rolled across the crowd. **"Cannalis, you are here to witness the birth of a god."**

Prickles ran up the backs of my arms. Trin stared at me sidelong. Who spoke?

The majority of those closest to the altar and the Stormlords ringing it were converts. We called them leathertongues. Rows of these lowly acolytes knelt, their hands upraised in mimicry of their masters. On tip-toes, I peered through the tumult. None of the Stormlords' mouths moved.

"I think...I think it's him." *The Great Archon.*

Trin's eyes widened.

"A god formed in my image. Lictor Laconius, it is time to be born anew. Come forth to receive my blessing."

A sea of heads bobbed and swiveled, searching for the source of the voice as well as the aforementioned lictor.

Burnished black plate weighed a man down as he departed from his brothers and hobbled to the line of Stormlords. Yellowed teeth split his smiling face. White hair trailed from his polished helm. A papery, well-veined hand clutched the hilt of a sword sheathed at his hip.

The altar burbled.

A fishy stench filled the air and dark, crimson-tinted liquid filled the altar's bowl. Quiet bubbling turned into a fountain of cascading blood. The crowd backpedaled in horror and cried out, but the Stormseye knights held them fast.

Trin's soft hand slid into my palm. "It's okay," she said.

I nodded. In Trin's first years of life, her father had been a wine merchant, and a highly favored one among the Brotherhood. Her earliest memory was of finding him dead, she'd said, three empty bottles at his desk. Their family's fall had come fast thereafter. The Stormseye seized her father's assets and cast them into the streets. Now, her mother slept with the smith and made her children work for him in exchange for shelter.

Trin had seen firsthand how power molded one into its selfish form. Her father's hedonism led her family into endless suffering. Ever since, Trin had commanded a purity of strength out of necessity, and a universal compassion born of stubborn resolve to never follow in her father's footsteps.

Until my mother's sickness, my family's deaths had only spurred me to greater fear. Until that morning, I'd never considered defying the fate heaped on me by the Stormseye Brotherhood. Courage itself seemed a crime I could be found guilty of.

No longer.

I pinned back my shoulder blades and squeezed Trin's hand. "Nothing about this is okay."

She gave a hesitant smile. "Oh, I don't know. This view isn't so bad."

Circumstances be damned; I laughed. Nothing shook her. I fell for her, then, a thing I'd done a thousand times before. A thing I hoped to do for the rest of my life if I should be so fortunate.

"Present your blade, Lictor Laconius."

The aged man did.

"Such weapons are for those with mortal flesh." A sound like creaking ice filled the air. The blade shattered. Laconius clutched his face and shrieked, a score of steel slivers perforating his flesh. A handful of leathertongues in the front row dropped to their sides, writhing and screaming with similar wounds.

"Drink from the fountain." Shaking, the lictor crawled to the base of it. Gnarled fingers clung to the lip and turned white as he pulled himself upright. Tears streamed down his cheeks. Undeterred, he plunged his face into the bloody bowl.

I cringed, turning up my nose as the man whipped his head back and gasped for air.

He groaned. Slivered steel plinked into the altar's bowl as his face spit out the shards. The wounds closed like tiny mouths. White hair darkened, became a light and nutty brown. He straightened, youth returning, shoulders broadening. Light flashed in his eyes as a dark line encircled his head.

Armor clattered to the ground, unbuckled by youthful hands. A pair of lictors swept up behind Laconius to wrap him in saffron robes.

"Death does not touch my children."

I eyed the altar of fountaining blood as it dwindled to a spitting nothingness. "A drop of that could save my mother," I growled.

"Would you really want to risk her turning into a monster like Laconius?"

I shook my head. "They could help everyone with their powers, yet they don't. They only help themselves."

The knights peeled off to let the crowd bleed back into their miserable lives. A resounding crack and flash heralded the disappearance of the Stormlords. Laconius's armor was left to rock on the curve of its shell in the dirt.

I stared at the altar, stared until everyone had left the plaza. Trin squeezed my shoulder then hurried off to help her family at the smithy.

If I possessed such power, I could control fate itself. I could save my mother. I could help Trin and her family—everyone in Cannalis.

I could make my fate my own.

CHAPTER THREE

THE ELDER

Near the ziggurat, the world had an aroma of shoe polish, rose water, and the coppery tang of metal. Smells of the rich.

As I neared my home, one beggar became two, became five, became dozens lining the streets. The stench was incredible, though not so bad as the slums around the Gate of Cannalis. Still, I woke every morning to air I didn't deserve to breathe. It stank of starving breath, human waste, and the occasional rotting dog carcass.

Rich air and poor air.

Worlds apart.

An old man and long-time customer of my family's business, selling stale bread for pennies, waved me down. "What's this? No crusty heels? No greenish heels?"

Trin and I called him the Elder. "I didn't have time. A knight chased me all the way to the ziggurat."

"Ah yes." He picked his nose, flicked it. How the Elder still lived was beyond me. No one derided the Stormseye Brotherhood more vocally than he.

A stained red cloak was clasped around ruddy-skinned shoulders, and of his tattered trousers, which may have once been yellow, only a few strips of cloth clung on below the knees. White and crusted feet, saturated by hardship and hard streets, matched his hands. Blood filled dried-out splits at the webbing.

"Another day in paradise under the Stormseye, eh?" The Elder pointed at his empty eye socket and nodded slowly. "You can't tell, but I'm winking."

A Stormseye knight trotted by. I stifled a laugh, dropped my gaze to the ground and whispered, "More caution, friend."

"Bah!" He slapped his bald, tan skull which shone under the midday sun. Subsisting on paltry scraps from my bread cart for so many years, the man was lean, though stunningly not yet emaciated. "I nearly forgot! I should be fearin' shouldn't I?"

The knight glanced back over his shoulder, brows knit as he turned a corner. Ringing filled my ears. My stomach flipped.

The Elder's tongue shot from his mouth as if he'd tasted curdled milk. "A noose of squalor they are. Ever tightening the rope so as to choke the life from each subsequent generation. What do I care if they kill me? Someday, the Great Archon will cinch the noose too tightly and choke himself. That'd be swell." He produced a browning apple core from a hidden pocket within his cloak, then offered it to me. I cocked my head. Where had it come from? A gap-toothed smile greeted me as he snapped off an end. "Gotta have pockets. Lots and lots o' pockets. Keeps a person alive."

Alive. The word stuck at the base of my throat. "I have to go. My mother is ill." I made to pass the Elder.

A skeletal hand clutched my elbow. "She's dying?" I froze, heart pounding in my breast. "You want to heal her?"

"Is there a way?" I spoke in a rush. "Like the Stormlords?"

He snorted and yanked tattered pants to ankles to piss in the street. His single eye narrowed around a passing patrol of Stormseye knights. Once they'd gone, the Elder smacked his gob and whispered, "There's always a way, El. Though I warn you, the journey requires curiosity. Have you that?"

The pain of circumstances outside my control called to mind a thirst for what might change them. I nodded.

"What about reading and writing, can you do that?"

I frowned. I'd not written much, but one of our neighbors taught school to the neighborhood children until a lictor caught her and ordered her execution. Trin's father had provided the best tutors until his death ten years earlier, so she had helped me continue my education. Countless nights had passed with each of us holding one half of a book and reading until our lone candle snuffed out. Trin had always waited for me to catch up before turning the page. "Yes."

"Good. You're a lucky one, then. The Stormseye has a stifling thumb and they press it where they can to keep Cannalis dumb." He glanced to either side. "I have a final question for you. Best I ask it elsewhere."

While my mother might already be dead, I couldn't refuse his offer of a possibility to save her. The Elder was a beggar and cretin, but I'd never known him to be mad. Besides, he had an air of mysterious power about him. It was as if his words of condemnation against the Brotherhood could be followed with action if it came to conflict.

I followed him to where he slept behind a butcher's shop and watched him rummage through a pile of meager belongings. With a curse he pulled forth a soiled scroll, glanced at me, then hesitated.

A silvery outline gave the scroll an eerie glow. I stared, my awareness swallowed by each passing second. Head throbbing. Pulse racing. I pushed down the urge to run as well as the impulse to snatch the scroll before I went.

Rolled pages trembled in the Elder's scarecrow hand. He studied me, lifting the eyebrow above his empty socket. "You remember what I've told you of Seekers?" Everything about the man had become tight and serious.

I rubbed my face and exhaled.

Seekers. The hopeful dreamers and adventurers who spent their lives in the Wildness beyond Cannalis. "They search for the Power and aspire to become wizards." I gave a nervous laugh. "But those are just stories you told Trin and I for entertainment. Legend and myth. No one survives the Wildness."

A wicked smile twisted the Elder's lips. "Do you always laugh when you fear you're wrong?"

"You're acting like it's real. The Stormlords say there are giants in the Wildness. Trolls and ogres, too. Only merchants who hire Stormseye knights for protection can survive."

The Elder spat. "Naught but truth from them, eh?"

He was right of course. The Brotherhood had two weapons they used for keeping the people downtrodden. While their blades could surely kill one's body, it was the Stormlords' terror-inducing sermons that killed the people's spirits.

I'd always wondered why the sermons were mandatory when so little of what they said had any impact on me. Repetition, it seemed, was more effective than I realized.

The Elder's words hung heavy truths around my neck, but still, I was tired of being strangled by the lies of old men. My accusing tone reflected as much. "How come I've never seen a Seeker, then? If they exist, why don't they ever return?"

"Because they're wizards now, you twit." The Elder rotated his hand, faint light pooling in his palm.

My mouth fell open. I glanced at his hand, then back at the scroll. "So, it's all lies. You've been to the Wildness and back haven't you?" I chuckled nervously. "It's safe beyond Cannalis. There are no giants, no monsters, no—"

"Let me finish." The Elder held up a suddenly normal hand, the light gone. "They're wizards now...or they're dead. Smashed to pulp by giants, or roasted over an ogre's spit, or feeding pups in a troll mother's den. Or maybe gutted by another Seeker desperate for power. A great many have burned, boiled, and bled at the hands of other wizards, too."

I swallowed back bile. "So that part's true."

The Elder winked, this time with his good eye.

Anger swept through me. The Stormseye had doled out punishment and cruelty my entire life, yet the lie that there was a possibility for another way, even if it meant a bad end to a worse life, stoked a rage in me I would do anything to unleash. It wasn't simply a personal betrayal. The Great Archon was a traitor to hope itself. Children's dreams for a better life, crushed. Parents' dying wishes that the next generation be free, unfulfilled.

Naive words bled through gritted teeth. "Then, I am a Seeker."

"Ha! You mean you wish to be one." The scroll rustled as the Elder took it in both hands.

"No. I *am* a Seeker. I don't care what happens to me but..." A tear welled at the corner of my eye. I grunted and brushed it away. "I'm tired of feeling helpless. Whatever it takes to avoid my family's fate, I'll do."

"Good. Because this is my final question. Are you fearless, child?"

Quite the opposite. I feared the Stormseye. I feared the beggars close to the Gate of Cannalis. I feared losing Trin, losing my mother, losing my own life. But more than any of that, I feared having no choice in the matter. And I would run from that fear even if it meant running straight through all the others.

"No," I said. "I'm afraid I'll die like everyone else born in Cannalis, pointlessly and with nothing but regret to show for it. So no. I'm not fearless."

The Elder clicked his tongue as he debated my answer for a painfully tense moment. "Only fools claim to be fearless. A little cynicism will serve you well, for this is no journey for fools." He brought his nose within an inch of mine. "In truth, you must know great suffering and you must be desperate to escape it."

Please. My mother's diseased form burst across my mind's eye. *My child*, she rasped. *Please.*

The Elder drew himself up. For the first time, I noticed he was a head taller than me—as tall as any knight. "Then consider this your summoning. You, El, are to go straight away to the Gate of Cannalis. Do not read the scroll before you reach it. If you do, your journey ends harshly."

My tongue darted over my lips as the scroll dropped from his hands into mine. It tingled where it sat. Energy raced up my arms and filled my chest with warmth.

The Elder continued. "Once there, the scroll will tell you what to do. You have until the sun sets to make it there. Otherwise..." he smiled, a gap-toothed thing. "Your journey ends harshly."

The back of my throat was raw from rapid breaths. Guilt flooded me, forcing me to turn away from the Elder. I stared at the scroll, awed by the power a simple scrap of paper held over me.

"Now? But my mother is so ill."

"Right now. You must make it there before dark." He thrust the scroll at me. "Once the sun sets, you will never get another summons. Squander it this eve, squander it forevermore."

I would be leaving my mother unattended. Alone in her suffering. Alone in the end. To leave her now would be a shame too great to bear.

My fist tightened, crumpling the parchment some as I pushed it back toward the Elder. "I'm sorry, I can't."

The Elder didn't try to convince me differently. Stoic, he simply nodded and stuffed the scroll into a hidden pocket of his cloak. A flash of blinding white light spread out around him, then condensed to a singular wink.

I threw up my arms, covering my face as the luminous flash trailed away into nothingness. The Elder had vanished, the scroll and my chance of ever being a Seeker along with him.

CHAPTER FOUR

UNTIL THE SUN SETS

The first thing I noticed was a clay pitcher tipped onto its side. The second was my mother's empty sleeping mat. Hollowness spread through my stomach. Cold sweat slithered onto my upper lip and the palms of my hands. Panting, I took a shaky step inside.

Moth-eaten clothing, stained through with sweat, lay crumpled beside the soiled mat and a bucket for her waste.

I turned in a slow circle. There was nowhere for her to hide, nor any reason to do so. In her state, wandering off seemed as likely as the possibility that a Stormlord had come along to heal her.

It was Idrinnia, I realized. The stories of the Everlasting Maiden she'd been telling. My mother's loose lips had finally caught up with her.

The Brotherhood had come to stamp out yet another ember of hope.

Wherever she was, my mother was dead. Was she terrified at the final moment, staring into the faces of cruel strangers? Had she felt alone?

My knees struck hard-packed dirt. A dreamlike sense of pain blossomed in my thighs from the impact. I gave no reaction, all feeling of self...stolen. My head hung deep, chin hovering above my collarbone.

I stared at trembling hands. I was fifteen, older than most ever lived to be inside the walls of Cannalis. I'd been working my father's bread route ever since he and my brother had succumbed to the plague. But in that moment, I was reduced to being a child again. Stripped of my family, I was naked before my fears.

And any opportunity I'd had to be something more than a pointless casualty had disappeared with the Elder.

Scabs of earth piled to either side of my fingernails as I clawed the ground and cursed. What could I do now? I knew only Trin and she was a smith's bad mood from the brothels or being forced to thievery.

Nothing changed. Nothing *ever* changed. Nothing would. The Great Archon and his Stormseye Brotherhood made sure of that.

Fate birthed me in the gutters and fate would one day give me back to them. Anyone foolish enough to hope for different deserved their destitution.

I sucked back snot, wiped my face and rose. There was at least an hour until sunset, which meant I could still earn a couple pennies before it got too dangerous. Beggars within days of starving to death couldn't be faulted when they killed for food. What easier prey than me?

Stiff bread loaves filled my hands. Fat tears plopped onto dark crusts as I slowly placed them in the handcart.

Just an animal acting one skittish step at a time to survive.

The cloth hanging over the entryway into my home furled, then snapped. Something or someone stirred in the alley beyond. I glanced at a makeshift dagger hanging on a nail on the wall. I used it for protection on my bread routes, though it wasn't much. When a knight's horse had thrown a shoe, a beggar beat me to it, but he'd needed my food more than the twisted hunk of metal and willingly traded for it. Since that day, I'd honed one end into a crude spike.

The cloth hanging lifted higher, revealing the statue-still shadow of a man on the wall of the alley beyond. I froze and waited. The man didn't move. My mouth went dry and my knees shook. The horseshoe dagger wasn't too far...

Blood rushed to my ears as I grabbed my weapon. "Who's there?"

A gust of wind made the cloth hanging snap violently. I retreated to a corner and held my dagger up in both hands. "Stay out!"

No one replied. Wind ripped the cloth drape from its nail. Light poured into my home, washing out the figure's silhouette in the alley. Energy crackled, roaring in my ears until I had to cover them. A deafening pop silenced it a moment later.

A buzzing quiet replaced the rush of sound.

My legs felt alien, my lips and cheeks stiff and bloodless as I muffled the sound of my breathing with one hand. Tremors overtook me. The dagger jumped around chaotically in my fist as I crept toward the alley. Jaw clenched, I thrust the horseshoe out first, then stepped from hiding.

I inhaled sharply.

There it was, shining and brilliant and hopeful.

The unfurled scroll flipped over, corners scrabbling across the ground.

A second chance for a new beginning.

———————————✦———————————

Reaching under my mother's sleeping mat, I felt the crush of leather and jerked it free. The jangle of pennies and a single silver. I tied it to my belt, making sure to keep it hidden inside my pants.

Outside, the sun hung over the horizon like a guillotine's blade waiting to descend. I left the handcart in the alley so I could say a final goodbye to my home.

A numb tingle rippled across my skin. I glanced at one corner, the one where my mother had told Trin and I the blasphemous stories of Idrinnia. The room spun as memories came to me unbidden...

I was half as old. I'd risen in the dead of night to urinate. When I returned, I watched my family sleeping. Moonlight washed over my parents, my sister and brother too. Gratitude had filled me—maybe the only time I can recall. It was a thing in short supply, almost more so than clean water or fresh food. Back then, I was surrounded by those who loved me. My older sister was killed weeks later.

The memory bled away. I clenched my teeth, jaw clicking. They were gone. Their deaths meaningless.

Now, I counted myself anything but grateful. Determined, perhaps. Bitter and emboldened, certainly.

A subtle warmth emanated from the area around the scroll where it rested in a trouser pocket. I patted it. "My fate will be different," I said aloud. I didn't believe their spirits lingered, nor that they'd hear me for that matter. I said it for myself.

I slung the horseshoe dagger through my rope belt. A little more than an hour separated me from failure. Determined, I locked my hands around the handles of my bread cart and heaved, trundling into the darkening streets.

Luckily, the Gate of Cannalis wasn't too far if I made for it straight away. But I had to see Trin first. If I left without saying goodbye...

No. I'd already lost my mother. I wouldn't miss Trin, too. That would only add to my guilt.

Bare feet slapped loudly on hard-packed dirt as I hurried to the black-smith's. Cold descended, numbing my toes and fingertips. Precious minutes ticked by as I weaved between the clutter of horses and piles of excrement. Beggars thrust empty palms, hoping for them to be filled by my generosity. Merchants selling rotted furs for warmth took one look at me and knew I was no sale.

It didn't matter. I ignored them all.

You have until the sun sets to make it there. Otherwise...your journey ends harshly. The Elder's words were less than comforting. I chewed the inside of my cheek as I went, praying to the Power that his offer still stood, frightening as it may be.

The Power.

The Stormlords had convinced all of Cannalis of the entity—that it had chosen them. That the Great Archon was a prophet of the Power. They used it as both a goad to drive the masses and a feast just out of reach to compel them. Only leathertongues were stupid enough to buy into such. Yet there I was, praying to it. I hated the Brotherhood more than ever for their fabrications. There was nothing left to have faith in.

So, I directed my prayers to myself instead. Made it a mantra.

"I control my fate. I control my fate. I control my fate."

Streaked with sweat and soot, the blacksmith was still hard at work when I arrived. An acrid tinge stung my nostrils. I threw my handcart to a stop inside the shop. Pausing, the smith lowered his hammer and frowned at me. Scratching his chin, he seemed to be weighing something. Then he motioned to the back of the shop. "She's there."

I found Trin oiling an old anvil. Her face swiveled toward mine, a smudge of grease on her porcelain cheek. A smile like the sun quickly clouded over when she noticed my expression. "What's wrong, El?" She came to her feet in a rush.

I stammered and rubbed my face. Trin moved toward me as if borne by a river's current, smooth and inevitable. I didn't realize how badly I'd needed her until that moment. Too much had happened. I wanted to tell her everything, to fall into her arms and weep, to feel the compassionate embrace of the last person I knew loved me. I wanted to break apart in my grief and have Trin put me back together.

But I couldn't.

You have until the sun sets.

Glancing furtively around the room, I noticed her mother and brothers watching me. The smith, too, had paused his work to stare judgmentally toward the back of his shop at me.

"Come." I pulled her into a shadowed corner away from eager ears.

I withdrew the scroll, and chewed my lip as I stared down at it. Trin's brow furrowed, a single line.

"El, tell me what's going on."

Utter madness dribbled through my brain. *The Elder is a wizard. My mother has disappeared. I'm fleeing into the Wildness. Did I mention I'm going to be a Seeker?* How could I say any of it without her thinking I'd snapped? And if I did tell her the truth, there was no time to convince her I was sane. I had to be brief if I was going to make the gate by sunset.

She took my hand gently in hers. "It's your mother, isn't it?"

My chin shot toward my shoulder. I grimaced and slipped the scroll back into my pocket. "I'm sorry, I don't have time to explain." My voice cracked. "I'm leaving Cannalis."

Our eyes locked. "What?"

"Right now. I'm sorry, Trin. I have to go."

She recoiled, hand falling from mine. "Why? How?" Simple words, yet they carried the density of storm clouds.

"My mother is dead. There's something I must do."

Trin and I had grown up together on the same stories but I couldn't bring myself to tell her the truth. She'd want to come, too, want to become a Seeker. If it was as dangerous as the Elder said, I couldn't risk losing Trin. "Alone."

Life under the Brotherhood was horrible but at least she'd be alive. And if I succeeded at becoming a wizard, I could return to free her and her family from squalor.

Tears welled in Trin's eyes. She thrust her chin out defensively. "Is that how it is? You're going to fly in here, tell me you're leaving, and give no explanation? You expect me to be okay with that?"

You have until the sun sets.

"I don't want to leave you." Pressed for haste, I spoke as quick as I could.

Trin mistook my urgency for hesitation. "So don't leave!" She shot a look back at her family. "Stay with us. We'll apprentice with the smith together. We need each other, now more than ever."

I sensed her fear under the surface. The smith would likely throw them out to live as beggars before the year ended and she knew it. Sadness tickled my throat and made my face heavy. If I proved useful, the smith might want to keep them around.

But that was no fate I wanted. I'd rather die young and daring than live to see my life lose all meaning. Even if that meant sacrificing Trin.

"I'm not staying."

Her upper lip bunched. "Looks like you've decided, regardless of my feelings." While it would make it easier to go if she was angry with me, that wasn't the way I wished to leave things. I couldn't.

"Listen, this is important." I licked my lips, hesitated. What if Trin was right? What if I was wrong?

"You don't have to go." She slid her hands onto my shoulders. "I know how it feels. She's gone. You're scared. But that doesn't mean everyone you love will abandon you." Her voice dipped low as she stepped closer. "I'm here, El."

Warmth emanated from her, filtering over me in waves. All I had was trust in the Elder and a wild hope that I'd been called to something greater. A tenuous thread at best but the only one I needed now. My resolve strengthened when the image came to mind of the white light trailing the Elder into nothingness. The man was a wizard, and even better, he wasn't a Stormlord. The knowledge he possessed could never be gained inside the walls of Cannalis. With every bit of my soul, I wished to grasp that knowledge. I was willing to sacrifice everything for it. Even Trin.

It tore my heart in half to admit it. To claim the power of a wizard, I had to leave her.

My eyes snapped open.

The Gate of Cannalis.

You have until the sun sets.

Time was running out. "I'll be back in six months." Empty words.

She sighed, pink lips quivering. After a long moment, she nodded. "I see."

"I'll be okay." I lied, as much for her as for myself. "I promise."

I drew her into a hug. That was the real reason I'd come anyway. To feel her one last time—not to make promises I couldn't keep. A lifetime of feelings merged as we melted into one another. Her skin was warm and damp with sweat. When I pulled away, her chest was flushed and red rimmed her eyes. "You're not to blame," I whispered, then rose onto my tiptoes to plant a kiss on her pale forehead.

As I turned to go, I choked back tears. My hand slid to her soft forearms, trailed down into palms, and then, a brush of fingertips before nothing. Only air remained between us. I left my heart behind, right there in the blacksmith's shop. Maybe my sanity as well.

Wooden steps carried me into the gloaming. Unfeeling hands groped for purchase on the handles of my bread cart. I heaved it forward, angled toward the horizon and the drooping orange sun.

Toward a fate to call my own.

CHAPTER FIVE

LAW OF THE GUTTERS

Heat rose like ghostly flame from the collar of the ratty cloth I called a tunic. Sweat blanketed me. I shivered. Shadows rose from the earth to grasp the city of Cannalis in twilight as the sun slid into the forested ranges in the distance. And with the thickening night came the cold. My hands were red and splotched with white. My veins, marbled blue.

The lanes of Cannalis whipped past as I creaked and trundled along. After a while, my feet were numb from pounding against the frigid ground.

I stopped and sucked in ragged breaths, arms slung over the crown of my head. A dark figure shifted in a nearby alley. I quieted my breathing, straightened, dropped my arms. I didn't want to seem tired or weak. I cleared my throat loudly and grunted, making a show of adjusting my horseshoe dagger in the process.

The farther from the city's center I went, the more dangerous things would be. Knights of the Stormseye didn't prevent anyone from leaving Cannalis—they didn't need to. Their stories were enough to deter any but the most adventurous traders. But their patrols would increase closer to the gate in tandem with the beggars and criminal entities.

Lanes and shadows and whispers drifted by. Once, a man spotted me and whistled. An answering whistle came, and a short time later, I saw another man with a scar running through his upper lip assessing me. Thinking they would follow me, I glanced back. The scar-lipped man had already faded back into an inky recess.

My life depended on my vigilance, now. I focused forward, never pausing, my hand never far from the dagger at my belt. I took up the mantra from before as I pushed my cart. *I control my fate. I control my fate.*

I entered the main street leading to the Gate of Cannalis.

Bodies lined the ditches to either side. Corpse crews only gathered 'customers' around the city's center. Where I lived, the dead rotted. Here was no different. Those who'd starved were bloated and swarming with flies. A handful were strangled, likely by the other downtrodden, while some others had deep slashes in their bodies. A gift of cruel mercy from the knights.

Beyond the Gate of Cannalis, I'd never been.

The Wildness was vast, a grisly death sentence for those without the resources or protection to survive it. At least, that's what the Brotherhood claimed.

I was pleased to find that the wheels of my cart drowned out the sound of buzzing flies, though it did little to silence the rows of naked and emaciated beggars calling for aid. Even the Elder had at least some lean muscle on his frame.

A young woman with protruding collar bones stepped into the street ahead of me. She smiled wanly. "What's in the cart, child?"

I ignored her—picked up the pace instead.

The Elder's words dogged my heels. *You have until the sun sets to make it there.* It had taken every scrap of will not to read the scroll before I reached the gate. Over the woman's cadaverous shoulder, a dark wood waited. I could almost see myself sitting among the trees' roots unrolling the parchment.

As I slowed, the scroll tingled where it rested in my pocket. I'd never touched anything magical before. The sensation was incomparable. An all-consuming itch, but at the same time, the relief of a good scratch as well. Pushing and pulling, irritating and satisfying, weakening and strengthening.

The embodiment of experience itself.

"Come on now!" she shouted, startling me. "What's in the cart?"

I pursed my lips and leaned on the cart, harder than before. "Nothing," I said without looking at her. "Get away."

A mistake.

She leveled a finger. "Liar. You got something." Other lice-ridden heads swiveled to regard me. Vacant stares, full of hunger.

For the first and only time in my life, I cast about, hoping to see Stormseye knights on patrol. The mere sight of them trotting down a street might scatter an entire mob. A single word of discord directed their way and this woman would be run through.

"Leave me!" I screamed. There were no others with handcarts in the streets. Not this late. No, they were smarter. I recited the law of the gutters—a proverb among the poor of Cannalis.

If not richer, bigger. If not bigger, quicker. If not quicker, smarter. If not smarter, dead.

In that moment, I was proving to be nothing but the latter-most.

I slipped by the woman. She pivoted after me and started walking calmly behind, like a predator stalking their prey. A stunted man with wiry white hair fringing his scalp hobbled toward me in silence. When he was close enough, I saw he had one foot. Despite this, he dashed forth, grabbing at the contents in my cart.

"Hey!" I reached back to stop him, but he'd already snagged a loaf and peeled off. Fewer than ten loaves in various states of festering remained, a meager cache to fight over. For me, it was the only food I'd have in the Wildness. I couldn't hunt, nor fish, nor fend for myself in any way outside the city walls. Going into the unknown as I was, I desperately needed it.

These people didn't care. They were dying now.

"Bread!" the woman shouted.

A young boy, naked but for a tiny cap hanging over his ears, leapt into my handcart. The sudden weight tore the handles from my grip which caused him to pitch forward and knock his face on a corner of the wooden bed. Blood blossomed. I reached for him, but he'd already found his feet again. Glimmering scarlet dripped from his nose as he scampered backward into the dirt and then dashed into the shadows.

A bouquet of grimy hands descended. I noticed the futility of my situation. For a moment, I thought about drawing my horseshoe dagger, but stabbing them would do little to stem the tide of starving, frantic mouths. Instead, I grabbed two loaves as if robbing myself along with them. Bitter hot breath filled the air. Shouts stabbed my ears. Brittle and broken fingernails scrabbling for food ripped at what little cloth their peers wore. Elbows beat at ribs. Someone cursed and clutched their face, blood welling between their fingers.

Someone's hand snared my shirt and tore it. My only shirt. I twisted away in a shower of crumbs as more hands fumbled for the bread cradled in my arms. Amid the fighting, a dagger glinted in the fading light. A severed finger flipped through the air. Shouts and screams melded into a singular, raging din.

Only a narrow strip of yellow remained above the horizon. *The gate!* *...Or your journey ends harshly.*

A horse screamed. Behind me, hooves thudded onto the mud-caked street. "What's the meaning of this?" called a voice soaked with outrage.

Stormseye knights.

They had little patience for an answer. The sound of steel biting flesh quickly followed, throwing the mob into a panic. I shouldered my way through the crowd, jerking my bread from grasping thieves as I went. I looked back. Blades flashed in downward arcs then rose, stained dark with blood. Bodies fell twitching and wide-eyed into fast-spreading pools of their own ichor.

I tripped. The bread didn't cushion the fall as a child might fantasize. My lungs seized. I rolled over—discovered the upthrust stone I'd struck that knocked the wind from me.

I sat up, wheezing until I caught my breath again. Ragged breaths returned. My bread loaves were lost in the fall. I patted myself down then clutched my crude dagger. *The scroll. It was gone.* Frantically, I cast about, but only saw a blur of filthy feet and hooves and lifeless eyes. I scrambled to stand just in time to dodge out of the way of a fleeing man who would have bowled me over.

Stormseye knights were cutting down any beggar close enough—and there were a great many of them. Crimson ribbons trailed the knight's swords through the air. Spears found their marks between exposed shoulder blades. Horses trampled the dead and living alike.

At the center of the chaos sat a lictor on a destrier, sneering commands. "Order, scum! We will bring you to order!" A flutter of movement caught my eye. Amid the destrier's clomping hooves, the scroll lifted then gently rolled over.

With each passing second, the sun faded and my chances of averting a meaningless life faded with it. As if about to plunge my head under icy water, I inhaled.

The lictor wheeled his horse in place as he watched his men violently restoring order. A gold amulet hung from round his neck, emitting a pulsating amber light.

Only a fool claims to be fearless.

I failed to see how dying at the feet of a lictor in pursuit of a roll of parchment didn't make me a fool, but the fear of not reading the scroll before I died outweighed all other considerations. Calm came over me. The hammering in my heart was a comfort; it told me I was more alive than I'd ever been. This fact lent me a strength of spirit I'd never known. Almost as if fate's steady hand held my own.

Then, it threw me forward.

I lurched toward the scroll, blades threshing air on every side, steam belching from the nostrils of grunting mounts as they wheeled their riders from one kill to the next. Terror threw palms upward in surrender, parched throats begging for mercy. In answer, blood spilled over diseased flesh and jutting ribs. A head rolled into my path and nearly tripped me. I hopped over it, barreling forward, through the hate, and the fear, and the reek of death and merciless carnage.

Only the scroll existed.

Just as I made to scoop it up, a knight turned his mount beside the lictor. Hindquarters slammed into my side, flinging me onto my wrists and knees. The scroll was within a short crawl. Like a rat, I scurried toward it, watched my hand wrap around it, and then pulled it into my bosom not unlike a mother rescuing her child.

Movement came from overhead as I rolled to one side.

"What's this?"

I felt an oppressive gaze settle on my back. I froze and glanced up.

Slate-gray eyes regarded me from a perpendicular slit in the lictor's helm—the single part of him that still seemed human behind the shell of armor. He spotted the scroll in my hand. "Stay where you are." He reached for his sword.

Instinct took over. My horseshoe dagger filled my other hand. Now that I had the scroll, no one would separate me from it. I punched up as hard as I could. The horseshoe spike bit deep, deep enough for my hand curled around its center to touch the horse's flesh. The mount reared with a scream as the lictor cursed and sawed the reins.

I bolted, feeling a blade cut the empty space behind me as I weaved through the swirling massacre. The knights had started to spread out as they continued their culling. Up and down the main street they ran down beggars, but some were fighting back as grim understanding dawned. The lictor and his knights meant to purge them one and all.

With gut-churning despair, I realized this thinning of the herd might be routine for the knights.

Just ahead, I saw the one-footed beggar crouched behind a barrel. A Stormseye knight galloped by, and as he did, the beggar hurled a dislodged cobblestone at his head. With a dull crunch, the rider tumbled backward from the saddle and met the earth with a thud. The beggar's victory was short-lived. A second rider broke off pursuit of an old woman and turned his attention on the cripple. "This rat slew Hollard!"

A pair of knights closer to the Gate of Cannalis answered their brother's call, clearing a path for me in the process.

"No! Fools, get that one!" The lictor's voice. I swiveled my head, saw his sword pointing at me.

I separated from the scattered crowd. The sun was a mere sliver now. A sprint to freedom or a harsh end—perhaps now it would be both. But I would read the scroll if it was the last thing I did.

I sprinted, though not very fast. One who ran inside Cannalis drew the Brotherhood's attention, so few ever dared it. I was nowhere near conditioned for my escape.

Fire wound up my thighs and down into my calves. For a moment, I worried my legs might give out, that I would fall to my face before setting foot in the Wildness, that the Stormseye knights would approach my failed body, laughing, and gut me.

You have until the sun sets to make it there. Otherwise...your journey ends harshly. Were the Elder's words prophecy?

I afforded a single look backward.

The lictor pursued me. A cloak of gold stitched with swirling eyes and lightning bolts billowed behind him, a knight trailing to either side. And they were gaining fast.

The horseshoe dagger tumbled to the ground with a vibratory ring as I stumbled, fingertips jabbing the earth for balance. I recovered. Fear tingled at the base of my skull. I shook it away and took up the mantra. *I control my fate!*

The Gate of Cannalis loomed ahead. I might make it to the Wildness, but it didn't seem like I'd go much farther. The knights were less than a stone's throw behind me now. The promise of a harsh end to my journey was all but guaranteed.

Hoofbeats thudded closer.

As soon as my feet had carried me under the gate, I opened the scroll. If I was to die, I wanted to at least know what I'd died for. Still running, my heart quickened as my eyes roamed the parchment hungrily:

From the Gate of Cannalis walk until you can go no farther.

That was all? No secret that would save me? Just a simple, vague direction? Useless.

My gut went numb, my face slack. I had thrown my life away for nothing. And yet it made so much sense. Who was I to think myself special?

"Stop!" shouted the slate-eyed lictor.

I paused on the Wild Road stretching from the Gate of Cannalis into a forest of mighty oaks, heavy with waiting shadow. My shoulders drooped as I whirled to face my killers. I would meet death head on, chin high, spine straight.

I'd gambled my life on the words of a crazy old beggar. My goodbye with Trin lingered like a pleasant scent. The warm feel of her would be a sweet thing to hold on to as the lictor's blade claimed my head.

From where I stood, I could have thrown a rock and struck the knights. If they wanted, they would be on me in seconds, swords and spears running me through.

Instead, they reined in at the threshold of the gate.

"Lictor?" one of the knights questioned.

I set my jaw and met the lictor's gray stare, the scroll crumpled in one hand. Blood dripped from his horse's belly.

"Shall I bring you a head, Lictor?"

The lictor broke his gaze from mine, glancing furtively at the scroll in my hand. He laughed. "I think not. This child is but a lure. I suspect the moment we leave the sacred grounds of Cannalis we'll be facing the Dark Waters Society or the Shadowgiants. Maybe even Cloudbreakers. No. For now, we'll leave the child's head where it is."

While I hadn't heard the names before—nor knew what they were—it sounded as if they opposed the Brotherhood. For that, they had my admiration.

The lictor folded his arms over his wounded mount's neck and watched me. For a few heartbeats, I was too scared to move. And then, I don't know why I did it, but I smiled. Perhaps it was fear begging me to do anything to break free of the crippling tension. Or maybe I wanted fate to know it had a student in me who was willing to be courageous. Or better still, did I smile because I'd won? The Stormseye Brotherhood's lies had failed to strip the hope from me. Finally, I had taken back control of my destiny.

And there was no greater testament to this than making a fool of a Stormseye lictor on his own doorstep.

CHAPTER SIX

THE FATE OF POSSUMS

Following the moon in the dark required all my focus. I moved at a snails' pace, for I may as well have been blind. Palms sought the solace of bark as I crept from tree to tree, my feet sweeping in forward arcs to avoid dangerous pitfalls. A twig jabbed my cheek. My finger came away sticky and warm with blood. I wished to see how much, but darkness swallowed the effort.

Night enshrouded me in a blooming discomfort. Monstrous fangs and dead-eyed abominations flashed through my mind's eye. It felt as though claws hovered over the nape of my neck. The Elder said fear was a good thing; I failed to see how.

A split in the canopy revealed the top of the moon and I angled toward it, making as much haste as a blind beggar. The scroll hadn't indicated a direction, but the last time I'd seen the moon, it hung over the horizon straight out from the Gate of Cannalis. Wherever I was headed, I assumed walking away from the Stormseye the best course.

I touched the scroll sequestered in my trousers. Euphoria bled around it and into my upper thigh.

Thinking of it quickened my heartbeat. I moved faster, any fear of monsters or injury momentarily forgotten. I had the scroll! The key to a new life. Nothing would stop me.

I was destined for something more.

Branches snapped as I barreled through the underbrush. A branch tore my trousers at the knee. Another raked my face. Half-crouching,

I swam forward, parting the thicket before me with wide sweeps of my bare arms.

From the Gate of Cannalis, walk until you can go no further.

Hours passed. I considered the strange names the lictor had mentioned. The Dark Waters Society, Cloudbreakers, Shadowgiants...

To say he spoke them with fear would be a stretch; more so, it seemed a healthy amount of respect. Trin and I had been secretly raised on tales of Idrinnia the Everlasting Maiden, but we'd also had the missives of the Stormlords drilled into us as well. Beyond the walls of Cannalis, dark creatures hunted for the blood of the unprotected.

Conditioning contended with recent revelation as I plunged onward, both excitement and primal fear giving me a surge of energy.

The canopy thinned, allowing the moon to illuminate my path. I straightened and progressed to a trot. Time's touch became a stranger. Silvery outlines stretched around tree trunks, stones, and my own feet. Color leaked across the earth. My breathing was labored and my legs ached. I was nearing my physical limit.

In a single night, I'd traveled farther than I ever imagined was possible. What wonders awaited me so far from home? I slowed to a stop, ready to find the answer.

Smiling, I unfurled the scroll.

Blank.

I frowned, stared, uncomprehending. Scratching my head, I flipped it onto its other side—nothing. I turned it upside down. I held it up to the fading moonlight, and then scratched at the paper like a baffled chimp.

Nothing.

My hands went rigid. The scroll drifted to the ground. I crossed my arms over the crown of my head, attempting to exhale slowly as panic swept into my chest.

But I couldn't go back. Exhaustion and self-doubt bore me to my knees as the first rays of sunlight peeked over the horizon. The entire night, I'd pursued a pointless endeavor.

Grief settled like a cancer in my bones, begging me to return to Cannalis. Would I ever see Trin again? Would I ever find out what truly happened to my mother? I'd barely started my journey and yet already I wanted to quit.

There was a chance the lictor wouldn't recognize me if I returned. Perhaps his pride kept him from reporting my attack against a representative of the Stormseye.

The Elder's voice chided me. *This is no journey for fools.*

No, fate had sealed that door with a smile. There was no returning.

My palm slapped down onto a patch of duff, clawed it into a fist, then slammed against the earth once more. Tears welled as I looked at the worthless scroll. Fueled by resentment, I crawled over to the soiled parchment on hands and knees. It crackled as I snatched it up and made to tear it in half.

I paused.

A faint word oozed across the page.

Walk.

Transfixed, I watched in awe as the letters darkened by the second, almost as if...

The sun climbed higher as I recounted my conversation with the Elder. When I'd read the scroll the first time outside the Gate of Cannalis at sunset, the lettering was faint. The Elder's words came to me in a flash of insight. *You have until the sun sets to make it there.*

Otherwise, the scroll wouldn't work! If I'd looked at it after the sunset, the parchment would have been blank. I would have quit before I started.

Staggering to my feet, I let loose a delighted howl, eyes flitting between the ensorcelled ink deepening on the scroll and the brightening sky.

Darkness and doubt peeled back. Renewed vigor pushed into my awareness. I'd been kidding myself to think that was as far as I could go. The scroll confirmed as much with its single word.

Walk.

As long as one foot found its way in front of the other, I could keep going. Still breathing, still moving, still hopeful, I slipped the scroll back into my pocket and ran.

\#

I was a Seeker.

It took me a while to put the pieces together as I navigated the towering oaks. Too much had happened too fast since I'd been forced from my mother's bedside. Her disappearance, the Elder's summons, my goodbye with Trin, the slaughter at the gate, and my confusion over the scroll's guidance—hardly a moment existed between points of turmoil for meaningful reflection.

But now I saw it. I was a Seeker.

I splashed over streams and brooks of varying sizes that glittered under the sun's rays. Fresh air and freedom parted before me with ease. The choking, clogging, cloying density of Cannalis's corruption was left far behind. Bare feet compressed the fast-warming duff with joyous abandon.

A line of quail sprinted from beneath a stand of wild plum bushes. I smiled and followed them to the edge of a cliff. An ocean of evergreens stretched to the far horizon as I worked my way along a ridge. A chipmunk perching atop a boulder darted into the shadows at my approach. Though it was well into midday, the moon was still out, a milky crescent hanging in the blue. A hawk soared across the sky, feathers stirring as it caught a swell then wheeled toward a range near the coast, a thin, hazy line in the distance.

The muscles in my legs no longer ached. Like the hawk, I found myself soaring over a land teeming with life. Fatigue failed to penetrate the subtle energy vibrating throughout my body. Anticipation, determination, purpose: these kept me moving forward more than food ever could.

I'd made it past the guarding lies laid by the Brotherhood, and now, I would become a wizard by any means necessary.

I, El, *was* a Seeker.

I sighed. Never had I been so proud of myself. Nor have I since.

Sweet day trailed into humbling night. The cold summer night's chill sank into my legs as I ascended a squat curtain of granite. Once over it, a bland meadow spread out before me. I took a single step then froze.

Two glowing orbs hovered a short way up the incline. Sweat rose to the surface of my skin, a chill lather, as the Elder's warning about ogres' spits and the dens of troll mothers rotated through my mind.

My fright was short-lived. I held my bladder long enough to recognize that it was no doom creature I faced off with, but a mere possum. My stomach growled. If not for the spasming in my bowels, I would have forgotten I hadn't eaten in a day and a half.

Wetting my lips, I bent to the earth and felt around until my palm fell flush with a stone. I straightened, spread my feet apart, and drew back.

Aimed...

Another set of eyes joined the first, slightly smaller and closer together—a baby possum.

A pitiful whine issued from my stomach. I grimaced, the stone poised to throw in a shaking fist. They watched me, then the mother turned away and bobbed up the hill, her offspring following close behind. The distance between me and my target grew. The moment came. Kill them and survive, or spare them and starve?

The moment went.

My shoulders slumped. I sighed, arm thumping back down at my side, killing stone slipping from limp fingers. What was I going to do with a dead possum anyway? Eat it raw? I told myself I'd do whatever necessary, yet couldn't. I sniffled. My mother had been taken from me. To do the same to that innocent creature would have been...

I pushed the sadness away. The Wildness surrounded me; it was no place for weakness or sentiment. Guilt gave me a duty to fulfill, a demand that my journey not be in vain.

The next possum that crossed my path would not be so lucky.

———————————

To my chagrin, no chance ever came. After my run-in with the possums, hunger drifted from a stabbing pang to a faint impulse. Glass shards riddled my shins. The places I'd been lashed while wandering through thickets stung with sweat. My low back ached, which was made worse by the press of my withering stomach sucked against my spine.

I couldn't feel my feet anymore, but it wasn't on account of the cold. Too many miles had left them as tattered, nerveless lumps. Despite the weariness begging me to stop, to hide under the nearest bush until someone saved me or death found me, I resisted.

Dusk sent forth its hazy pall while the crescent moon grew more luminous by the minute. I withdrew the scroll in anxious ritual, stared at it with a futile longing in my heart right until the moment the words faded with the last rays of sunlight.

Walk. Do not stop until forced.

The second part was new, and continued to be so all fifty times I checked the next day. The words mocked me with their familiarity. With a curse, I tucked the scroll into my pocket and refused to look at it again.

The feel of moisture on my lips became a vague memory as I pushed on, every part of me constricting around the desire for a sustenance that never came. Desperation transplanted food first, and then water.

Time became slick.

Minutes bled into hours. Hours hemorrhaged into days. I blinked at the sun, the dark, the sun again, eyelids rustling over dry eyeballs every time. Starving, exhausted, and dehydrated but still able to walk, I entered somewhat of a meditative state.

Consciousness swirled into a quiet void and left me as a body swimming in sensation. The hum of the world filled my ears. Scent guided me, a tickling thread as the veil between myself and nature thinned.

I didn't need to fall down and die to begin the process of decomposition. I simply needed to walk into the unknown and allow my life to drain away step by step into the soil. I've experienced many unbelievable things, but the act of dying while in motion—of edging toward oblivion while moving to its harmonious tune—stands forth as one of the most contented. A soulful bliss, only otherwise achieved on the cusp of death.

A root snagged my toe. For a single terrifying second, I hung suspended, touching nothing but air as the world was slingshot around me. Then, I plummeted.

My arms did not lift to brace against the impact. I struck my shoulder first. My head snapped against the ground. The world rang, darkened. When I commanded my legs to pull up under me, they failed to listen. With great effort, I rolled to a seated position, a rag doll pulled up by the shoulder, and then came to rest with my back against a boulder.

A groan dribbled from sundered lips as I stared out over a cluttered meadow ringed by forest.

With my legs dead and splayed out before me, I sighed, finally able to confirm to the scroll with confidence that I could go no further. The time to wait had finally come.

Chapter Seven

SEEKER

Useless legs make waiting easy. My arms, too, refused to function. Without water, I'd die soon. Maybe that's what I waited for...death. If not for lack of moisture, I would have cried. Never again would I see Trin. Never would I become a wizard.

The wind moaned over me. I glanced around and realized it was me moaning. Eager to shift my attention to anything other than my battered body, I inspected the meadow stretched out below. A handful of stumps and fallen logs lay scattered about a shallow hump of earth at the center of the clearing. Specks of white trillium blossoms lined veins of cobalt that threaded the grassy expanse.

One of them sparkled.

Water.

I squinted, rubbing cracked lips together. Dead skin hissed for succor that I could not grant. I wheezed out a laugh, head dropping back against the boulder propping me upright; it hurt but so did everything.

Blistering rays of sunlight bore into me. Heat percolated in waves through my torso. My pulse throbbed in my fingertips. Jabs of feeling returned to my feet as the day wore on. The clearing dissolved into a blurry mass of brown and green...

Clipped memories danced with hallucinations.

The Stormlords danced naked around a dead giant, its chest burst open. A ribcage of twisted oak poked from the wound and eyes like cratered moons stared blankly at the heavens. The Stormlords chanted,

"Eat! Eat! Eat!" and dipped their hands in the giant's moss-colored blood.

White smoke poured over the earth.

Out of the cloudy vision, the Elder stepped forth, a dozen years younger and three teeth richer. His single eye shone mischievously. "Do you know Idrinnia the Everlasting Maiden?"

Trin appeared at my side. "El's mother told stories of her. My father did as well."

"You have good parents." Tears coursed down his cheeks. "Fewer and fewer of those any more. Too afraid of the Great Archon and his Stormlords. Too busy scraping life together. Too resigned in their despair to hope."

The Elder grinned. "Much like you, Idrinnia was raised in Cannalis. Back then, dark and cruel masters ruled the lands of Kelundar, and they sucked the life from their people the same way the Stormseye Brotherhood does now."

Trin snorted derisively, an action oddly out of place. "No one could be as bad as the Brotherhood."

"They were worse," the Elder hissed. "The rotten bastards killed Idrinnia's family. As a young woman she spent a year alone, living on the streets. Then, she disappeared into the Wildness."

The Elder hunkered low, the specter so close I could have touched him if I'd had the strength. "Decades passed. Then one day, she arrived at the gate. She'd changed, of course—drastically. She rode a moonstag twice the size of any warhorse. Its pale fur and translucent horns commanded every eye; wherever its hooves touched earth, a patch of ice was left. She herself bore a twisted staff that held the red light of dawn in a jewel at its head. Seashell-pink robes swathed her lithe form. Atop her head sat the Crown of the Heavens, a mantle of twined gold and azure sky."

I blinked in confusion. "Were you there?"

"This was over two hundred years ago." He flicked my nose. "Don't be thick. Now, where was I? Oh yes. Some of those among Idrinnia's company bore similarly powerful trappings, though nothing so dazzling as she. Not by half."

"Why tell us this?" Dark silhouettes stalked slowly from the white smoke. They wore helmets and armor and carried swords—knights of the Stormseye. Panic set my heartbeat to a dull hammering as they edged in behind the Elder. "We'll be in trouble with the Brotherhood just for listening."

The Elder humored me with a smile. "Life's full of trouble, don't you know? Worry about the trouble you want to find more than the trouble that's sure to find you. Do that, and you'll be better for it." The Elder twisted around and assessed the knights. "Do you know *why* they do the Stormlords' bidding? Why they would kill rather than disobey?"

Trin sat down at my side and interlaced her fingers with mine. "I do," she said. I whipped my face toward hers, stunned.

"Do tell?" The Elder tapped a fingernail against a yellow tooth.

"They're Seekers," she said. "Just like El. Just like Idrinnia and her company."

As if slapped, I jerked back from Trin, my fingers slithering out of her grasp.

"And what do Seekers seek?" the Elder asked.

Trin's voice was a haunting echo that slid into my ears and down my spine. "The way of the wizard."

✦

When I finally woke, I wished I hadn't. A dull ache pressed against my skull, and not from the boulder. Arm trembling, I put a hand to my head, wincing on contact.

Six sunrises I'd seen since fleeing Cannalis, and shortly, I would see a seventh. My neck, back and shoulders were fiercely stiff as I pushed to my feet. Gelatinous spots edged into my periphery and my heart beat painfully in my chest, stealing my breath as I straightened through the knees. A thousand pinpricks nearly felled me but I leveraged the boulder for balance.

"Fool," I choked out. My throat was drier than sun-baked clay despite the dewy gloom. I glanced at the bright halo of sky layering the horizon. The scroll unfurled with a lazy snap of the wrist.

Wait.

There it was. A single glorious word. "Wait," I wheezed. "Wait. Wait. Wait." The words tumbled from cracked, bleeding lips. The word echoed through my soul, tasted sacred as it left my mouth. It danced through me, that word.

"Sure." I laughed, scorn-laced notes rolling over the clearing. "Sure. I'll wait right here." A spasm of pain shot down one leg. I winced then tipped backward like a falling tree. A portion of stone jutting from the boulder struck my hip, causing me to cry out. Stars flanked my vision. I forced myself to breathe slowly as I battled a rush of blood that threatened to drag me back into unconsciousness.

I grit my teeth, snarled like a trapped wolf, and shoved back to my feet. I was done waiting. Whatever my fate was to be, I preferred to die searching for it rather than wait for it another second. After a few more steps, the stiffness in my limbs eased, allowing me to walk almost normally but for the injury to my hip. Rest had done wonders for me. Sleep, it seemed, was the main culprit of my wrecked state. Water had been scarce, but I'd found it enough times over the course of the trek to persist—though my kidneys did ache. At that point, I'd grown at least somewhat accustomed to starving.

Fog caressed the fallen logs and tumbledown stones clogging the clearing. A family of deer worked their way across, studying me when they weren't chomping at the grass. Crows alighted in the trees farthest from me. I'd always had an affinity for birds, so I endeavored to follow after them. Wherever they fled to, I would go, the scroll's guidance be damned.

After a single jaunty step downhill, I caught motion at the treeline on the opposite side of the littered meadow. Startled, the murder cawed frantically and fled. The deer froze a moment, then bounded away as a figure strode to the raised island at the center of the clearing.

Was I hallucinating still?

At first, they appeared as a floating head under fading moonlight. Then I noticed they were bedecked from neck to foot in inky robes, blending them with the night. A white mask encased their skull and most of their face, leaving only their mouth and chin uncovered. Bored-out holes gave the strange figure ominous dark pits where eyes should be. A shiver prickled the flesh at the backs of my arms. Was this who I waited for?

The figure swiveled their chin abruptly over a shoulder, gray ponytail flipping behind. A line of twenty warriors or more, men and women both, emerged from the trees to take up position behind the masked figure. These also wore black, though leather armor instead of cloth robes. Steel studs glimmered on their vests and down the sides of their legs. Weapons filled their hands: bows, daggers, swords... all manner of blade. Ready for battle.

They were swathed in shadows. Black hoods were pulled up around black sashes covering the bottom half of their faces. The only spot of color on their persons seemed to be a circle of white paint around one eye, with two more, each smaller than the last, trailing down their cheeks directly beneath the first.

They stopped short of the white-masked figure. Most sheathed their weapons. They seemed to be staring at me. My pulse throbbed through my skull. A chill swept through me. They were there to fight. I scrabbled back to hide behind the boulder.

Who their opponents were became apparent an instant later.

I heard them before I saw them. A tumble of rock somewhere behind me and low-spoken words drawing closer by the second.

Crouched low, I watched them descend, at least a dozen, maybe more.

Over leather armor, they wore gray tabards with bolts of lightning stitched into the fabric. These were cinched at the waist by thick belts bearing an array of weapons similar to those carried by the dark-robed gang on the other side of the meadow. From beneath gray headbands, a streak of painted lightning descended down the temple before branching out onto either cheek.

A wave of sensation passed through me. The hairs on the back of my neck stood up. The air came alive as if a storm approached. A dark, foreboding feeling made me shudder. Power lurked nearby. Not a storm…

A Stormlord.

I shifted, readying to flee for my life, and as I did, I dislodged a chunk of rock at my feet. It hurtled down the rocky slope end over end into the clearing below.

I held my breath.

A woman at the head of the group of gray warriors whirled toward me, open hand flying skyward. Three archers fell to a knee, arrows notched and aimed at my hiding place.

With nowhere to go nor the strength to get there quickly, I stepped into view, hands buoyed in surrender.

"Distra," came a smooth voice.

My skin tingled. The voice carried with it an air of implacable confidence, as if by word alone, it held absolute power over the person it named.

"Distra," they said again. "It's just a Seeker."

The woman dropped her hand slowly. The archers stood, bow-strings easing. Distra turned to the slope behind her and made a series of harsh guttural sounds accompanied by a flurry of distinct hand signals.

"No." A man emerged from the shadows. "The Order of Odd is accounted for as we see it laid out before us. That one is alone. And certainly no threat."

All I could see of the man's face was a trail of dark beard, too well shadowed under a tall, wide-brimmed hat. Much like the white-masked figure waiting in the ravine, this man wore a robe, though it was gray rather than black. One sleeve had been removed, revealing a lean arm tattooed with white lightning from shoulder to wrist that gave off a preternatural glow under the moon's light. Leather straps crisscrossed his torso, holding pouches and glass vials tight to his body. A deep blue crystal hung around his neck, giving off a sparkle in the quickening dawn. "Come closer, Seeker," he said peremptorily.

On shaky legs, I complied. The bearded man sighed. "Hopefully you're more brains than brawn." He turned away, striding down into the clearing below. "Distra, best to recruit before you shoot." His warriors followed.

She grabbed me by the tattered collar of my shirt and dragged me along behind. For the first handful of steps, my legs forgot how to work and I stumbled. The woman, Distra, eyed me harshly but slowed when she noted my condition. She took me firmly by the elbow, supporting me until I was able to walk under my own power. While sleep had done me well, the rigors of the Wildness and lack of food still very much affected me.

They came to a stop at the edge of one of the trickling foot-wide streams veining the meadow. Like a puppet with their strings cut, I was dropped to the earth. Distra crouched beside me, pale eyes roaming and assessing my sorry condition.

She signaled at me with her hands. When it became clear to her I had no grasp of their meaning, she huffed in frustration. "You're a Seeker." Her speech, if you could call it such, was broken and weak, as if her words were brittle husks that lost all density before reaching my ears. Air with a hint of shape and tone.

She indicated my miserable legs. "Why?"

I couldn't make sense of the question.

"Here." She brought a water skin to my lips. I drank greedily until she traded me for a hard biscuit. "More food at camp."

"Camp?"

The gray warriors spread out into a crescent formation as the man with the tall hat claimed the hump of earth at the center of the clearing. He stopped a hundred paces shy of the white-masked figure who stood at relaxed attention on the other side of the raised strip of earth.

Distra stood, tracking my eyes to the pair of robed figures. "Omatuu is too strong. He will win." She nodded grimly. "He's a better wizard than Vethati. Maybe the best."

A wizard!

Warmth spread from my chest down into my arms. My stomach flipped with excitement, giving me a boost of energy. Omatuu was a wizard—maybe the best one.

And I was a Seeker.

Distra stared down at me. Unable to wipe the smile from my face, I met her gaze as she jammed a thumb emphatically against her breastbone. "We are Cloudbreakers."

My mouth hinged open. The Stormseye lictor was right—there were Cloudbreakers in the Wildness. And they appeared quite dangerous. If the Brotherhood worried over them, I was partial to liking them already.

And if Cloudbreakers were real, that meant there might also be a Dark Waters Society and...

I pointed at the other clan dressed all in black. "Shadowgiants?"

Distra snorted, shook her head. "Order of Odd."

Although understanding Distra's broken speech came with great effort, my senses were hyper-focused. Too many exciting things were happening and I refused to miss any of it.

She pointed at the white-masked leader of the Order of Odd. "She is Vethati. Come."

We approached the Cloudbreakers' line. The wizard, Omatuu, faced the midnight-wrapped Vethati. Warriors on both sides had their weapons sheathed. Most looked relaxed, which stunned me.

"Are you going to fight?"

"Only wizards duel," Distra croaked. So, she was a Seeker like me. They all were.

The dueling wizards fell into defensive postures: Omatuu a balanced squat; Vethati a deep angled stance with one leg outstretched. They raised their hands. Peeking sunlight outlined the curving sheen of Vethati's bladed hands. Omatuu, meanwhile, thrust one clawed hand in the direction of his opponent, and held the other behind his back in a fist.

Laughter rang as sudden as a thunderbolt across the clearing—Omatuu's. He spoke in a mocking tone. "This is exceedingly unwise, Vethati. I am years your better. A Prime. You are but a Second. Have you already grown tired of the wizard's life?"

Vethati's masked head cocked to one side. She glanced at those behind her, seeming to consider something.

"Ah." Omatuu's mocking tone shifted to musing. "So, it's your Seekers who've forced your hand. They can get quite desperate for a wizard's knot, can't they? Personally, I wouldn't know, for I keep my Seekers happy."

I had no clue what a wizard's knot was nor why Seekers might be desperate for it. But I promised myself I would find out.

Omatuu started circling his opponent, and she moved in step with him. Both maintained their postures like expert dancers. "You know, Vethati, there are other ways to come by wizard's knot. Why don't we join forces, hmmm? We could visit ruin upon the Dark Waters Society this very night. I shall take Khemetri's topknot, and you, that of her Second. Surely, that would satisfy your cabal?"

Vethati gave no response as she stopped creeping slowly to one side. Her hands drifted out to the sides...then faded. I gasped as I watched the color drain, turning them into ghostly outlines.

Rage tinged Omatuu's voice. "You think she's more powerful than me, don't you! A dire mistake." He snorted. "Suit yourself. You'll know who the true terror of the Wildness is soon enough."

The air around me felt as though it were being sucked away. Goose-bumps covered my skin. Sweat broke across my brow and my heart raced in anticipation.

I blessed the scroll and the Elder. If I'd had the moisture and energy to spare, I might have cried for joy.

Wizards. Seekers. Alive in the Wildness. In my mind, I spoke to Trin, shouting to her from a different world. *Trin, if only you could see that it's real. If only you knew!* Our entire lives we'd thought Stormlords were the only ones who held the Power.

The door of possibility was kicked open before me.

"Watch, now." Distra looked as though she'd eaten something bitter. But her eyes were unblinking, dark and expectant, gleaming in the bright morning light. I glanced sidelong at the others arrayed in a row to either side and saw in them something that unnerved me—an insidious hunger. It was as if nothing existed, as if all else was a passing blur and the only thing that mattered was the duel and the longing to be a wizard.

But it wasn't their primal desire that worried me. It was the knowledge that, I, too, shared the same yearning to see their magic unleashed.

Even if it meant one of them would die.

I swallowed dryness at the back of my throat and watched my destiny unfold in the duelists steps, in the subtle movements of their ghostly hands. Violence and death all in the name of edification.

The combatants' hand's flew toward each other and the world flashed.

Chapter Eight

DUELING WIZARDS

In the split second of silence before the fighting started, Omatuu's breath quickened to a sudden, rapid pace. I saw it, a rhythmic yet forceful swelling of the chest. Though faint, I could hear Vethati doing the same in the distance.

Omatuu struck first, whipping the clawed hand in a forward arc at his opponent. Tendrils of blue flame sprang from each fingertip, gathering into a scintillating orb an inch above his palm. It shot forward, a crescent of blistering fire.

As the blast hurtled across the clearing at Vethati, the rush of displaced air blew my hair back. My eyes stung from the heat and began to water.

Vethati was ready. Limp hands weaved back and forth across her body. For a moment she sparkled—then the flames consumed her.

"Ice," Distra grunted.

Steam rose from the Order of Odd wizard. Then she cut forward with a series of bladed hand movements swiping in all directions. Omatuu countered, throwing his hands overhead and to either side of him. A dull boom of force meeting force accompanied each sweep of the Cloudbreaker wizard's arms, like a gale wind striking a wall. The hems of his robes whipped one way, flattened, then wrenched in another. Leaves swirled at his feet before violently dispersing.

Vethati spun around, hand sweeping high, and then suddenly low to the ground. Omatuu cursed and sprawled to one side, flicking out a palm to block the rush of wind. Her attack caught him midair and sent him grunting and tumbling over the uneven earth like a skipped stone over water.

A searing sound, like fat sizzling over a cookfire, came sharply to my ears. A ball of molten flame roiled toward Omatuu. He came to a knee, translucent fists dragging up into the air. At his side, a log rose as if carried by some invisible giant. He threw his arms forward and the log shot into the oncoming fireball. Just as the blazing sphere was about to overcome the wizard, he lunged at it, ribbons of light trailing his fingertips as he swept them in an upward arc to split the inferno harmlessly around him.

I shielded my face in futile warding against the scorching mass flying past. No other Seeker moved. This wasn't the first duel they'd witnessed. A section of earth a hundred feet behind me burst into a geyser of rock and smoking mud where the flaming gout struck.

With phantom fists, Vethati had been prising a chunk of granite from the earth when she recognized her doom racing toward her. The log, now afire, had gone unseen, blocked from view by her own plume of magic until it was almost upon her. With no choice but the one she'd already committed to, she heaved at the stone slab. At the last second, the log exploded against the raised column, saving her life. But a shower of embers flew into the wizard's face. She stumbled back, slapping at the burning bits assaulting her masked face.

Omatuu sliced upward with one hand. A ripple of energy closed with a stumbling Vethati across the way and knocked her onto her backside. He cut the air in a downward arc, slamming her in place. She gave a pained scream. Almost, I'd forgotten she was human.

Singed beard smoking, Omatuu licked his fingers and casually snuffed out a glowing ember as he covered the distance to his downed opponent. He pressed his fingers to his temples. An onyx sphere blossomed between his eyes. It swirled, expanding, then snaked toward the prostrate Vethati, disappearing into one of the eye holes of her mask.

She writhed, palms clapping the sides of her head.

Omatuu laughed.

Desperate, she tried to rise, but another blast of wind slammed her back to the earth. The white mask tumbled away.

The Order of Odd Seekers ran.

"Over," Distra said.

Omatuu waved his Seekers to his side as he loomed over his inert opponent. When I straggled in behind the others, it was clear Vethathi was in a state of torment. She moaned and shook as if cut in a thousand places and then dipped in salt.

I'd been thrilled to see the battle commence, but now, seeing the result, I felt ill.

"Worry not, I've broken her." Omatuu clasped his hands behind his back. Hands capable of hurling logs, summoning fire, and calling the winds. A thrill spitted me as I considered having the same powers.

Omatuu continued. "I must admit, you surprised me with that simple maneuver. For a Second, your basics are exceedingly strong. Too dull-witted to be a Prime though." He sighed. "You should have listened to me."

Distra stepped closer to him, a long, curved dagger in hand.

"My Head Seeker," he said. "Please relieve Vethati of her wizard's knot."

Vethati whined, sucking in breaths like a terror-stricken child.

Omatuu chuckled. "You put up a better fight than expected, so I'll not kill you outright." He looked to the surrounding woods. "It never hurts to put a thorn in the sides of the other cabals every now and then, does it?"

"Won't a thorn given be a thorn returned?"

Omatuu whirled. "You're still here, Hellas?" Spiteful incredulity dripped from his words. "I thought you died in your cups last night. Or maybe that was the night before? Regardless, you'd make better worm-food than you would a Seeker, so do me a kindness and withhold all further...*wisdom.*"

The rest of the Seekers fell silent. Chin jutting resolutely, Distra made her way behind the moaning wizard. She crouched and gathered a handful of silver hair before sawing it free. *What value could an old dead ponytail have?* I bit back the urge to start asking questions. Beyond their willingness to engage in consensual violence, I didn't know these people.

Vethati whimpered and then her eyes snapped open, flashing white moons to match the face paint of her Seekers. She gazed skyward, her mouth opening and closing as if testing an injured jaw. Rising on unsteady legs, she pitched forward, chest leading her, vacant eyes fixed on the horizon.

"A wizard's mind *is* their life." Omatuu addressed the rest of the Cloudbreakers. "You need only lose one to lose the other. Something you would do well to understand if you're to survive."

I swallowed. I'd never met a wizard and this one had just condemned another to a life of madness and laughed about it. Ever since the moment he'd appeared on the slope, my fear of the man had grown. Watching him dismantle Vethati hadn't helped.

Omatuu turned and gave a perfunctory nod to Distra. "Congratulations."

Hellas clapped the Head Seeker on her shoulder. Distra did not smile, though I got the sense she should be celebrating.

Lifting his chin, Omatuu turned to regard me. It seemed he'd forgotten I was there. He removed his hat a moment, giving me my first glimpse of him in the light. Sharp—that was my first thought. His eyes said it all, cutting into whatever he looked upon with unwavering focus. A volcano could have erupted behind him, and still, his gaze would have remained, boring into mine.

His hair was bundled atop his head, tied in place by his own strands. He traced a finger along the inside of his hat then drew it out for inspection. "Blood...from my tumble, no doubt." With a sniff, he placed the hat back on his head.

He stepped toward me, blocking the rising sun and swallowing me in his shadow. "You're young, and by the look of you, a woeful ingrate equal in measure to Hellas."

Fear held me, tighter than a coffin. From what I'd seen that morning, one thing was clear: do not cross Omatuu. "I...uh." I searched the ground for answers.

"Stop," he said. "Your stammering only lends evidence to my conclusion. To top it off, you look nearly dead. Why didn't you visit a bloodtrader? They would have given you respite."

A bloodtrader? I'd never heard of such a thing. My earlier conversation with Distra came back to me—she had looked me up and down and asked, "Why?"

It appeared I'd missed something in my journey to become a Seeker. "I don't know what you're talking about."

Omatuu glared. "You wandered into the Wildness without knowledge of bloodtraders?"

I shrugged, sending a lance of pain through my neck where I was still horribly stiff.

Hellas was the first to laugh, slapping a hand onto his immense belly. Others joined. Even Distra wheezed—her version of laughter.

A grin hooked up under one of Omatuu's cheeks. "I'm mistaken. You're a fool by degrees of magnitude such that it makes even Hellas's stupidity pale in comparison. If it were not for the wizard's edict, that all Seekers must be given sanctuary in a cabal, I would not take you." Omatuu paused and stroked the long braid of charcoal beard descending his chest. "By the Power, you *are* a Seeker, aren't you?"

In that moment, wilting beneath a true wizard's inquiry, I didn't feel like it. Did Seekers have to know what a bloodtrader was, or the use of a wizard's knot for that matter? I didn't, and it made me worry I'd just thrown my life away when I could be back at home helping Trin and her family.

Every Seeker watched me. Distra spat. A gentle breeze stirred Omatuu's gray robes, but he was as impassive as a block of ice.

In the distance, Vethati scrabbled over an outcrop of rock and out of view. Everyone's journey had to end somewhere. Mine, I decided, was not here. The part of me that questioned my fate had died with my mother. This was what I meant to do. As awed as I was by Omatuu, I refused to let his degradations sow further doubt in me.

My fate was my own.

"I *am* a Seeker." My heartbeat quickened. I balled one hand into a fist. "But you're wrong. I'm no fool."

Hellas shifted, eyes darting back and forth between Omatuu and I. He feared the wizard, which in my estimation made him smarter than Omatuu claimed.

The wizard Prime of the Cloudbreakers smiled mirthlessly. "Young, near death, and stupid. What more could I ask for in a Seeker but perhaps arrogance?" His expression turned placid. "It's brazen correcting me like that. Some might even say suicidal. What's your name?"

"El." Anger stirred in me and my tone betrayed it. I trod dangerous ground, speaking to him like that. But I'd already decided Omatuu was worth hating. I may have been young and half-dead, but he was self-righteous, cruel, and a killer.

"From here on, you will no longer be known as El. You'll be known as Jester. Now...*Jester*, how long have you been out here?"

"A week," I said flatly. "I think."

Someone gasped. The other Seekers glanced at each other in surprise.

Omatuu arched an eyebrow. "Are you also a liar? That long on your own in the Wildness without supplies? And you never visited a bloodtrader for help?"

I nodded.

"Interesting," Omatuu said. "Well, despite your flaws, you have the courage to be a Cloudbreaker. And some luck, it would seem." His voice took on a formal tone as he waved a hand dismissively. "Jester, do you consent to joining the cabal known as the Cloudbreakers? Or will you return to your life as a walking corpse?"

Looking around, I didn't fathom there was much choice to it. The Elder had fired me like an arrow into the unknown and I like to think I'd finally struck my target. Images of dueling wizards flashed through my mind. The desire to wield such powers ached in every part of me.

I control my destiny.

"I will be a Cloudbreaker."

"Then it's agreed," Omatuu said. "My part of the bargain maintained by the cabals is done. You're on your own now. Sadly, time will prove to both of us that I'm right about you. Only fools contest the wisdom of their betters. And there is none here who is more my lesser than you, Jester. Luck may have gotten you this far, but you'll end up like Vethati." The wizard sneered. "She thought she could beat me—her superior in all ways. Arrogance was her downfall. Remember where it got her...or don't. It matters little to me. You're destined to share her fate all the same. And sooner than you think."

CHAPTER NINE

HARSH RECKONINGS

The journey back to the Cloudbreakers' camp was not how I pictured it. I thought I might find solidarity among the Seekers, a kinship born of shared danger and desire. Then I recalled the Elder telling me it wasn't just giants and wizards I must worry over. Other Seekers would gut me if it brought them a step closer to magic powers.

Still weary from my days in the Wildness, I drifted back from the front of the long column to the middle despite pushing myself to go as fast as I could. Already, I was demonstrating weakness after Omatuu's scornful declarations. Nowhere near ideal.

The Cloudbreakers were like any group of humans. Some were terrible and some were less so. Belefi was the former. In the same spirit as Omatuu, she seemed to delight in tormenting me with self-elevating barbs. Given she was two years my elder and previously the youngest Cloudbreaker, I assumed she hazed me because she herself had been the most recent recipient of such treatment.

An older man joined her as I lagged. Then another. Their worn faces split into scummy grins as they belittled me. I acted like I didn't hear them and convinced myself they sought to hurt me because they'd become jaded with their own failures.

But they saw through it. They wanted me to know they were stronger.

"Do you hear something?" Belefi gripped my shoulder, one hand cupped to her ear. She may have been as tall as Trin, but her looks matched her hideous personality. "I think I hear tinkly bells!"

Jester...I hated the name. And I hated Omatuu more for giving it to me.

One of Belefi's followers strode past. "Nice motley, Jester!" He plucked the tattered shirt hanging around my shoulders. "You trade a pig for it?"

Suddenly, the man flew to his face in the dirt, shoved from behind by Hellas. My eyes went wide as I leaped to avoid the man rolling in the dirt. "Aye, it was your mother's shirt! Nasty old hog, just like her boy. Now piss off," Hellas barked over a shoulder.

Belefi scowled and helped the man to his feet. I turned to Hellas who smiled broadly. "I can't believe no one told you about bloodtraders. Here, eat this." He handed me a bread roll which I bit into greedily.

The heavyset man brushed back a cascade of red-gold locks. I'd been listening to the conversations of Hellas and the others all morning—when I wasn't busy being harassed—and from what I gathered, Omatuu's condemnation of the man was misplaced. I suspected he'd been labeled as stupid by the wizard Prime because of his joviality. Of all the Cloudbreakers, he smiled and laughed the most. The man put me at ease and I found myself trusting him. Although from the way he carried himself, I suspected the dagger and ax at his belt weren't just for show.

"Thank you," I said, keeping my eyes forward.

"Give me any reason to cuff that asshole and I'll take it." He paused. "I thought bloodtraders were the only way anyone ended up out here. My uncle knew a bloodtrader. Used to buy ogre blood from him by the barrel. Put two drops in every tankard he sold. One cup was all it took to keep them addicted and coming back for more. Crafty bastard, my uncle."

I threw Hellas a sharp look. "How were you summoned to be a Seeker?" Did everyone get a scroll? I hesitated in telling him about mine. The hierarchy of leadership within the cabal wasn't yet clear to me and I didn't trust Omatuu. I had already decided I wouldn't tell him anything I didn't have to.

"Same as most. Skinmap to a bloodtrader. From my uncle, like I said." Hellas shook his head. "Never thought I'd have to tell someone in a cabal about this. You don't know what a skinmap is either, do you?"

I didn't.

"Once you get to a bloodtrader, you give them their skinmap back so they can hand it out again. They're made of treated troll flesh. Can't be burned and the ink never fades. Then they give you food and drink and send you back out to find a cabal." Hellas squinted at me suspiciously, but before he could ask about my unique summoning, I fired off a question.

"What *is* a bloodtrader?"

He shrugged. "It's pretty much what it sounds like. They trade in blood, mostly. Ogre's blood to brewers in the cities, keeping the populace dull for the Brotherhood, or selling troll's blood to Stormlords and rich merchants so they can live longer. What you really need to know about them is they'll help out anyone—for the right price, of course. See, they know if they can create good relationships with a lot of Seekers, the lucky ones will become wizards someday. Any group of armed and daring warriors can take down an ogre or troll on occasion. But wizards..."

Hellas stretched his arms high overhead and yawned. "They can tackle much bigger game. They're the ones who bring in the more rare and valuable wares."

"Like what?"

"Body parts from dangerous creatures. Plants from other realms. Sacred books, sacred this, sacred that. The list is exhaustive, and once you hit the bottom, that's probably only the start. Just trust that bloodtraders, whether you love them or hate them, are the hubs for all things magical."

He looked at me with a funny expression on his face. "It's truly crazy for me to hear you didn't know about them. Every Seeker I've met has been called into the Wildness because they have some distant connection to a bloodtrader. Other than that, I've never heard of anyone just wandering out here and living." He clapped me on the shoulder. "But hey, now I have!"

We wound through a forest of charred snags and scorched earth. Hellas heard an attack had been carried out on a wizard from another cabal. "Wizard won." He gestured at what looked at first to be the gutted remains of a tree stump.

Frowning, I peered closer—flinched back. A skull stared back at me. Three more piles of ashen remains dotted the clearing.

Hellas sighed. "Seekers lost."

No one had bothered to bury them. I chewed the inside of my cheek as worry surged through my belly.

We trudged on through the fire-scorched area in a sort of reverent silence. As we neared a line of healthier trees, I asked Hellas, "What made you decide to become a Seeker?"

"No one decides to become a Seeker. They decide to become a wizard. To possess the Power. Same as everyone. Being a Seeker's just part of the necessary cruelty we all endure along the way."

"What about the Stormseye?" I cast about furtively, my old habit of worrying over being caught by knights unrelenting. "They say the Power is a sacred destiny. Don't we risk their ire by pursuing it on our own?"

"We're about as much of a threat to them as a pack of wild squirrels is to us." Hellas arched an eyebrow as he pushed out his lower lip. "Our relationship with the Brotherhood is somewhat...parasitic. Without Seekers and wizards supplying bloodtraders with blood, the Stormlords would have to spend too much of their own time tracking it down rather than discovering ways to become more powerful. So they let us do it for them."

I thought about that a moment before asking my next question. "Why don't they just get their own Seekers?"

Hellas smiled. "What do you think Stormseye knights are?"

I nodded slowly, understanding dawning. "They keep their cities in squalor. Then they make everyone go to sermons and force-feed them drivel about the Power being a divine gift for the few. With our lives in such poor condition, the hope for something better gets the Stormlords recruits. Every leathertongue aspires to be a lictor one day, don't they?"

"Sounds about right," grumbled Hellas. "Ain't much different than it is out here. Except we actually do become wizards once in a while, unlike those sad ingrates scraping out their Stormlord's chamber pot."

I watched my filthy toes float forward in silence. "I never knew."

Hellas lowered his voice to a conspiratorial whisper. "It's okay, El. You grew up under the Great Archon's rule—everyone in Kelundar has. Only once we become Seekers do we start peeling back the lies."

The muscles in my jaw tightened. I balled a fist, crushing the last bit of roll into a flaking mess. "The Great Archon...why doesn't anyone do anything about him? Why don't the cabals unite and bring him down?"

"If the Stormseye went to war against the cabals, it'd be over quicker than a hummingbird mates. Even without the Great Archon, the Stormlords would obliterate us." He rubbed his russet and gold beard. "But, it might weaken them just enough that they'd be susceptible to the Illuminated Path. Neither would risk that war though. Naught but cinders and worms would remain. Instead, the Brotherhood just accepts the bloodtraders and allows them to go about their business. They fear the Path. Not us."

Illuminated Path? It felt as though every answer only led to more questions. Discovering a world outside the one I'd always known was dizzying.

Hellas took note of my disoriented state. "You'll get there. It takes time. I won't say this life is easy, but waking up every day knowing you could have a wizard's knot by nightfall—that's what keeps me out here. It's what keeps us all going." A somber look fell over him. "Not easy at all. You'll see and do things...things you'd never wish your loved ones to know about." Sorrow deepened the lines of his expression. "You seem like a good kid. So you should know this now because you're free to go at any time. You don't always get a wizard's knot like Distra did last night. Wizards only challenge each other in special circumstances. Otherwise the only way to get a wizard's knot is to hunt them." He grew quiet, his gaze settling on the ruined patch of forest where the skeletons lay. "You have to kill a wizard, El."

You seem like a good kid.

The contradiction held me in its breathless embrace. A moral bear trap biting into me. Either I carried out murder to gain magic power or I died with nothing like my family had.

Debate raged within. What was bad? What was good? Savage beings ruled the world I'd always known, and for them, there was no cure but death. Someone had to liberate the dying mothers and starving children; the beaten men with shattered dreams lining the streets, bartering dignity for scraps of food. If I had to kill a stranger in order to gain the power to save countless lives, I would do it.

For how else was I to slay the Great Archon?

His was the hand that choked the life from Kelundar. His sermons that suffocated autonomy and progress. His oppressive and violent doctrines that led my family to their graves!

In that moment I knew, I would stop at nothing to end the Great Archon's reign.

Nothing validated this more than my reaction to Hellas's declaration. When I heard I'd have to kill a wizard, my gut did not turn. My heartbeat did not quicken. My legs remained steady, unshaken by fear.

I felt nothing but resolve. Purpose.

No hesitation.

You seem like a good kid.

Nothing at all.

CHAPTER TEN

CLOUDBREAKERS

The burden of my training fell on the Head Seeker. As soon as we returned to camp, I was Distra's problem.

She tossed a bundle of crude poles wrapped in canvas in the dust at my feet. A hammer and a half dozen pegs followed. We stood at the edge of camp, just inside a circular berm planted with rows of gashbrush and dotted with fir trees for cover. Anyone seeking to enter the camp would have to come through a single entry point, or hack through six feet of thorn-covered branches. Gashbrush—nasty stuff.

Distra instructed me on how to get my tent set up. I thanked her. Before she could go, I asked a question that had been burning inside me ever since she'd sawed off Vethati's ponytail.

"What will you do now that you have a wizard's knot? Aren't you done?"

Distra turned slowly back to me. "I find a tower...trade food for the secret location of the Spirit Gardens. Not done." On the last word, she flicked a hand sign, punctuating it.

"Spirit Gardens?"

She strode off, ending the conversation.

I sighed and watched the Head Seeker cross the grounds.

Ramshackle tents encircled campfires in clusters. Logs had been rolled into place for sitting at various points and rudimentary chairs were cut into a handful of stumps. The camp wasn't as advanced as a street row in Cannalis, but it didn't need to be. The basics for living were all there: a well for drinking water; a pavilion for butchering and smoking meat; a small garden and an area for carpentry. I got the impression the Cloudbreakers were doing better than most of those still living under the Stormseye Brotherhood's thumb.

A few larger tents, presumably for storing weaponry and food, sat near a massive mound at the camp's center where Omatuu lived. I'd never seen a structure quite like it. Exposed roots burst forth from its base like the legs of a monstrous spider, then sank back into the ground after a half dozen feet. More branches twisted skyward from the mound to form Omatuu's quarters, a latticework of roots shaped like a tulip.

There was no apparent entrance.

That is, until Distra ascended the steep mound and Omatuu parted the squat fortress's walls for her.

Footsteps thudded up behind me as I gawked.

I'd never set up a tent before, so it was a relief to find Hellas standing there offering to help. He nodded toward the Head Seeker as the roots slid back into place. "Distra has a way about her, doesn't she?"

"What do you mean?"

He held two poles together, then motioned for me to tie them. "For starters, she's not one for making friendly as you can tell."

I shook my head. "I like Distra. She's...not mean. Not like the others."

Hellas smiled. "I don't even think Distra likes Distra. You may be the only one who does."

"But she's Head Seeker. Doesn't that make her our leader?"

"Sure it does." With a loop of rope in hand, Hellas handed me a hammer and peg. "Distra is a combination of intimidating and efficient. A group like this needs a hammer to nail it into place on occasion. Can't be someone everyone loves. Omatuu's a lot of things, but stupid isn't one of them. He knows what a Head Seeker needs to be like. That doesn't stop us from being jealous of her, though."

"Jealous?" I hammered the peg into place.

"Head Seeker always gets the wizard's knot after a successful duel. Our Prime beat the Order of Odd's Second. Now, Distra's done with the hardest part. Only a few steps away from being a wizard herself. The rest of us..." he scratched behind an ear. "We'll have to get lucky and score one on our own."

I looked up from where I knelt on the ground. "Once you've got a wizard's topknot, that's it right?"

Hellas stepped back alongside me to survey my tent. "This is looking fair."

I nodded.

He wiped his nose. "Alright, so it goes like this. First, get a wizard's knot. Then, find a wizard's tower. When you do, you'll have to trade them food for the secret location of the Spirit Gardens." A thought seemed to strike Hellas as he raised his eyebrows. "You could do those in reverse order, too, I suppose. The only problem there is that once you know where the Spirit Gardens are, you'll be desperate to get there. That means you'll be desperate to get a wizard's knot. But desperate Seekers are stupid Seekers and stupid Seekers are dead Seekers. There's what's left of the last Cloudbreaker who got desperate." He jabbed a thick finger at Omatuu's earthen fortress. A fire-scorched headband hung on the rugged filament of a burl. "I don't recommend such a gambit. Wizards are a crafty lot and Omatuu's one of the craftiest. They take precautions."

My throat tightened. With effort, I swallowed and tried pushing confidence into my voice. "Understood. Kill a wizard. Claim their topknot. Find a tower. Trade them food for the secret of the Spirit Gardens—"

"Damn. Hate to say it, but I skipped a step. The Occuli Rift. Before you get a seed from the Spirit Gardens and raise your own tower, you've gotta drop the wizard's knot into the Occuli Rift. In return, it'll spit out a Tome of Callings. That's your lifeline to the Power, and it's the only way you'll learn to fight. *Then* you get a seed from the Spirit Gardens." His hand flipped back and forth lazily in the air as if he was bored of listing tasks. "Plant seed, grow a tower, hope a Seeker finds you, study for months to learn the war callings and the Hand of Life spell..." He sighed. "...Tower slowly shrinks to the ground, step out, and poof, you're a wizard! Not too hard now, is it?" He winked.

My shoulders slumped in resignation.

Hellas punched my shoulder consolingly. "Nothing's too impossible if others have done it before, right? You're young. Might take a couple of decades, but you'll get there. Maybe start with learning how to kill wizards, eh?"

———————————————+———————————————

The child of yesterday needed to be smothered, a way made for the wizard that would be. In thought and action, I could no longer be the 'good kid,' as Hellas saw me. I had to adopt an attitude that allowed me to cast away my fears in the face of death like a cloak that over-warmed me. I had to sacrifice my morality, to think of killing as a way to save lives. Others needed to be treated as stepping stones on my path to the Power if I was to someday bring about the fall of the Great Archon.

But first, I needed to kill a wizard.

And that meant I needed weapons training.

The first month was difficult. Between twice-daily training sessions and hours of chores, new blisters covered my hands by nightfall. Sometimes they throbbed so painfully, I struggled to fall asleep. My joints, especially where forearm met bicep, were in a constant state of aching stiffness. Whenever I climbed into the ring, I climbed back out moments later, utterly humiliated by my opponent and cursing my body's betrayal—I could hardly hold the weapons I was meant to master.

The first month went so badly that by the second one, Distra had cut back my chores so she had time to instruct me privately, though I often wondered why. Most of the time, she treated me as a fruitless obligation...as if I would be dead in a matter of months like Omatuu claimed. Once, Belefi disarmed me in the practice circle in three moves, then pinned me to the ground with her knees to slap me gently as a ring of others watched and laughed. Nothing about the moment had hurt more than when Distra had grunted in disgust and stalked away.

But I'd been dealing with pain my entire life. While Belefi's ridicule paled compared to Distra's indifference, neither stopped me. On the contrary, such things fueled me to train harder.

I wasn't going to convince Distra she was wrong about me with my words. She needed to be shown.

I refused the reduction of chores and instead woke well before sunrise in order to have them finished with enough time for my training. Once I'd received my Cloudbreakers' garb, I tore a blood-stained tunic I'd pilfered from the storage tent into strips and wrapped my hands. Blood still dripped from my fingertips by day's end, but each time I winced, I grit my teeth and told myself I loved the feeling because I had chosen it. I even went so far as to convince myself I wanted more. If I grew accustomed to trivial pains, they wouldn't distract me in a future duel with another wizard, or when defending myself against hunting parties of Seekers.

Day after day, I soaked in the lashing, aching, dull throbbing pain. At sunset, when the others found their seats at the fire or roamed the perimeter on guard duty, I snuck off to an orchard to practice more. A master would strive for nothing less, and my best chance at killing a wizard was to be a master.

Being the sole person who believed in me was a lonely endeavor. Night after night, I searched the faces of my peers sitting around the campfire, awash in its flickering orange glow. Women and men old enough to be grandparents. A few close to my age, like Belefi, though none younger than eighteen like me. If the Cloudbreakers were a reflection of other cabals—which I suspected they were—then I would be competing against Seekers with more wisdom, strength, and speed.

The law of the gutters sang through my mind.

If not richer, bigger. If not bigger, quicker. If not quicker, smarter. If not smarter, dead.

But what of ambition? I had that in abundance.

It dragged me out of bed each morning; it numbed the pain in my bloody hands; it acted as a soothing salve to my ego each time another Seeker knocked me to my backside. And on the rare occasions I glimpsed Omatuu, it blinded me to his contempt.

At the end of the second month, Distra alone saw a fire in me worth feeding. Hellas was convivial whenever our paths crossed, but I was preoccupied with training and he was too busy drinking around the campfire each night. Distra, however, offered more of her time to help me. Where she used to grunt in displeasure or shake her head each time I messed up, she now motioned vigorously at me whenever I did something well, too.

Two more months came and went, as did the variety of weapons that found my hand. Axes were heavy. Swords were too fine and too rare to waste on a new Seeker. Bows...I was nightmarishly bad with those. Distra suggested daggers, but the spear made the most sense to me. Its reach removed the weakness of my height and it was versatile; I could throw it if need be. I wanted to train solely with the spear and told Distra as much.

"Too complex." She went on to explain that in a fight with a lot of hiding, and dodging of fireballs, the spear was unwieldy and as likely to get me killed as save me. Yet to me, the spear came naturally. I practiced with it every night in the nearby apple orchard. This led me to belabor my position on its superiority for weeks. I pleaded with Distra to let me quit the other weapons in favor of the spear.

"No," she said, terse but restrained in her annoyance as I dogged her heels near the orchard. "Train more with ax. Make you stronger. Flail right, kill easy."

I let out a frustrated growl, turned, and hurled my weapon. The spear slid soundlessly through a hanging apple then embedded into a tree with a schlunk.

Distra stopped, eyes narrowed around the wobbling haft where it stuck in the tree. "Fine. Split time between dagger and spear."

I stifled a smile. "Thank you." It was then that I noticed a pack slung over her shoulder. "Where are you going?"

"Hunt." Her hands moved in tandem with her hollowed-out voice. "Wizard sighting."

I begged her to take me with her but she refused. "Beat Belefi first. Then you go."

CHAPTER ELEVEN

LESSONS IN FRIENDS

One advantage to having so few friends was having more time to myself. Belefi was stronger than me, so I took Distra's advice—at least some of it. I continued my regular training with the spear, but instead of splitting my hours with the dagger, I started using the ax to build more power. Stumps and dead trees fell beneath my chopping blade until they were naught but pulpy sinews. Afterward, I carried dismantled logs in a circle around the encampment, breathing heavy from exertion. One day, I hauled them up Omatuu's mound but that quickly ended when the wizard flew from his fortress with a crazed expression. He'd not needed to say anything for me to know it was time to complete my strengthening exercises elsewhere.

As the weeks wore on, I got the sense that the older one became in the Wildness, the more likely they were to adopt the Seeker's life as simply that: life. Not just a sign on the road to something better. Even with my increased strength, as well as hundreds of hours accrued since my last sparring session with Belefi, I believe it was this slow creeping resignation that gave me my edge over her.

Swaying with confidence across the circle from me, she held one hand behind her back, and the other on a wooden ax handle. If she struck me as hard as she could in the skull, it could do serious damage, if not death. Headshots may have been against the rules, but I wasn't putting anything past her.

She sucked in her lips as if about to tell a joke. "Before we start, I have a gift for you, Jester." Her hand whipped around in an arc. A bundle flopped to the ground before me. It was a strip of leather with a few bland pieces of cloth sewed into it.

A jester's hat.

Half of the Seekers who'd gathered to watch the fight roared with laughter, while the other half smirked and shook their heads at the childish taunt.

I gave a thin smile, scooped up the hat from the dust, and placed it on my head. "You'll look the greater fool here when I beat you while wearing it."

The laughter trailed away.

"Teach her a lesson, El!" Hellas bellowed.

Belefi's ugly face twisted into a sneer. She spat, and I made a face of mock fear. In truth, fear had made my legs heavy and my hands unusually damp. Belefi didn't need to know that, though. Confidence always cowed people like her.

I fell into a crouch as she strode toward me, her face a mask of bloody intent. I sidestepped and ducked as the ax handle flew overhead, a blow I wouldn't have soon recovered from if it landed.

I shot the blunted end of my spear at her throat, striking it square. Her eyes went wide. She paused and gulped, clutching at her throat. Putting all my strength behind the blow, I took a step and twisted, slamming the haft into her lower legs. She upended onto her back with a thud.

Then I was on her, clutching my weapon with both hands as I pressed it down against her struggling hands and neck. "Who's the fool now?"

Belefi gasped, air finally returning as Hellas jerked me back off her. "Easy, El."

Someone whistled low as I broke free of Hellas's grasp, tore off the jester's hat, and flung it away before stalking from the arena.

I snatched up my iron-tipped spear on my way to the orchard. I'd done what I needed to but that didn't excuse me from my aspirations of mastery. There were apples in need of earnest skewering. I imagined them as the heads and hearts of wizards as I slashed and stabbed myself into a state of sweaty contentedness.

Later in the day, Distra returned from her hunt to find me still slaying juicy foes. From the way she glared, I knew her hunt hadn't been successful. Her hands whirred. "It's foolish not to be practicing with bow and daggers most."

Over the course of our time together, I'd come to understand her hand speech to the point that it took little time to interpret.

"I want to master the spear first." I nicked an apple with a stab. "If I'm to be included in hunts now that I've defeated Belefi, I need to be proficient with something, and this is what works best. Being half-terrible with daggers or worse with a bow seems less helpful than being great with a spear."

"You're not great," she wheezed, then worked her hands. "You may have beaten Belefi, but you're still not ready. Two Seekers died yesterday because we didn't work well as a team. There's no room for selfishness on a hunt."

I looked at Distra, sniffed, then slashed a trio of apples in a single swing. "Is that really the reason?" I thought she meant to scare me into agreeing with her by telling me about the death of the Seekers, but I hadn't left Trin, nearly died in the Wildness, and trained myself to the bone for four months to be limited in what I was allowed to do. I'd left Cannalis for freedom and power. "Or is it because you think I'm too young?" My spear snaked out, piercing fruit-flesh. "Or too weak?" An apple clung to my spear's tip as I swung it to a stop in front of Distra. "Apple?"

Her mouth became a flat line. Quick as a flash, her dagger left her hip and sliced a distant apple in two. The halves dropped to the ground.

"A no, then," I murmured.

Distra was in no laughing mood. She whirled on me, gesturing wild-ly. "If you're hunting wizards, you should be far enough away to shoot them with a bow, or close enough to stab them with a dagger—any distance between is a death sentence. When you're good with both bow and dagger, you get to hunt. Understand?"

She whipped back around, casting a second dagger after the first. It thudded into a tree, shivering in place.

Omatuu emerged from the shadows behind the tree. I held my breath and took an uncertain step back.

"It doesn't matter, does it, Distra?" He stopped beside her knife and traced the length of the hilt with a fingertip. "How many hunts do you truly think Jester will survive?"

Only a wrap of loincloth covered his manhood. Gray robes and belts were slung over one arm, and he clutched his wide brimmed hat in one hand. From the dampness of his charcoal beard and lustrous dark hair pulled back into a topknot, it was clear he'd been bathing at the nearby river. What surprised me was how strong he looked. Cords of lean muscle covered every inch of his wiry frame. The white lightning tattoo stretching the length of his arm glowed, even during the day.

He didn't look at me—not once—as he spoke with Distra. If he meant to stir hate in me by ignoring my presence, he had succeeded.

Distra shrugged. Her eyes found mine and I sensed some compassion in them, as if they were saying, "I'm sorry." As Head Seeker, I knew she had a better understanding of the wizard than any other. Her pale blue eyes told me I would not like what came next.

Like a stalking tiger, Omatuu approached. "Of course, I could be wrong as I was with Hellas. He has survived far longer than I predicted. Fool and drunkard he may be, but the man has shown a surprising skill for not dying."

My response was unwise, but certainly, it felt good. "You mistake Hellas's kindness for foolishness."

Beads of water flung from Omatuu as his head whipped toward me, smooth voice both excited and harsh. "Oh but it is, Jester! There's nothing clearer." He gave a fake smile. "Let me tell you a story. When I was a Seeker, I was not quite so young as yourself—though of an equivalent ego—when I found a wizard's tower. I'd already whetted my blade in the blood of a wizard, so I had a topknot. As one does, I went to the city of Ferrek to fetch the wizard food. Yet I made one mistake. Ignoring the warnings of the Death Bard's wizard Prime, I invited a friend along to help me. I'd spent years in the Wildness, and this person had become like a brother to me, so of course, I wanted him to receive the secret location of the Spirit Gardens, too. I knew the years had been difficult on my friend. Delusions of us claiming the Power together were...misguided."

Omatuu leaned forward until his face hovered over mine. "It was kindness that had me do something so dull-witted. See, he didn't have a wizard's knot of his own. So with all the pieces set up before him—by me—there was but one thing left to do. Under the cover of night, he held a dagger to my throat and told me if I didn't give him the wizard's knot, he'd cut me ear to ear without a second thought." Omatuu's voice jumped higher in register as he repeated his last words. "Without a second thought. That part hurt most. For me, at least."

We stared at each other for a long time. A twitch of one of Omatuu's eyelids was the only betrayal of emotion under the hardened man's mask.

"Tell me, Jester, did I give him the wizard's knot?"

I shook my head.

"Right you are. It was his life or mine. Kindness is a fool's dream. Best to kill it before it kills you." Omatuu's chin shot into the air as he squared his shoulders to Distra. "I want you to take Jester on your next hunt. I need troll's blood." He smiled at me. "This brilliant lesson has prepared you, I imagine. You are ready, aren't you, Jester?"

I worried that Omatuu had the power to see a person's future, or some arcane object that told him who was or wasn't made to be a wizard. The truth of his malicious intent was likely more mundane but no less damning, I realized. Years of watching Seekers come and go, live and die, ascend to wizard powers or grow old and useless in the Wildness, had given Omatuu confidence in knowing who might cut it and who wouldn't. This time, he was dead wrong.

"I am," I said defiantly.

Distra snorted and looked away.

Omatuu chuckled. "Oh you're ready, alright. The only question is what you are ready for. I suspect it will be a most unpleasant surprise." He waved dismissively. "Goodbye, Jester."

I glared holes into his erect spine as he strode away, whistling to himself.

Distra slapped the back of my head.

"What?" I said.

"Idiot!"

That night, I mentally prepared for my first hunt. It would be a lie to claim I wasn't terrified. The thrill I had imagined as I practiced with my spear in the orchard winnowed inside me as I lay awake in my tent. I tried talking myself into a state of calm but failed. I'd already heard too much about my quarry. Fangs. Snake-like reflexes. Tough skin. Sinewy arms and deadly claws.

Belefi was one thing.

But trolls were an entirely different breed of danger.

Three nightmares assaulted my sleep, ensuring I would wake for my first hunt far from refreshed.

In the first, my mother was still alive. "Please, El. Please!" She gasped and wailed and reached skeletal fingers for me but I didn't move. For what seemed hours in the time of nightmares, she screamed while I stood in silence in the alley beyond our home, unwilling to move my feet and go to her side. Nothing impeded me from doing so. I wanted to see her but my dream self was unwilling. By choice alone, I stayed rooted in place listening to the final gurgles of her dying.

The sound...

The sound of it. There are things in this world neither potion nor spell can eliminate.

My second nightmare was a simpler kind of fear made manifest. What I imagined to be a troll gripped my arms, then bit my head off. I shouted for help as its jaws descended. No one heard nor cared. It was like being in Cannalis again, I realized days later. Just meat for those more powerful than I.

In the third nightmare, the Cloudbreakers were arrayed before me in a line with arms and legs bound. I stepped before each one and laid my spear blade on their shoulder and asked, "Who is your god?"

Tears in their eyes, they said, "You are," before I slashed their throats. Horror stretched the lines of their cheeks as their mouths gaped and their eyes rolled to white. Shocked expressions paled at the understanding of my betrayal. Hellas, and then Distra, were last to die, but die they did.

Omatuu laughed when I asked him who his god was. "You?" he sneered. I thrust with all my strength but may as well have been stabbing solid iron. His laughter built to a singular pitch that drowned out all but a painful ringing. My useless spear fell from weak hands. Helpless, I dropped to my knees amid the dead and covered my ears as the ringing intensified. When I looked at them, my fingers were black with alien blood.

I woke up doused in sweat and wheezing. With a head full of cotton, I quickly prepared for the hunt.

"By the Power, Jester, you look like a mid-morning latrine." Hellas folded over his own belly as he whipped aside the tent flap. "Nothing a little ogre's blood won't cure."

I blinked at him dumbly.

"Here." He handed me a thin, stoppered vial.

I popped the cork, sniffed it, and then jerked away. "Smells like roses and carcasses."

Hellas laughed. "Yup, that's ogre's blood for you. But it'll keep you awake and alert for most of a day. In a pinch, it can also wake someone who's taken a beating. And it helps with digestion, so it'll get things going, if you know what I mean."

A rancid, sweet taste pooled at the back of my throat. Disgusting as it was, it seemed to have its uses. I shoved it into my pocket.

Dressed in Cloudbreakers' livery—a gray headband and a tabard cinched around my waist by a thick leather belt—I grabbed my spear. Distra made sure I had a dagger but didn't push a bow. A Cloudbreaker named Gorik with more wrinkles than a tree has bark painted a bolt of lightning from my temple to my chin.

"This'll protect ye," he said. I sincerely doubted it. Only my spear and my wits could do that.

Gorik didn't go on hunts anymore; he was relegated to face painting and camp defense. No more than a third of the Cloudbreakers were allowed to leave the camp at a time but that didn't mean the ones who stayed for defense were the best of them.

Hellas fell in beside me to whisper, "Happens to more Seekers than I care to think about."

Not me, I thought. I will not be Gorik. The old Seeker had a gentle hand and easy smile. Yet, I had no doubt that he'd kill me if it got him closer to the Power, just as Omatuu had warned.

Kindness is a fool's dream—best to kill it before it kills you.

A score of Cloudbreakers passed beyond the camp's wall of gash-brush. Omatuu remained behind, as did another fifty Seekers of our cabal.

"Your first hunt!" Hellas tested the point of my spear with a fingertip. He winced, then sucked at the place it pricked him. "A spear, eh? Interesting choice for troll hunting. Bastards are quick as snakes and got a ridiculous reach. Better to use bows, but if we have to get close, you'll be wanting to score big cuts. Damn things heal quick."

I forced a laugh, but inside I whimpered, my courage all but gutted. My hands had started to shake. Then I remembered the ogre's blood in my pocket. If all it took was a swig of putrid drink to ensure my first hunt wasn't ruined by shaky nerves, the momentary discomfort of a single taste was worth it.

I pulled forth the vial and unstopped it. But before it touched my lips, Distra appeared at my side and seized my wrist. "No."

I looked to Hellas but the man hung his head and jogged toward the head of the column. Distra watched his fleeing back with narrowed eyes.

"What's wrong?" I asked.

She held out her hand and waited for me to give her the blood. I complied.

"Good," she grunted. "Don't."

Knowing Distra, that was all I was going to hear on the matter so I changed the subject. "Why don't we have any other wizards in our cabal? I keep hearing about Seconds. Why do we only have a Prime?"

Distra whistled, directing the Cloudbreakers to follow a goat trail up a butte to their left. The column angled their way up the slope, and it wasn't long before we were surrounded on all sides by oaks and cedars. A jay chased another of the same through the undergrowth as Distra finally regarded me.

"Because," she said with her hands, "Omatuu is a very strong Prime. Still, it's very dangerous to forgo a Second or even a Third. Only a matter of time before the right wizard challenges him, or our camp is faced with an all-out assault."

I blinked at her, my question evident.

"Because, Omatuu is also very greedy. He doesn't want any other wizards around his studies. He doesn't want anyone else uncovering the Night Bridge."

"Power save me," I said. "This isn't something else I must do to become a wizard, is it?"

She shook her head. "This comes after. Discovering the Night Bridge is the key to traveling freely between Kelundar and the Golden Lands. Maybe other places, too. Most wizards who discover the Night Bridge disappear. Forever."

Freedom from the lands of Kelundar? Access to other lands? The thought that I could go anywhere if I surpassed a wizard of Omatuu's standing stoked longing in my breast. It dispersed the lingering pall of my nightmares. I rolled my shoulders back and allowed myself to soak in the possibilities.

Why couldn't I outstrip Omatuu in power and find the Night Bridge? I was one of the youngest people to ever set foot on the path of a Seeker. That had to mean something about me. Something within me slid into place. Not only would I be a wizard, I decided, I would be one of the greatest who ever lived. Reaching the Night Bridge before Omatuu fanned the flames of my ambition. I framed my newfound goal as a personal competition between us. One I vowed to win at any cost.

"How does it work with two or three wizards in a cabal?" I chewed a fingernail on my free hand. "Who chooses who duels?"

"The weaker ones, those freshest from their towers, are eager for combat after learning the way it's done. But they aren't ready. Prudence, practice, purpose—these are the best words for those newly come into the Power. If they aren't ready, death comes swiftly." She sucked at her teeth. "Besides, a Second or a Prime challenging a Third? They would appear weak. Everyone would attack them. Among Seconds and Primes though, all challenges are fair."

I nodded. "So in other cabals, their wizards work together?"

"In a way. When a cabal loses too many warriors, or their wizards appear weaker for some reason, there may be a battle. Stir up enough chaos around a wizard and it's easier to get in a kill shot. Obviously, open battle between cabals isn't a dream for Seekers. More of us die that way, and even if we come out on top, our numbers might dip too much and make us vulnerable to another attack."

"So Primes, Seconds, and Thirds work together to fight off attacks?"

She nodded. "But that's even more rare than duels. Vethatii challenged Omatuu because her Seekers were getting desperate. They could have disbanded or tried killing her in her sleep. She had to challenge someone. Might as well test herself in the process. They say a Prime must only beat another Prime once to beat all others. Omatuu's in the clear. Only a fool would come for him now."

Someone named Jester, perhaps?

I shifted my spear to my other shoulder. "Do you have any friends, Distra?"

"Bad idea. You heard Omatuu." Her hands signed as she shrugged. "He was right about that. There are no friends in the Wildness."

"That's sad." The nature of the wizard's way was a treacherous one, where friends were as likely to kill you as help you. But I refused to go through that alone. Hellas's bulky swagger came into view a short distance ahead. "I think Hellas is my friend."

Distra grimaced. "Poor choice."

I paused a moment, then signed, "You're my friend, too." I nodded, as if confirming the fact to myself. "When I become a wizard Prime, I want you and Hellas at my side. You're good people. Others underestimate you."

A smile twitched onto one of her cheeks. "You as well," she signed, then rushed forward to lead the column.

Chapter Twelve

THE HUNT

On the fourth day out, we reached the crest of a butte and began our descent to a marshland. Distra, Hellas, and myself fell to the rear.

I caught sight of motion miles off in the distance and froze. I struck Hellas with the back of my hand as I came to a halt. "Did you see that?"

Treetops stirred and then thinned as what appeared to be a clutching wooden hand broke through the canopy a second later. Sound carried to us. Rumbling. Booming. Snapping.

The thick man hissed as he grabbed Distra and pointed. "Look," he whispered excitedly. "One of us should go. You've got the wizard's knot...I can lead the group the rest of the way if you want to—"

"No." She stared at the claw-like wooden tower in the distance. "It's too far. A half-dozen other Seekers will reach it before nightfall." Then in what seemed an attempt to convince herself, she added, "It's too far."

A wizard's tower!

All of a sudden, the journey of becoming a wizard felt far more real. I stared at my goal. My purpose. My fate. It was the very thing that would transform me from lowly Seeker into a wizard who wielded the Power. A pathway to controlling life's fundamental energies and unlocking its most pressing mysteries. Domain over life and death stared back at me from the intervening distance.

I wasn't prepared for how upset I would feel at not being able to reach it. Distra seemed to feel similarly. She booted a rock down the butte with a curse.

"Damn." Hellas looped thumbs through his belt and then trotted down the trail, muttering about not wanting the secret location of the Spirit Gardens before he got a topknot. "Good way to drive yourself to madness."

I placed a hand against the Head Seeker's back. She jolted like a startled horse.

"Sorry," I said as I withdrew the attempt at comfort. "I just wanted to say...if anyone deserves it, it's you."

Grim-faced, she nodded, then made her way after Hellas.

Of all the Cloudbreakers, I decided, I liked Distra best.

———————————————+—————

Silence fell over the Cloudbreaker hunting party as they piled in to crouch behind a log. At the center of the shadowed woods sat a fen. Peat spread out over ankle-deep water, the mirrored surface broken here and there by errant strands of horsetail. Marigolds, the color of lemons and blood, marked the barrier between fen and forest's edge. Somewhere close, the River Wild added a persistent shushing to the quiet.

The only sound was the swish of fabric and creak of leather as Distra spoke in furious hand-sign. "Wizard. You know the drill. The killing blade gets the topknot."

She paused, glanced quickly, then sucked at her teeth. "Bows first," she signed. "On my signal."

My pulse pounded in my skull; I felt the pressure of it in my ears. Sweat slicked the spear haft in my palms. With my back against the log, I leveraged my shoulders against it to sit a little higher, then peeked out over the top.

The wizard's throat and the lower half of their mouth was painted completely black. Otter skulls pinned a cloak of raven feathers in place at each shoulder. A black hood hid much of the wizard's face, and a shirt of chain their form. Light glittered off an emerald-green amulet on their chest and they held a steel scythe, another viridescent stone fixed at the juncture between blade and black-bone handle.

"No trolls today," Hellas whispered. "Far bigger game. Khemetri, the Prime of the Dark Waters Society."

I nodded. It was said she was nearly as powerful as Omatuu—maybe more so. I gripped my spear like a prayer.

Distra began counting down from five with the fingers on one hand. The Seekers shifted, tongues darting over dry lips, fingers twitching where they hooked around bowstrings. Spit stuck in my throat, refused to go down.

"Five."

I regretted forgoing bow training. On the cusp of bloodshed, I wanted to remain as far from the wizard as possible.

"Four."

The last tangible thought I had was spent wondering if I'd missed my birthday. Was sixteen too young to die?

A cacophony of motion stole the answer from me as Distra reached three. I'd expected everyone to shoot when she said one. I was mistaken. This was no ordinary game they hunted. Tactics upon tactics were necessary to end a wizard's life.

They loosed the first volley on three. I looked to see if the arrows struck their target.

Khemetri's head swiveled toward the log we hid behind. Unlike Omatuu and Vethati, she only worked her magic with a single hand. Turning her body sideways, the Dark Waters Society Prime swept her scythe upward. Arrows skittered off a shield of air. She backpedaled in the murky fen as she drew up a curtain of water from around her ankles. Our second volley loosed on the count of two but ricocheted harmlessly against a wall of ice, the earliest shot frozen halfway through.

Distra cursed. Seekers fanned out to either flank at a sprint, while our archers—a third of our number—remained. These angled their bows, aiming to clear the wall of ice to their target. They shot one after another in a tattoo rhythm, raining arrows to keep Khemetri on the defensive until the others reached her.

The rest of us rushed to close with hand weapons.

I stumbled. Hellas reached back, grabbed me by the shoulder and pulled me along. I circumnavigated logs, clusters of gashbrush, and sucking mud. I glanced across the fen to where Distra led a group around the other side.

I glimpsed the wizard's silhouette behind the wall of ice just before it shattered. She threw out her hands. A jet of flame streaked toward the log we'd launched our attack from. It burst apart as liquid fire splashed against it, consuming two bowmen in the process. They dropped to their knees in squealing pain, then fell limply into the water with a sickening sizzle and gouts of smoke.

"Cloudbreakers!" someone screamed.

My chest ached. My lips stuck to my gums, dried out from heaving, fear-fueled breaths.

Khemetri moved gracefully, a fluid yet focused dancer. She deflected arrows, spun around, returned a blast of wind and lancing flame.

Branches clawed at me as we crashed through the undergrowth. Cover was the only thing that would save us now. I wasn't aware others followed us until Belefi tripped over an exposed root and cried out.

Khemetri whipped around, spotting us. Her scythe punched the air then slashed at an angle. A gale of wind slammed Hellas into me at speed as the rest of the group raced past us. He and I tumbled over the earth like ragdolls, a clipped cry escaping my lips just before my breath was struck from my lungs. We rolled to a stop. Dazed, I looked up. Two saplings were laid low by the wizard's attack. An oak swayed dangerously...

Its trunk emitted a deafening crack—a handful more in rapid succession.

I shoved Hellas. "Move!"

He was a split second behind in recognizing our peril. With a startled shout, he scrambled off me. I rolled then lunged in the other direction as the oak tree crashed down, sending up a fountain of earthen detritus.

Stumbling to my feet, I retrieved my spear.

"Way not to die," Hellas grunted out. "Come on!"

We resumed our charge. Blood matted the hair on the back of his head. I was sure I had injuries, too, but the rush of danger overwhelmed my senses, deadening pain in the shadow of survival.

Seekers closed in on Khemetri from all sides. Their legs churned the shallow waters as they whooped and hollered to disorient her. An arrow lodged into a ring of her chainmail near one hip. She jerked it out and threw it at impossible speed into the forehead of the Seeker who'd shot it.

Heart pounding, sweat pouring down my face, we broke from cover at a sprint, Hellas brandishing his ax, and I, my spear.

Maintaining her deadly dance, Khemetri shouted, "Look for trolls, find Seekers! What a shitty day!" Her scythe spun in her hand, hurled a wheel of green flame in every direction. Those that were closest dove into the fen for cover. Khemetri slashed at a prostrate Cloudbreaker a dozen feet away. Concentrated air sheared his head from his shoulders like a nipped rosebud.

Someone closed with her from behind, but at the last moment, she sensed the attack and whirled. Ax met steel scythe. She slapped the emerald amulet on her breast. Green smoke billowed from the gem to swallow the Seeker's face in a voluminous cloud.

He crumpled to his knees, clutching his throat and gagging. Dark sores erupted along his temples. Khemetri decapitated him then swept her hand around her in a protective halo, deadly vapor trailing it and the Seekers retreated from the pestilent nimbus.

Hellas and I came to a halt at ten arm spans. The others paused too, casting furtive glances at Distra who shifted from foot to foot. Even I saw our attack had been stalled, but too many were already close, unwilling to let a topknot slip through their grasp.

Indignation stitched Khemetri's words. "You think I wander unprepared?" She slammed the butt of her scythe into the fen's murk. The emerald in the black-bone haft gave off a blinding flash. Vibrations rippled the water's surface. An inhuman groan rolled over us, sending a chill down my spine. The sound of tumbling rock and shifting earth assaulted my ears, and my teeth clattered together as the ground shook. Behind Khemetri, something bulled through the underbrush.

Two somethings.

The wizard retreated into the dark of the forest laughing, and for a moment, the joy was hers and hers alone. Then, another booming laugh, bassy and resonant, like it passed through a hollowed-out tree bole, joined her. Then another, just as deep, coming from a thick, inhuman throat.

Two monsters stepped from the forest, half again as tall as Hellas but carrying four times the girth. Swarming around slabs of candle-wax fat and buried muscle, flies heralded a smell I'd not soon forget. It struck my nose like a bolt of lightning. The scent more than the sight of them nearly caused me to faint; any who have fought them would say the same. Homunculi bubbled from their bodies, a baby head sat next to one of their slavering, moon-round faces, while the other had three dugs and three arms, each with three stodgy fingers—a toothless face on one thumb.

"Ogres!" bellowed Hellas.

A wizard alone was dangerous. With ogres at her side, though, Khemetri was unbeatable.

One heedless fool failed to realize this and charged anyway, a half-hatched battle cry on his lips. The three-armed ogre tore a branch free with a meaty hand and swung. The blow struck the charging idiot so hard he wrapped partially around the limb like a blood-soaked rag. The ogre rumbled with laughter, fat jiggling as it stepped forward to shake the Seeker off the limb and into the fen.

Crackling bolts of flame shot from the shadows of the forest from behind the ogres. Unseen, Khemetri was neither done nor gone.

I froze. If I ran, was I giving up on my ambition to be a great wizard? I looked around, found Distra backpedaling and snatching at the tabards of the Seekers nearest to her. *Flee.* My legs wanted to agree with the other Cloudbreakers but refused to move. Hellas was gone too.

The baby-head ogre fished around under the water's surface, then came back up with a massive stone in hand. It threw the anvil-sized chunk of rock at the first Seeker it saw: Belefi. Her chest burst like an overripe melon when it struck and flung her limp body into the murk. I stared at her ugly face, vacant eyes momentarily visible as lapping waters settled—and she was gone.

From the shadows, Khemetri sent spikes of ice after the faltering Seekers, skewering legs or torsos. The fen was naught but blood and screams, and terrible laughter.

Unable to move, I waited for death, a stone, or fireball, or spike of ice. All seemed just as likely.

"Flee dammit!" The voice was close, familiar, but I could only watch in horror as the baby-head ogre sighted me. It searched for another boulder under the water's surface while its three-armed comrade chased Distra, tree branch swinging after her. Thankfully, the ogre was slow, and it was clear Distra would outstrip her lumbering predator on her way to the treeline.

A rush of air—something heavy—lifted my shoulder-length hair. A splash followed, just behind me. The ogre roared, and the baby face on its shoulder contorted with anger. He'd missed. I felt naked, but impossibly, still alive.

Then a hand was gripping my tunic, yanking me backward.

"Run!" they screamed. I think it was Hellas.

I did. I ran and never looked back.

It is without shame that I tell you I did not stop running for a very long time.

Chapter Thirteen

ONLY THE RIGHTEOUS

Out of nearly a score of Seekers to leave the Cloudbreakers' camp, only nine survived our run-in with Khemetri. They sat around a campfire, the weight of defeat heavy on every shoulder. Each of us stared into the flames, watching the day's images through a different facet of the same horrific jewel.

"Klent," someone said.

All nodded. Hellas spoke in a hoarse whisper. "He was a good Seeker."

"Fendra." The hollow thump of Distra's voice pecked the darkness. "Aylor."

Nos, one of the men who'd hazed me along with Belefi, wept. "Belefi."

More names were cast like ash into the dark, then drifted away. Being a Seeker was an ever-evolving tragedy few saw past. We were as one in that moment, acknowledging the ease with which life was snuffed out by those with greater power. Grateful, too, for luck alone stayed death's icy touch.

After a long silence, a woman stood sharply. "I'm..." Wild eyes roamed the fire. "I'm done. I'm going home. Back to Cannalis."

"What about the Stormseye?" I said.

Unblinking, she seemed to gaze through me. "A bad life is still a life. With or without the Power, I'm keeping mine." She cast her headband into the fire and then stumbled off into the night.

The others said nothing. They just let her go. I assume they empathized with her decision. Distra sniffed disdainfully then straightened.

Despite the fear I fought to shake free, returning to Cannalis was never an option. I did, however, think of Trin. Six months, I'd told her. I'd been in the Wildness four, and only just gone on my first hunt. Bitter sadness pumped through my veins. Who would she see if I returned? Could I, having watched abominations and wizards slaughter my peers before my eyes, even be the same person to her? I'd worked hard to kill the childish, innocent El she grew up with.

While it wasn't comfortable to claim it, my time in the Wildness, though short, *had* changed me. Whether or not it was for the better was worthy of debate. I was stronger than I'd ever been. Skilled with weaponry, and knowledgeable of otherworldly powers, I was a survivor. No longer just another casualty-in-waiting in the press of bodies within Cannalis's walls.

I was a Seeker.

Yet, I aimed to commit murder. I was immersed in killing and nightmarish deeds. Trin, on the other hand, was a righteous champion of doing good. Our reunion, if it ever occurred, would be nothing more than a shock of reality between strangers.

More names came and went, an interval of brooding silence following each. When there were no more dead to honor, the Cloudbreakers closed their eyes in solemn reverence. It felt wrong, hearing the names of the fallen whom I didn't know. It felt wrong to give them honorary silence. In most cases, I couldn't summon a face to match the name.

I ground my teeth in brooding silence then rubbed my hands together over the fire. They went from warm to hot. I held them there, blossoming prickles on the skin telling me I still lived, guilt burning through me. When it felt as though glass shards pressed into my fingertips, I retracted my hands with a pointed intake of breath.

A gray-haired Cloudbreaker named Laertha broke out a wineskin. She was a knobby kite of a woman, all flapping skin and angularity. Her first instinct was to be helpful to me, but never without a drop of criticism. "Some of it leaked out when the ogres attacked. Should be enough for a gulp apiece."

Distra waved the wine away. Hellas took a longer pull than he should have. After he passed the wineskin to the next Seeker, he turned away from the fire and fiddled with something in the shadows. I caught a glimpse of a vial flashing in the firelight as he knocked it back.

Ogre's blood. It dawned on me that the man might be an addict. Given my brush with death, I thought of Trin. She loomed like a titan in my mind as I recalled how her own father's selfish acts had led to her family's suffering.

Across the fire, Distra watched Hellas with hard eyes.

I cleared my throat, sought to break the tension between my only two friends. "What do we tell Omatuu?"

"We failed," Hellas bellowed. He squared his shoulders to the fire. "What more is there to say?"

"Isn't it odd Khemetri was all alone?" I said. "In the middle of nowhere?"

"Ah, deary." Laertha was sweetly condescending, as if she spoke to a toddler. I wanted no such treatment. "The wizards do many things alone out of sight of their Seekers. It's one of the only ways we catch them outside of a duel. If you do not seek greater power and knowledge, you ain't no wizard."

Distra's hands were a blur of tracers in the radiating light. "They play a game of secrets, some of which we lowly Seekers understand, some of which we can only guess at. Rest assured, there are a great many more we cannot fathom."

Chubby fingers raised, Hellas pinched each in turn, ticking items off a list. "Hunting for Soul Stones. Visiting a bloodtrader. Hunting for the Night Bridge. Performing rituals so they can summon dread beasts like Khemetri did today."

Distra signed. "Tracking down wizards who cross over from Mahjiri." That was the other name for the Golden Lands.

Hellas's hand drifted slowly to his side. "Aye, that especially."

"Wizards from the Golden Lands come here?" I frowned at Distra. "I thought you said the Night Bridge was a wizard's key to freedom from the Wildness."

"In a way, it is," said Hellas. "It fuels a magical exchange between Kelundar and Mahjiri, which allows wizards access to more knowledge, more secrets. If a wizard from Kelundar can follow a wizard from Mahjiri, or vice versa, they might be able to steal something valuable or learn another secret."

At that, the other Seekers nodded.

"Yes," Hellas sighed. "Wizards do love their secrets. Anyway, the Night Bridge is freedom from the cabals because anybody that finds it becomes strong enough to stand alone. They can continue pursuing more Power without need for the protection offered by a cabal." He shrugged. "Could also be used to start a war, though."

"War?" My voice cracked. "But Kelundar hasn't gone to war for—"

"You're thinking in terms of armies of peasants with sharp sticks, Jester," Laertha said. "You think that matters in a battle between wizards? The Great Archon alone could sweep away the whole of Cannalis like a wave sweeps over a sandcastle."

"No peasant armies." A rigidness fell across Hellas's expression. One eye twitched as he hunkered forward over his girth to stare intently at the fire. I assumed the ogre's blood was doing whatever it was meant to do. "The wars of wizards are waged in places unseen. Unknown battlegrounds. Rifts in the fabric of reality. Other dimensions..."

A gust of wind slapped at the fire, laying it low and sending smoke and embers into the faces of those across the way. They scattered, finding new seats in which they wouldn't be harried.

A chill crept up my spine. *Other dimensions...*

The idea was thrilling even if I could barely conceive its scope. I recalled the way the Stormlords had transported to the blood altar when they'd risen Lictor Laconius into their ranks. "Is there anyone who could stand against the Great Archon?"

Distra's voice was gravel poured through a horn funnel. "Illuminated Path."

"I'll save Distra the strain." Hellas proved ever willing to talk. "The Stormseye Brotherhood rules the lands of Kelundar as the Illuminated Path rules the Golden Lands. Two sides of the same coin. Ask me the differences?"

I frowned at Hellas. "Okay. What are the differences?" Excitedly, I added, "Who is their Great Archon?"

Hellas shrugged. "No clue whatsoever. Like Distra said, there's a lot we Seekers don't know. What we've discussed here is but the first page in a never-ending book of knowledge."

"The only thing we know for sure," said Laertha with a yellow smile, "is how little we actually know."

Between the day's disappointing outcome and the fact that I'd only just begun my journey, I felt impatient. From there, despair came naturally.

Silence fell around the fire. Seekers rubbed bleary eyes then drifted away from the fire. It wasn't long before their snores joined the crickets in a grating symphony.

Distra rose to add a log to the campfire. I sat in silent vigil, digesting memories like stone with the handful of those who remained.

Other dimensions...

I was barely able to grasp the one I was in. I considered the possibility of dueling a powerful wizard someday in another plane of existence. It seemed as far from possible as becoming one of the Great Archon's Stormlords; as unlikely as resurrecting Idrinnia the Everlasting Maiden and marrying her.

Suddenly dizzy, I looked to the stars wheeling overhead, impossible specks pinning back the darkness from creation. Trees stirred in the dark canopy, moved by gusting winds. For a moment, they frightened me, but once they stilled, they became a source of comfort.

Light and shadow. Stillness and motion. The dance of everything between.

I let sit the mind-churning questions raised by the previous conversation, opted instead to break the silence with something plainer. One step at a time, I would take in all the information I could. Tonight, survival seemed the most pertinent thing to discuss.

"What if ogres attack us again?"

Laertha chuckled. "Frightened, are you?"

"Weren't you?" My voice was low, full of rage. I'd had enough of her offensive tone. "I wish to know my enemies for the next time we meet."

Laertha shot me a cool glare and didn't speak again.

In a seeming attempt to cut the tension, Hellas cleared his throat. "In the wild, ogres ain't much. Easy to track. Then you just pepper them with arrows for a bit until they bleed out. As you saw, they're slow, too, but with a Prime at their back you always run. Bastards are as strong as they are brutal."

I scoffed. "You mean you don't just stand there staring stupidly?"

Hellas laughed. "Not your fault, El." I appreciated the times he called me El instead of Jester. He continued. "Freezin' up happens to the best of us. Sometimes, the brain gets overloaded and there's nothing you can do but shut down. People aren't supposed to see what we see. The mind ain't always ready for it. Laertha knows that, too."

I smiled, appreciating the support.

Talking about the horrors of the day wouldn't normally be my first choice, but I felt a ball of discomfort sitting inside me like lead; it needed to be released. Too many such balls, I predicted, might slow me on my way to becoming a wizard.

"It's not always like that." Hellas reached over to rest a hand on my back. "Seekers who volunteer a lot experience a lot. It's never easy. How do you feel?"

"I'm just..." I thought of saying, 'happy I survived' but the words melted in my throat. Relief broke through me.

I cried.

The others looked away as if seeing me might make them weaker by association; more vulnerable to their doom, even. Luck's great gift of survival was a numbered thing. So, they refused the possibility of their deaths, clinging instead to willful ignorance as if it could invoke invincibility. Always, it would be the person beside them who would die. Not them. This denial, I realized, was what permitted them to return to the hunt time and again.

I swallowed hard. Distra alone met my gaze. She had the courage to face pain and suffering like me. Her fate was sealed in the Wildness, and so, it kept her in its embrace. Despite knowing she could die, she faced ogres, trolls, and wizards. She and I, we rode the razor's edge of 'what if?'

In my estimation, we possessed the Power already.

Slowly, Distra came to stand. She wended her way around the fire then stopped before me.

"Up!" she barked. When I stared dumbly, she grabbed a fistful of my tabard in one hand and hoisted me upward into a plume of smoke filtering into the night sky. Our noses were almost touching. Roughly, she wiped the tears from my cheeks.

"Good." Glacial blue eyes bored into mine. "It's out now."

With a snap of her wrist, her knuckles forced my chin into the air. "Stand straight. Not weak. You're a Cloudbreaker. A Seeker. Stronger now."

She stepped back, hands whirring in the space between us. "If you weren't, you'd be dead. You're not dead are you?"

The tears stopped as I shook my head. "No."

Distra nodded. "Stay that way as long as you can. You're a survivor now. Show it in your spine."

A swell of pride entered my breast. She was right. Death hadn't chosen me. Not yet. Merely, it had reminded me I was on a path that required comfort with such encounters. And when I let her words sink in, I did feel stronger. When you've done things the majority of the world hasn't—things you never thought you could—you can't help but feel a sense of being better than before.

A long time passed as I stood there. I could feel the awkwardness of the other Cloudbreakers watching me, but I didn't care. Strength was building in me, warm and fluid and concrete in every limb, stretching me taller, filling my muscles. I looked around...looked down on the rest of them.

I was chosen for greatness by none other than myself.

Pride and ego drove me. A wizard had to wear an impenetrable badge of conceit. Otherwise, they would falter. In this, Omatuu had the right of it. For little did I know, there would come a fork in the road. A divergent path all wizards face on their road to power.

Chapter Fourteen

BLOOD AND BREAD

The Wildness climbed without end. A far shorter line of Cloud-breakers than that which set out ascended the steep hillside. Yellow grass and tumbledown stone spread as far as the eye could see. Beside me, Hellas labored dramatically. I was surprised to find my chest tightening in anger at his wordless whining. Every grunt emphasized, every wheeze drawn out overlong—it grated. At the source of my frustration was his addiction. I saw it as a lack of dedication which was swiftly transforming into personal affront.

He was my friend and he was making the wrong choices. The harshness rising within reminded me too much of Omatuu, so I refocused on my feet and sped ahead, far away from Hellas.

I may have been one of the smallest Cloudbreaker Seekers but youth had its natural advantages. Where strength and wisdom eluded me, curiosity and vitality filled the empty space.

Meanwhile, Hellas continued to struggle. "Damn your pace, Distra!" He bent at the waist, slapped a meaty palm to a knee, and called for a stop. "We'll lose half again as many Seekers to walking as we did to Khemetri if you keep this up."

With Distra's hearing so reduced, she didn't seem to make out Hellas's words as she turned around. One look at the weary group was the only communication she needed to understand the shouting. I made sure I stood straight when her gaze swept over our line. She waved a halt.

I removed a satchel from my shoulder. I rarely hungered, even when I should have. Living in Cannalis had trained me well in that regard, but after a day of battle and the previous night's rough reflections, I would have eaten an ogre's foot to calm the ache in my belly.

Hard bread would have to do.

I bit into it and felt it instantly sap the moisture from my gums. A sharp corner stabbed the roof of my mouth. Salty, coppery blood gave the bland bread some flavor. Despite its stiff and tasteless qualities, it was still one of the best things I'd ever eaten.

Blood and bread, the dietary staple of every Seeker.

All around me, mouths crushed, tore, and snapped their food into manageable bites, then washed them down with eager gulps of their waterskins. No one talked. Distra set that tone. She sat higher up the slope than the rest of us, eating slow and deliberate as she stared unflinchingly at distant trees.

The Head Seeker paid me no mind. I watched her in silence until a curse from Hellas drew my attention. At the end of our diminished column, sitting on a broad stone, the heavyset man fumbled with something at his side. He glanced furtively up at Distra, then shifted so his back was to the group.

Hot in the chest, I rose, the haft of my spear filling my hands. Out-pacing wisdom, I marched downslope to where Hellas sat, casting a shadow over a far larger and more seasoned fighter. If I'd been a decade older when I watched the vial of ogre's blood touch his lips, I might have delayed the impulse to swing the butt of my spear at his hands.

But I wasn't.

Hellas wore a quizzical expression. "What?"

I swung, whacking his knuckles and sending the vial speeding into the grassy unknown. It took only a moment for his shock to wear off. For wrath to overcome the sting.

His eyes went flat, lips curling into a snarl. A chill rippled down my spine and I stepped back as he stood.

Rage seeped through his teeth. "You little pissant."

"You need to stop." I spoke with far less sureness than I'd needed. "You—you can't keep taking ogre's blood like that."

He took a step forward. "You think you get to tell me what to do, little troll's cunt? If it wasn't for me, you'd be a crispy husk at Khemetri's feet." He loosed an indignant grunt. "And you repay me by doing something stupid like that."

"I don't care if you saved my life. You'll never be a wizard if you keep drinking that swill." The brandished spear in my hands felt a fearful act, so I stuck the butt of it into the ground, then attempted to emulate its straightness. I found steel in my voice. "Consider what I just did as a favor returned."

"A favor?" Hellas's lips twitched. "That was my last fucking vial. A week's worth, at least."

"A week closer to being a wizard, then," I said. "You know I'm right."

Fists clenched at his sides, Hellas stared at me from under a soiled, gray headband. Wind rippled across the yellowed grass of the hillside.

I was getting through to him, hitting him where it hurt most, I thought. "As long as you rely on ogre's blood, Omatuu will be right about you." Emboldened, I raised my voice. "You'll remain a fool, and then, you'll die a fool."

At this, Hellas's hands came to his belly. Mean laughter rumbled forth, his long blond hair jumping as he shook through the chest. He turned to the others, smiling and motioning at me. I relaxed, feeling my own edges softening as my fellow Seeker seemed to hear me.

I looked at Distra. She watched our exchange impassively, as if it were nothing more than a conversation about the weather. She was the last clear thing I saw for a short time. Out of the corner of my eye, Hellas swiveled around in a blur, his malevolent smile replaced by the clipped image of a balled fist.

My vision flashed.

Then darkness...

Three Hellases stood over me, pointing down, spittle flying from their lips. Muffled words were drowned out by the ringing in my ears. Vaguely, I felt stiff grass along the back of my neck and hands.

Time seemed a singular moment without end until words finally won through, clear and comprehensible.

"Only thing Omatuu's right about is you, Jester. A joke. A pathetic, sad little joke." Hellas pursed his lips, then his chest convulsed.

A wet gob struck my cheek. Distra appeared at Hellas's shoulder just as he merged into a single him again. She jerked him away, leaving me with nothing but blue sky to orient myself.

Perhaps it was fate for me to lose all of my friends.

***

Once recovered, I kept far away from Hellas; it didn't keep him from shooting me baleful looks whenever I let my gaze wander in his direction. I didn't relish the idea of being knocked out again. Besides, he was right. Perhaps I was the foolish one.

A short time after my trip through the abyss of consciousness, we reached the ridgeline of a hill.

Distra hissed and raised a fist at us to stop. Weapons whispered forth. I searched the wooded area below. Sunlight gleamed off a row of golden hoods bobbing at the base of the hill, the hems of red cloaks trailing them.

"Who are they?"

"Death Bards," said Distra. "Another cabal."

My stomach lurched. Distra appeared surprisingly calm in the face of impending violence. "What are we waiting for?" Sweat filled my palms, forcing me to grip and regrip my spear. One at a time, I wiped them on my trousers. "We have bows and the high ground. Shouldn't we attack?"

"No." Distra slung her bow over one shoulder. "No wizard. Come."

I frowned, swayed anxiously as the others put weapons at ease. We followed our leader on a course to intercept the Death Bards. Wary, I brought up the rear, strangling my spear in both hands.

The Death Bards were nothing if not ostentatious. I thanked whatever powers had led me into the company of the more simply dressed Cloudbreakers. Each of their fifteen Seekers had one hand painted gold, the other red, to match their cloaks and hoods. Wearing breastplates, earrings, and nose studs, they looked altogether very out of place in the Wildness. Better suited as a troupe of street performers in Cannalis, perhaps. The only similarity we shared with them was our weaponry: daggers, bows, a few hand-axes. A single spear jutted from the Death Bards' column. The young woman bearing it raised it slightly as if giving cheers with a tankard and smiled at me. In a show of solidarity, I returned the gesture.

The two groups drew up short of each other. The Death Bard leader strode forward, an exceedingly tall man with a gold sword at one hip. Distra went to meet him. Everyone else fell quiet.

Laertha came up alongside me and spoke in hushed tones. "If there's no wizard, we've no cause to risk our lives. Everyone out here is trying to survive. Seekers know killing each other gets us nowhere fast. Even wizards don't like senseless scuffles since it needlessly reduces their buffers. Besides, it keeps our wizards honest when we show some Seeker unity here and there." She pointed at Distra and the towering Death Bard leader. "They'll trade news now."

The system of keeping everyone in the Wildness in check was a morbid one. The threat of violence loomed over every head. Betrayal, every heart. I looked around, seeing the faces of people I might need to someday kill. A duel, a camp attack, a knife in the night—the how of it made little difference.

"Why make friends with them when we might need to kill them? Or duel them—if we become wizards?"

Laertha made a disapproving sound. "Survival happens one step at a time, Jester." That was her problem. She thought only of survival. Becoming a wizard happens fifty steps at once.

Out of earshot, I watched them confer. Laertha leaned down at one point, her breath stale. "Distra will tell them of Vethati, the Order of Odd's Second wizard who Omatuu defeated."

"I know who she is."

"Was," Laertha corrected. "They'll want to know about that, because if they raid the Order of Odd, they'll only face a Prime and a Third rather than the entire damn trio."

"What about Khemetri?"

"Oh, Distra'll tell them about that, too. If the Death Bards decide to track her down and take a crack at her, they could get her. Since she's the Prime of the Dark Waters Society, that means they'd be left with only a Second wizard. We could pressure Omatuu to do a raid."

"Why would we need to pressure him?"

"Well, he just earned Distra a wizard's knot, so he might not be so keen to go risking his life for a long while now. It's all a game of keeping us on the brink of desperation. They could care less whether we succeed." Laertha chuckled. "Or die for that matter."

I watched the exchange more intently, wishing I could read lips. The Death Bards' towering Head Seeker was quick to smile and nod as Distra spoke. Once she'd finished, he rambled on for some time. Excitement filled me as I watched, knowing I'd soon be privy to the gossip of the other cabals. No food could satiate me so completely. My curiosity was ravenous.

The Head Seekers returned to their respective warbands. The Death Bards wound their way up the hillside, offering nods to the Cloud-breaker line as they went past.

We continued on into the woods.

"Do the cabals know where each others' camps are?" I asked Laertha.

"Sometimes," she said. "Sometimes not. They move on occasion to throw the other cabals off. If a wizard's got important business else-where, we move then, too. We've moved a half dozen times since I became a Seeker and that was a decade ago."

It was the other 'business' that got my attention. I decided it would be a good idea to spy on Omatuu whenever I had the chance. If I was going to be a wizard, I had to think and act like one. That meant discovering secrets wherever I could, and at any cost.

CHAPTER FIFTEEN

THE DISAPPEARING HERON

From the fated run-in with Khemetri in the marshlands, it was a four-day journey back to the Cloudbreakers' camp. On the last night of our return, we found a ring of stones near a narrow strip of the River Wild. Hellas led conversation around the fire, which meant I kept to myself on a soft patch of forest duff until sleep descended.

I slept fitfully, waking on occasion with a puzzle on my mind for long stretches of the snore-blasted night. I was gaining greater evidence by the day for a worrisome conclusion: there seemed to be an inverse correlation between how long someone stayed a Seeker and their chances of becoming a wizard. The puzzle I sought to solve was the same one that dogged me every night I spent in the Cloudbreakers' cabal—how might I leverage my strengths to become a wizard faster than the others?

I recited the law of the gutters. I wasn't rich or big, and while I was quicker than many, it hardly felt like a deciding force in my fate, so that left me with smart or dead. While I didn't possess the wisdom of experience that Distra or Omatuu might call smart, there were many kinds of intelligence. In raw intellect, I was only above average. In that regard, Trin had always been my superior.

Memories of my journey from Cannalis to the Cloudbreakers peppered my awareness. I held them all together, let them blur until they winnowed into a singular, satisfactory word: willingness. The uncompromising vision of myself wielding the Power had pushed an eerie focus to the fore. That was what separated me. It sounded like a paltry thing to lean into for achieving something so grand as magical powers, yet the more I considered it, the brighter my path shined. If I wanted the fate I thirsted for, it wouldn't be when I was Laertha's age. Powerlessness didn't serve me, much less the life of a Seeker. Wizards had seemingly created a clever form of slavery in which the slaves volunteered themselves, and I refused to remain in shackles longer than necessary. Living by Omatuu's arrogant whims was a fate worse than death.

So I would take the risks others wouldn't. A razor's edge of chance separated the daring from the idiotic, but I had to trust myself without question if I was to succeed. I had surrendered Trin to live as a wizard, not die a Seeker.

As the first rays of light filtered through the forest canopy, I rolled to one side, having barely slept, and withdrew the scroll. Surrounded by the others so much on our hunt, and wishing to hoard secrets of my own, I'd foregone my nightly ritual of looking at it, but with my solitude assured in that moment, I quietly unrolled the parchment.

Do what is needed.

Why did I even bother? The scroll, truly, was an outrageous, willful devil. If I had an ounce of pride, I should have torn it to shreds a dozen times by that point.

"Do what is needed." I repeated it under my breath, then noticed a full bladder compelling me to oblige. Only Distra was awake as I tiptoed through camp. We exchanged a quick nod before I walked a few hundred feet to the River Wild's banks to relieve myself.

I picked my way down a short, rocky slope, then covered a pebble-littered strip of land to a clump of bushes. I went about my business, head sweeping the surrounding area. Being raised in a city, I struggled to feel comfortable in the Wildness during my most vulnerable moments. Time saw this instinct dissipate slower than desired. My appreciation of nature's beauty grew daily, interrupted with diminishing frequency by those pervasive thoughts of impending death from creatures unseen. Still, I glanced at my spear, glad to have it with me.

Sparrows raced from the trees on one bank to the other. Sunlight fleeced the river's surface as I finished and stood to lace my trousers. To my right, the current curved out of sight behind a copse of foliage overhanging the water. A heron took up position on a shallow strand by the nearest shore—dense undergrowth blocked my view just after.

Tranquil and patient, the heron let the river bring it what it needed rather than hunting it down. It made ready by positioning itself in the right environment, and then took what came. It forced nothing, showed no desperation.

A warm tendril trickled through my heart. The muscles of my face went slack in that moment of calming bliss. I sighed as I saw what the scroll had meant. "Do what is needed," I said aloud. I had to be prepared to bring all my skills to the right place at the right time and then let the rest flow to me.

A lean-muscled, cobalt arm stretched forth tentatively, silent as a creeping cat behind the wading bird. My heart caught in my throat, legs going wooden. The heron rubbed its head under a wing, completely unaware. Black-clawed fingers snaked out the last few feet, viper-quick. The heron loosed a clipped squawk. With its prey seized, the rest of the monster's body vaulted into view. Legs tucked under its torso, it hung in the air a fleeting moment as it used its other sinuous arm as a stanchion in the river's current. The heron honked in death as the predator—with dark-blue flesh the color of a stream at dusk—came to a stop and rammed it into gaping jaws. Donkey-like ears twitched atop its grotesque, misshapen head. Knots of back muscle bunched around an articulated spine as it feasted.

My mouth went dry, my hands numb with fear. I swallowed hard, watching the heron's stiff, slender leg poking up over the creature's flexing shoulder.

Distra's description of a troll had been spot on.

Something in me shouted for action, but which action, I didn't know. I was freezing up again, just like with the ogres and Khemetri. If I'd fought then, would I have died? Or could I have been clever and daring and focused, and earned a wizard's knot?

I exhaled slowly. *Willingness, that's my strength. That's what separates me from the others. I must be daring.* The scroll's words from that morning buoyed my thoughts.

Do what is needed.

Troll's blood had been the Cloudbreaker mission, though a failed one. But that was Omatuu's need. The scroll spoke to me and me alone. So what did I need? I needed to become a wizard faster than any other. I needed to take risks.

Waiting be damned, I was no heron.

I was the hunter.

The haft of my spear was warm in my hand as I plucked it from where it leaned against the birch tree. I squatted, once, twice, attempting to get blood flowing into my legs again. My arms shook, jostling the spear. I worried I might make too much noise and either spook the troll or invite its ire.

Despite the urging in my pulse to turn back and alert the rest of the Cloudbreakers, I took a step, then another, making my way toward the dense copse of trees and undergrowth. In retrospect, I could have chosen a far less noisy place from which to approach, but my terror at the thought of the troll seeing me outweighed better judgment.

I pushed through a tangle of branches then pointed my spear at the monster. It had already turned around, having smelled, seen, or heard me. Lupine eyes, intensely gold, fixed on me as I emerged. The heron was no more than a spatter of blood and feathers around the creature's gaping maw. Thick slabs of lip molded around a pair of upthrust canines. Propped up on apish haunches and arms twice the length of a man's, it stared at me.

Licking my lips, I took my first step from the shore into the icy rush.

The troll growled, low at first, but terminating in a high keening sound as its fist rose, dripping, from the shallows. It padded toward me slowly on fists and shortened legs like an ape. After a few feet, it emitted another threatening, guttural sound.

I bent my knees and stepped to meet it. There was no time for fear, and so, it left in the rush of imminent violence. I felt as though I watched the actions of another. I know now this is how the body prepares itself when faced with death. The soul hangs back to await the outcome.

And in most cases, when facing trolls alone, it never returns.

The beast took two quick steps forward, haunches swinging through the air and then landing with a splash.

I took a single step back for better position then stabbed the air. The troll paused, lips splitting into a menacing snarl of black-gummed teeth as it stretched to its full height.

I gulped. The gesture was meant to frighten me off without a fight and it nearly worked. At half the troll's height, the idea to take it on alone seemed a bad one. But I was determined to risk my life and the beast had already given all the warnings it would give before deciding a threat needed to die.

So our dance began.

To protect my flanks, I retreated back into the woods, spear leveled, blade wobbling in the air. The troll followed. It lurched forward. I barreled backward into the dense underbrush, a cobalt arm snatching at the air where I once stood. Branches snapped as I regained my feet. Before me, the troll was no more than a shadow as it ducked under the dark canopy. I flicked my spear tip at it and missed by a wide margin. It snarled. Black claws shot out to steal my weapon but I yanked it back just in time and clung to the haft with a burning grip.

Frantically, I pumped the air with the blade tip, felt it score rubbery flesh—once, twice. Enough to kill? A momentary thrill passed through me. Then the troll stalked into the light and I continued my backward flight onto the pebble-strewn banks. Gray-green ichor seeped from the gashes I'd given it along its forearm and the webbing between sinewy fingers on one hand. Despair was kept at bay only by the dim realization that I'd managed to hurt it at all.

But the troll ignored the wounds and came onward. Already, the cut on its forearm was healing. I grimaced. Death by a thousand cuts was out of the question, it seemed. A kill shot or death; those were my options.

It lunged for my spear again, seeking to disarm me, but missed. Panting, I stepped behind a tree, hoping to keep it between myself and the monster. The creature lunged, raking a shower of bark into the air before circling away. A fragment stung my eye. I cursed, blinking hard.

The troll lunged again. This time, I narrowly dodged a slash of claws sure to have disemboweled me. It swiped at the air again, another attempt to take my spear, I thought. Instead, it grasped the small birch I hid behind in both hands and pried it from the ground as easy as a child might pull up a weed.

My mouth fell open. But wasting no time, I rushed forward, spear tip aimed at its heart. The troll shifted at the last second and I buried my blade into its bicep. The creature yowled and threw the snag at my feet. I leapt back to avoid a collision, knee striking rock as I stumbled away.

I spun around to find the troll in pursuit. It feinted at my spear. When I made to stab its hand, the clever monster's other hand looped low. Clawed fingers hooked my heel and jerked my leg out from under me. A blur of earth and sky. My back struck hard ground, knocking the wind from me. A black-gummed maw sped toward my face, bloody drool trailing in viscous ropes. Still clutching my spear, I swept it in a short arc, slashing the troll across the nose. It screeched and reeled, giving me just enough time to find my feet.

"Jester!"

In the distance, I could hear the other Seekers arguing about which way my screech had come from.

"Here! Troll he—"

The monster was on me, cutting off my cries of alarm. The gush of gray-green blood from the wound along its bulbous snout had already stopped as its claws whooshed at me in rapid succession. Splinters flew from the haft of my spear. Talons scraped the metal blade, giving off sparks and a clip of black nail. I circled back and away to create space, striking at its throat when I could, but it was too fast. It swung high, then low. Claws raked my calf. With a pained cry, I fell to a knee.

The troll swept a fist—struck my elbow numb. My spear clattered to the rocks at my feet as the troll reared back with deadly obsidian talons to slash my throat. One of its ears twitched.

There was a shout, then a thrumming noise followed by a quiet thud. The troll craned its head around. Arrow fletchings sprouted from its shoulder.

I snatched up my spear from the ground and gripped it tightly. With all my might, I pressed a knee into the earth and thrust. I was small and physically weak, but my aim was true. It was enough.

The blade tip sank through folds of taut flesh around the troll's heart. It swung its head back around, the cobalt skin around its golden eyes tight with pain. I fell back as it threw a half-hearted blow at my head, though still enough to shear flesh if it connected. More arrows thudded into its back. The troll barely reacted. From the way the creature's eyes were quickly losing focus, I could see it was already dead, its heart split in half like an apple.

Its head sagged to its chin. Then the troll fell face first into the dirt at my side. I sat back beside it.

Led by Distra, the Cloudbreakers hurried over, weapons brandished and warily eyeing the troll carcass stretched out at my side.

"Jester!" Distra shouted. "You fool!"

The others looked at each other in wide-eyed astonishment. Hellas stepped forward and booted the troll's limp body.

I winced as Distra helped me to stand. She slung an arm around my waist and gripped my belt to help bear the weight of my injured leg.

"A damn brave fool," said Hellas.

"Sorry." I said between heaving breaths. "I needed...to relieve myself. It was in the way."

Hellas laughed. "I take it back, El. You're no fool, you're absolutely insane." He looked at the troll carcass and pursed his lips. "By the Power, you really took this thing on alone."

I fixed him with a long, hard stare, and said nothing. Hellas shook his head. Distra gently smacked my cheek with her free hand. Her outrage, it seemed, had ebbed. Admiration filled the hollowness of her strangled voice. "Stronger now."

Chapter Sixteen

BEHOLD!

Upon my return to the Cloudbreakers' camp, I was outwardly humble.

Inwardly, however, my ego exploded with the feeling of unbridled achievement. I'd successfully killed a troll—alone, no less. That's what I told myself, at least, all the while ignoring the part of the story where if Distra and the others hadn't come to my aid and distracted the thing, I would have met the same fate as the heron.

Instead, I'd seized a fate of my own.

Youth being what it is—a half-blind scramble through one's own psyche—I illuminated my part in the triumph and tamped down the role of all others involved. Hellas, my momentary enemy for all of a day, helped little in the matter of my overblown pride. When we arrived at camp, he hoisted me onto his shoulders as if he played a pivotal role in my ability to conduct such a feat. A hero by association.

"Behold! Jester, the Fearless! Jester, the Trollslayer!"

Dozens of Seekers crowded in around the group with furrowed brows. Some asked what happened. Many asked where the rest of the hunting party was. Others thought it a jape.

Laertha and the rest set them straight.

"Faced down Khemetri and a pair of ogres."

"Took a punch from Hellas—and lived."

"Slew a troll singlehanded!"

Shocked expressions swept the knots of Cloudbreakers hemming in on all sides. To say I loved the attention was an understatement. I'd not tallied the events of the past week myself but hearing them stated as evidence of my might amplified my ambitions tenfold.

When I looked back at the others of the hunting party from my seat atop Hellas, Distra's half-smile greeted me. Then, she saw something up ahead and it faded. I swiveled around.

Omatuu stared flatly, arms clasped behind his back. A hush fell over the Cloudbreakers' camp. I tapped Hellas's shoulder and he let me down. Whoever had been holding my spear returned it to my palm as the hunting party came to a stop.

Omatuu made no attempt to hide his hostility. Wizards covet their secrets, yes, but they also covet their conclusions. While the prospect of battling Vethati may not have scared Omatuu, seeing one of his predictions proved so wildly false horrified him.

Everyone knew what he thought of me. My survival alone would have been enough to wound his intellect. Yet, I'd gone a step further. In a way, I'd beaten him by sowing doubt among the suppositions that tethered him to confidence.

Omatuu laughed, bringing a hand around to stroke his charcoal beard. "Please tell me you saw this happen, Hellas, that you've the blood to show for it? If it's Jester's words you trust, then I daresay—"

"Here," came Distra's strained voice. She stepped forward bearing a once-empty water skin, now bloated with troll's blood.

A dozen more plopped to the ground in a swirl of dust after the first, filled with the fishy sweet, stinking ichor. During the butchering, I'd wretched at least twice. But because I'd delivered the killing stroke, Distra made me bear the brunt of the processing of the beast as well. We could have brought back twice as many full waterskins if the rest hadn't been lost during the fight with Khemetri. I had been urged to drink as much of the troll's blood as I could stomach, and in doing so, marveled at the speed my leg wound healed. Afterward, I'd felt stronger, my muscles fuller, my senses sharper. The next day, I found myself at the head of the column, barely breathing while the rest of the hunting party lagged. I saw why Omatuu needed the liquid. Why the Stormlords let the bloodtraders and the cabals persist to produce more of it. We'd harvested as much of the troll skin as we could carry; it would be used for leather armor, I was told. Hellas had made me a necklace of the same onyx talons that nearly tore out my throat.

And now, Omatuu strode forth to gently lift it. He let the necklace drop as he inspected me. "You survived." He raised his eyebrows, then sighed. "Of the twenty Seekers I sent on this mission, the Power has deigned it necessary to return you to me. Tell me, was it this troll that killed so many of my Cloudbreakers?"

"Khemetri," Distra grunted in explanation. As Omatuu's gaze settled on her, she signed the word for ogres.

"Ah, well, perhaps if you'd sicced Jester on them first, more of you would have lived. Clearly, Jester is a ferocious warrior, far more capable than I first thought. And only...how old are you again?"

I suddenly remembered a birthday had come and gone in the months I'd spent in the Wildness. Without a mother to celebrate such a thing, its importance was easily forgotten.

The Power. That was all that mattered now.

I could never go back to the days of ignorance and innocence, when the most I looked forward to was the one moment in the year when my woefully poor mother showered me with the only thing the Stormseye Brotherhood couldn't suppress: love. Even now, centuries later, with the Power at my disposal, my heart yearns to see a meager slice of sweet bread presented in her hands.

I swallowed hard. "Sixteen."

"Jester..." Omatuu stared upward as if searching his own thoughts, rocking heel to toe a few times before coming to a rest. "I take back the name I gave you. It was ill-conceived, as were many of my judgments."

A deeper silence than before spitted the throng of Cloudbreakers. They were just as stunned by the admission as I was. Distra stepped up beside me, a hand cupped over my shoulder. I waited for the jab. None came.

"So, I'll let your peers choose one for you." Omatuu turned to go, voice trailing away as he went. "When you're finished, come see me."

Once he strode out of earshot, my peers began.

"Fireheart!"

"Trollslayer!"

"Ironsoul!"

"I liked Jester!" The others shoved and booed that Seeker from the group, Hellas delivering a parting boot to their backside.

Countless suggestions came and went. It was too many to track, and regardless of the merits of the names, all of them sounded far better than Jester.

Seekers less interested in my aggrandizement started peeling away from the pack. The suggestions, too, dwindled as the energy of the moment ebbed. I chose to remain quiet amid the rain of validation. Some seemed to view my lack of desire to pick a name as a way to continue at the center of attention. In truth, I was simply indecisive. If I picked one, I might offend the others. Having just gained their respect, I was in no hurry to make enemies again. The young are social creatures, rendered stupid by their aversion to being disliked.

Soon, only a handful remained. Cookfires crackled nearby where Seekers broke into conversation. Flagons of drink slammed together, a bell tolling the end of my night's glory.

Just as the suggestions came to an abrupt halt, Distra said, "Truespear."

I liked it a great deal. More than the other names mentioned, it gave credibility to my unique choice of weapon as well as the skill I'd worked to hone with it. Not only that, coming from her, it meant substantially more. Her trust in me, for once, may have matched my own.

"Truespear...yes." I hesitated. "Thank you." Justice and pride begged me to take back that which was stolen. "Though, I'd like to just be called El again, too."

Hellas shrugged, chuckled, then wrapped an arm around Laertha. The pair wandered toward the fire to start their routine of heavy drinking.

Distra bowed her head. "El."

I chewed my lip as I stepped over an exposed root and climbed the steep mound to Omatuu's fortress. The headband of the Cloudbreaker who'd grown too desperate hung from a thorny hook. I arrived at the base, where the roots jutted upward from the mound at a forty-five-degree angle toward the sky. To my surprise, a hair's breadth of space separated each gnarled timber of the latticework.

There was no entrance.

I took a breath. What could Omatuu want from me? Slung around my neck and shoulders, a dozen waterskins taut-full of troll's blood weighed me down. Distra had made sure I took them straight to Omatuu.

My palm came to rest against the wood. It was red—warm and slick like a manzanita tree after a heavy rain. Suddenly the wood groaned, sinewy branches bending to either side to form a portal. I stepped back in a hurry and nearly fell backward down the mound. A canvas flap hung within, stirring gently. A handful of roots creaked as they eased together, crisscrossing into a series of steps. I mounted them slowly, careful not to let the swinging troll's blood throw me off balance.

The canvas flap slithered aside. Before I'd fully stepped through, Omatuu was back to haranguing me.

"I've little time for chit-chat, but I'm curious what name the others have chosen for you, so speak quickly and do so without all the 'umms' and 'I thinks' and 'I don't knows.' You proved yourself a viable Seeker. Try acting it for once."

I immediately stammered and hated myself for it. Omatuu was bent over a desk, eyeballing the contents of a green glass vial. After a moment, he snapped his fingers in rapid succession, an imperious demand.

"Truespear," I blurted. "But really I just want my old name back. The one you took. El."

Omatuu glanced at me sidelong then returned to his vial. He lifted a second one filled with a ruddy liquid, then poured half its contents into the green. "El it is, then. I'll let the others call you Truespear when they fancy. I find such a name..." He waved a hand in the air. "Overwrought."

With utmost caution, he slid the green vial into a tall iron stand. His hands drifted backward tentatively as if giving space to a cobra, ready to strike if he moved too fast.

Omatuu turned around to face me. "Now, El, I see you are above your peers."

"What do you mean?"

"You won't fool me with humility, El, so stop fooling yourself. I know you think you're better than the others. And maybe you are. You're half, even a third their age, and in a matter of months, you faced ogres and a wizard Prime, and then killed a troll."

Despite my agreement, it felt shameful to have him speak my thoughts out in the open. Jaw clenched, I nodded. "Each of them milks their doubts in different ways."

"But not you." The wizard paced over to a pile of scrolls. "You've not given over to despair yet. You know time is of the essence—the pursuit of the Power is a mission requiring singular focus without distraction." He brushed the scrolls aside then lifted a thick tome. "Do you know what this is?"

I didn't.

"This is a Tome of Callings," he said. "War callings, to be specific. Here, try reading it."

He handed me the thick book. Its covering was smooth, a different kind of leather than I'd ever seen. A hard, off-white material bound the spine as well as the edges of both front and back covers. Giddy with excitement, I pulled it open to the middle.

Blank.

I frowned and flipped through to the back, then backward to the front. Through and through, every page was unmarked.

"This, young El, is what you seek. When you take a wizard's knot, you'll journey beyond the Seething Sea to the Occuli Rift. There, you'll climb down into the crater and drop a wizard's knot into the abyssal well. That's where the Power lies and where it originated. And this..." Omatuu hefted the tome from my hands, lean bicep muscle swelling. "This is what you'll get in return. All the knowledge of the wizard whose life you took, and in their own words, the war callings. Secrets...flesh and bone and blood made ink."

His final words stabbed at me. I eyed the whitish material clasped around the book, as well as the leather that was not leather. My stomach went sour. "Why are you telling me this?"

"It's what all Cloudbreakers must know if they're to serve my purposes. What good are you to me half-informed? How content would you be to remain in my cabal if your questions went unanswered? By offering you these important scraps about your desired destination,

I give you no reason to venture far. I secure your loyalty." Omatuu smiled, a fake thing. "Isn't that right?"

Luckily, my nod came quicker than my doubts.

Omatuu stepped closer, looming. "To have survived this long at your age, there must be a great deal more to you than I first assumed. I'm not often surprised. Yet here you are. In truth, I thought I'd sent you to your death, not on some glorious crusade."

The shift in the Prime's attitude toward me caught me off guard for the span of heartbeats. That was as long as it took to see through the facade. His words and actions were misaligned. He played my ego for some personal benefit which I did not see.

That was the second time I suspected he feared me.

"You have greatness ahead of you, El." A stiff, avuncular hand dropped onto my shoulder. "Thusly, I have a task for you."

He flicked one of the bladders of troll's blood still draped around my torso. "You're to take eight of these to Dags Grimjaw, a bloodtrader. Exchange them for the items on this list."

Omatuu plucked a thin scroll from the table at his side and handed it to me. I tucked it into my trousers; paper rustled against paper as it slid into place next to my other scroll. I froze.

The Cloudbreaker wizard narrowed his eyes around the source of the sound. Eager to move beyond suspicion, I bowed forward, breaking his gaze. "I'm honored to be given such an important task. I won't let you down, Omatuu."

"Yes." The Prime's lips pursed as he turned away slightly. "I'm certain you won't."

Before I could turn to go, Omatuu snared my arm. His grip was like steel; it took everything in me to stifle a shout of pain. When I looked into his face, I could tell from his relaxed expression that this was only a fraction of the pressure he could apply.

"One last thing." His tone dropped, a bottomless well of dark intent. "If you do not return within two weeks' time, I'll hunt you down and kill you." He wafted upward with a hand. A chilly gust billowed in through the canvas flap behind me, wormed down the collar of my tunic and set goose prickles to standing along both arms. "I need the items on that list as soon as possible. So, on the off chance you find a wizard's tower, ignore it. Understand?"

I did.

Over the course of years spent as the sole wizard in a large cabal, Omatuu had developed clever tools for manipulation: degradation, fear, obligation, flattery, and any mixture therein. I was certain he saw physical abuse as beneath his efforts but not beyond them if it got him exactly what he wanted.

Manipulations, however, worked only on the unsuspecting.

I nodded. "I understand." Then I slipped out into the cool night beyond Omatuu's fortress.

Chapter Seventeen

BLOODTRADER

I spent three days alone in the Wildness on my way to the blood-trader's outpost; it came and went in a blur of blustery nights and overcast skies. I'd started my journey from Cannalis just before the start of summer, and now, autumn's blight bled across the land. For me, it was a welcome change. I found solace in the seasonal transition and the beauty of the dying—so long as it wasn't my corpse nature feasted on.

Propped up with my back against the trunk of a sprawling cherry tree, I removed the ropes holding the tiny cask of troll blood from my shoulders, then drew forth Omatuu's list. I'd already read it a half dozen times.

With no knowledge to relate them to a purpose, I contented myself to memorize them for future reference. "Iron Summoner's bowl treated with hydra venom. Boneshard of..." The next bulky word filled my mouth "...humungalor. Touchstone from the shores of the Blue Colossus." The last snared my imagination and I repeated it over and over in my mind.

The shores of the Blue Colossus? It sounded like a creature, yet what creature was large enough to command an entire shore? The size and scope of the world within the walls of Cannalis withered to a pinprick with each passing day spent in the Wildness.

After a while, I wrapped the rope tethers of the cask about my torso and heaved myself to my feet. Distra had drawn me a map that was now spread between my hands as I stumbled across a shallow creek. Indifferent to the squelch of water in my boots, I surveyed the area ahead. So far, the directions she'd given me were impressive. Clearly, she was accustomed to this kind of thing and had done it for others.

From what I'd heard, Omatuu's discovery of the Night Bridge was inevitable, and that meant he would need things from the bloodtrader at increasingly frequent rates to prepare for the unknown dangers awaiting him once he left the cabal. Being far too fixated on mastering my spear, I'd never paid much attention to the comings and goings of the other Seekers in camp, but I assumed Omatuu sent them on clandestine missions like mine with some regularity.

At least, that's what I would have done.

I imagined there was only so long a big fish might last in a pool of similarly hungry, smaller ones. Omatuu was on borrowed time—I think he knew this best of all.

Yellow light poured over the horizon as I descended into a small clearing ringed by pine and spruce trees. A squat two-story cottage, with a long lodge attached, sat at the clearing's center. On my way toward it, I slowed beside a pond full of strange two-headed fish and three-eyed frogs to read a sign. It said, 'Bloodtrader Outpost.'

A funnel of smoke crawled into the blue-gray sky. Steam covered the interior of the windows in a thin layer, diffusing dancing candle flame within. I circled the cottage in search of a front door, but the awnings submerged the landing in impenetrable shadow.

At a steady pace, I moved closer.

When I was within twenty feet, a dark, angry face filled a window, startling me and propelling me backward onto my ass in the damp grass.

"You there!" the creature barked. "By the Power, if you're not prepared to explain your damnable creeping, you best ready yourself for consummation by horrors unimaginable. Now talk, and faster than you walk!"

I gaped at the furrowed brow in the window. From the look of the creature's face alone, I would have expected a less human-sounding voice. But the only thing odd about it was the twang accompanying the harshness.

"I—I'm a Seeker," I stammered, then, motivated not to be eaten, shouted, "sent by Omatuu of the Cloudbreakers!"

A door dragged upward with a rumble, disappearing somewhere in the cottage roof. My jaw dropped open. I'd seen magic and monsters, yet this simple engineering trick stunned me; perhaps because it was wrought from simple hands rather than those destined for some slice of godhood.

I rolled onto one side, the sloshing blood around my torso making my movements awkward as I came to stand.

Light framed the figure in silhouette. A broad upper body tapered into slender hips and short legs. He appeared to have cloven hooves for feet. "Disgusting little pipsqueak, aren't you?" the bloodtrader said. "Woulda given my humungalor indigestion if I'd let her eat ya. Woulda wasted every drop of troll's blood you brought to make her gut right again, too."

Hesitantly, I searched the trees behind me. I didn't know what a humungalor was except that Omatuu wanted a shard of its bones. And apparently, one could eat me.

A high-pitched laugh came from the bloodtrader as he noticed my worry.

I steeled myself, puffing out my chest. After all, I was El Truespear. "How'd you know I carried troll's blood?"

"'Cause it's always troll's blood." The creature stepped to one side. "Now get in here. You're soiling my good grass. And wipe your damn feet! Who knows what fecal this or that you got clinging to ya."

A woven mat of coarse hair lay outside the door. I followed the creature's direction, then entered. When I got a clear look at the bloodtrader for the first time, my heart jumped to the back of my throat. I stepped back as if my bare feet touched hot coals.

In more ways than gave me comfort, Dags Grimjaw resembled the troll I'd slain less than a week prior. Cobalt skin, the very same; a long, heavy nose and ears like a donkey. If he'd had golden eyes, too, I might have bolted. The terror of my fight with the troll was still very much alive inside me.

Thankfully, there were a few vital differences. One of the bloodtrader's eyes was brown, the other ocean blue. Where the troll had been lean and long-limbed in its upper body, this creature was compact and stodgy. And it helped calm my nerves immensely to see him dressed like a human. A rich one. Dozens of sparkling rings adorned root-thick fingers while gold loops hung from fat lips and drooping ears.

"Walk into my damn cottage and won't even look me in the eye, eh? Feckless turds, that's who Omatuu sends me. I'm surprised he trusted ya with such a large cache."

"I'm—I'm sorry," I said. I looked him in the eyes for a moment. "I just...I wasn't..."

Instead of sharp canines jutting from a wide lower jaw, Dags had a row of flat, non-predatory teeth, which were now lining a broad, unsavory expression. "Expecting Idrinnia the Everlasting Maiden were you? Porcelain skin, pert teats, flaxen locks. All that was what ya hoped for, eh?"

"No, no, I—"

"Well, worry not your brainless head, I'm no troll. Though, as you been so quick to reckon, our species ain't too far off. The Power only knows what I am—besides an abomination, I mean."

The word 'abomination' was spoken as a matter of fact rather than with any derogatory intent, which sparked my curiosity. "What do you mean, you're an abomination?"

He raised a heavily ridged brow. His tone mocked my own, "What do you mean, you're an abomination?"

My fear ebbed as we spoke. I set my feet and stared him down. "For a hermit, you're about as hospitable as a cow pie."

"See, there we go. A real person. Humans try to fake so much of who they are. Honesty, when ya'll manage to come by it, is the best part about the lot of ya." He wiped his protuberant nose with a fat finger, then smiled. "As ya no doubt already realized, I'm Dags Grimjaw, and you'll be happy to hear, I decided I like ya—just now. But I am surprised you're surprised by my demeanor. The humor and mood of Grimjaw's Bloodtrade is part of the experience. I like to think wizards and Seekers come here to bandy words as much as they do to exchange valuables. Omatuu shoulda told ya to expect a bit of a tongue-lashing."

I adjusted the tethers strapping the blood to my back. "He told me little."

"The man won't be winning many popularity contests, that's for sure," Dags said. "Not that I'm one to talk. Though it is hard for me to imagine my rough play with words fails to charm even the touchy ones."

"If not your words," I said, "your face surely wins them over."

Dags Grimjaw shot me a stunned glare, then burst into wheezing laughter. He took me under a shoulder, which I expected to smell worse than it did—the troll I'd fought smelled of fish and mildew. Grimjaw on the other hand exuded the smell of pine needles and smoke.

"Come on then, tell me what ya need, my young jackanapes. Maybe Omatuu needs a dried ogre cock to warm his puckered backside." Dags helped remove the cask from my back, then held it up to one ear with ease to slosh it. "Eight liters, shy two points. Here, you'll want some tea. I've a cot in the back for ya to rest the night. Don't expect to keep me up talking though. I go to bed early and bend that rule for none." He winked. "Beauty sleep, you know."

With a smile, I fished the scroll with Omatuu's items from my trouser pocket. After unrolling it, I fidgeted with it a moment.

"What?" Dags Grimjaw said. "Still learning to read?"

"No." I looked at him expectantly. "I just wish I knew what some of these things were."

"Lemme see." The bloodtrader took the scroll and held it daintily between thumb and index finger. He brought a tiny spectacle up to an eye—the blue one. "Judging by your puny frame, I expect you're a new Seeker, then?"

"I am."

"Of course you are." He returned the spectacle into his multi-pocketed vest. "Any Seeker with a few years' experience would know what these things were. Come."

Dags gave me no choice as he snagged me firmly by the collar and dragged me unceremoniously around his shop. Three long tables took up the majority of space in the lodge. If I had to categorize them myself, one held tools: bowls, goblets, hammers, and weapons of various make and age. Another bore liquids in hundreds, if not thousands, of vials. Bladders of every color and hue covered the table. Casks sat underneath between the legs in rows three deep.

The third and largest table was more mysterious, a sort of catchall for anything else. Mushrooms, powders, jewels, scrolls, tomes, bones, and even a tree branch lay strewn in haphazard arrangements. It was here that we started.

Dags Grimjaw plucked a tan sliver from a pile. "A shard of bone from the thigh of a humungalor. You know what that is?"

I shook my head.

"If you become a wizard, they'll be your best friend and your worst enemy, outside of other wizards, that is. Humungalor are scions of the

Fey, a family of giants who protect the earth from those who'd do it harm. They, along with the other Fey, were here long before the Power."

I frowned. I'd heard of giants before—never referred to as humungalor. "How did you get a shard of one's thigh bone?"

"When wizards fight, they sometimes bind humungalor to them as thralls. They're kind of like slaves. By kind of, I mean that's exactly what they are. Anyway, if two wizards duel and both have humungalor, one is sure to die; even if their wizard dies first, honor compels them to battle to the death. On rare occasions, other things can kill them, but those instances are few and far between. Humungalor are not to be trifled with."

"You called it a scion of the Fey. Are there other such creatures?" I touched a curved horn as long as my arm. "If I'm to be a wizard, I want to know everything."

Sheer disbelief twisted Dags's face. I didn't blame him. Having been summarily shunned for so long by my comrades in the Cloudbreakers, as well as my wizard Prime, I lacked all knowledge beyond what it took to become a wizard. The volume of information that flowed my way was but a trickle of what I needed.

To this day, I am thankful for my friend, Dags Grimjaw. Though his barbed words came in ample quantity, so too did his willingness to share what was important.

Dags shook away the expression dramatically. "Annoying as you are, Omatuu rankles me more. For whatever reason, the righteous twerp deemed it necessary to keep ya ignorant. 'Twould bring a warmth to my heart to undo his intentions there. I've always been one to stick thorns in sides where they're least expected."

I smiled. "And I thank you for it."

He chuckled. "Aye, just make sure you don't strain yourself overmuch. I'd hate your brain to leak from your ears. As ya can see, my floorboards are exquisitely tidy. Now what's your question? You're so damned ignorant, it's hard to keep track. Scions of the Fey, was it?"

I nodded. "Yes, you said humungalor were a family of giants dedicated to protecting the earth. I assume you mean 'family' as in different kinds of them."

"Careful now, you're getting smarter." Dags winked at me. "Yes, giants, minotaurs, the cyclopeans, all protectors of the earth. Equia'raxa guard the waters of life. The Avilar rule the skies. And the Draco are keepers of the flame, and that includes lightning. A scion of the Fey for every element. They were here long before the Power came along and wizards started binding and enslaving everything they damn well could."

I ran a hand over a series of axes. A desperate face appeared on the reflection of one blade. I leaned in close, inspecting it. The image of the man pounded against his steel prison, causing the ax to jump. I jerked back my hand.

"Look out for that one. Mad man, he was."

I gathered myself and said, "I thought the Power had always existed. Like air or water."

"Stormseye Brotherhood garbage, that is." Dags Grimjaw scoffed. "They want ya to think the Power is the only source of magic—an eternal one that only they control. At this point, that's becoming truer every day. But it ain't so yet. As long as the abominations exist, and the Fey exist, the Power is dispersed and made accessible to the likes of you, me, Omatuu, the Illuminated Path. Bet you never heard of half this stuff before when you were living in Cannalis?"

"I never told you I lived in Cannalis."

Dags huffed. "Didn't have to. Anyone living outside the Brotherhood's reach knows these things. The Fey and all the rest... it's all just a matter of fact for those livin' in the world."

"I thought the Stormseye Brotherhood *allowed* the cabals to exist?" I thought back to my conversation with Hellas. He'd made it sound like the cabals were permitted by the Great Archon, rather than a final hurdle to seizing absolute domain. "Don't the Stormlords need the bloodtrade? Don't they use the cabals as protection against the Illuminated Path?"

Grimjaw shrugged. "Sure. That, too. But the Great Archon ain't as powerful as folk like to think. The cities of Kelundar are ensorcelled. That keeps out the most powerful scions of the Fey and subdues any magic but the Stormlords own within their walls. If every last wizard wasn't so damnably selfish, they could utilize the Fey to break the high and mighty Archon's grasp on Kelundar."

The Stormseye Brotherhood weren't as strong as people said. I could hardly believe it. My entire journey to that point was done under the false impression that I was allowed to do so at the Brotherhood's consent. If what Dags suggested was true, if the Great Archon could be brought down using the Fey...

"Is the Fey stronger than the Stormseye Brotherhood?"

Dags wagged a cobalt finger, a ruby sparkling in the candlelight as he did. "Don't get hasty, young un'. I didn't say that. I only said it was possible. Think more one-in-a-million than a one-in-ten chance. And the time for that possibility grows short. The Fey weaken with every passing year while the Great Archon grows stronger. Look here."

He turned my attention to a small porous stone, black as the night sky and marbled through with iridescent blue. Before he said what it was, something inside me already knew.

"A touchstone...from the shores of the Blue Colossus."

Dags frowned. "Not so dumb as ya thought you were, eh?"

I never thought that.

He brought a candle flame up next to the stone. Lightning rippled within, throwing rays of dazzling light outward wherever the fire passed. "This stone comes from the area around the nest of the Blue Colossus. It doesn't matter how powerful the Great Archon gets, if someone figures out how to kill that titanic creature they would supplant the high and mighty turd in a wink. Stones likes this one—hundreds of miles from the Blue Colossus—contain immense power, for it is the father of all abominations: trolls, ogres, hydras. It birthed all of them. Myself included, whatever I am."

I gawked at the blossoming energy within the stone. "What *is* the Blue Colossus?"

"A behemoth. Its head scrapes the heavens, and its shoulders span the ocean. It's as ancient as the Power itself. A god. And there's not a thing in this world more valuable than its blood."

I was entranced. I knew then I needed to see the titanic creature. For how long I stared at the stone, I did not know. Eventually, Dags nudged me. "Here, for Omatuu." He thrust the stone into my hand.

"What—uh—what does it do?"

"Depends."

"On what?"

"Whatever you want." He left it at that as he loaded up the other two items on my list, then hefted a glowing white disk. "Time for bed, now. Don't bother me further." A grim mood fell over the bloodtrader and we fell into silence. He'd already given so much, I decided not to push my luck.

With grunts and hand motions, he showed me where I'd sleep for the night in the lodge then disappeared to his own quarters in the second story of the connected cottage. It was clear he wasn't worried I'd steal anything. He didn't need to. The absence of a warning was warning enough.

I lied awake long into the late hours of the night. From my place on my cot, I watched candles gutter, evoking spokes of luminous blue light from the onyx touchstone from the shores of the Blue Colossus.

"Whatever you want," I whispered. Then, I fell soundly asleep.

Chapter Eighteen

REVELATION

I woke to the sound of Dags Grimjaw sweeping his floorboards. I lay there unmoving as he worked. Since the fight with the troll a week earlier, I'd been lugging blood through the Wildness, and had yet to find a spare moment for solid rest. Sharp tongue or no, Dags made me feel comfortable, and so, for what I assumed to be a few short minutes, I fell back asleep.

A loud splash preceded flecks of liquid striking my face. I sat up in a rush to find the bloodtrader shoving a mop across the floor. "Did I wake ya?" After a couple thrusts and drags, he submerged the tangled threads in the bucket once more. "Apologies. Lot of work to keep the place tidy. Gotta start early."

I rubbed sleep from my eyes, and then set about loading my pack, making sure the first things in were the ones on Omatuu's list. The touchstone's smooth surface cooled my palm. I slowed, staring at it for a long moment before bundling it in a cloth and shoving it into the pack.

The bloodtrader stopped his work to offer me a biscuit and fish head.

My nose wrinkled. Fish in Cannalis was never something you ate, and I'd seen the three-headed ones in Dags's pond. I waved it away. "It's a bit early for fish."

"And yet, there's no time like the present to be a complete and utter imbecile." Dags narrowed his mismatched eyes. Unlike our other moments of banter, this time he was legitimately offended. "Who taught you to refuse the generosity of a host? Bad manners. Besides, I'm the best cook in the Wildness and—"

I snapped up the cold morsel and tossed it in my mouth. A burst of salt, tender flesh, and flavor tightened around my taste buds as I chewed. My eyes flicked to the biscuit. With his expertise well established, I was eager for that taste as well.

"Always trust what I say," said Dags.

"It tastes okay," I said with a smile.

A low growl filled Dags's throat. "You know you're a feckless turd?"

"So I've been told by my betters." I laughed. "And I trust what they say."

The abomination clapped his hands. "Now you're talking sense." He frowned. "I just realized I never got your name."

Mouth brimming with buttery, flaky biscuit, I chewed a moment, finger hovering over my lips, then swallowed. "El. Though I was recently given the name Truespear. And before that, Omatuu had everyone calling me Jester."

Dags grunted. "Omatuu always dubs someone 'Jester.' If ya do become a wizard, you'll be the first of those he's named to do so—the first to live longer than six months, for that matter. He's a bastard, aye, but he's got a knack for picking out the Seekers who die quickest."

Annoyance set the muscles of my neck and shoulders to twitching. "I suppose I've two months left to prove him wrong, then."

Leaden sadness sagged through me. Already, I had been in the Wildness over four months. My promise to Trin of returning in six would go unfulfilled, just as I knew it would when I had said it. A hot barb of guilt jabbed at my heart. Our goodbye had been laced in lies—all of them mine. If anything had befallen Trin or her family, the blame belonged to me. I could have helped and didn't. There were no words that might soften or excuse my betrayal. I was doomed to live with my choice regardless of whether I attained the Power.

My appetite lost, I put the food down and gathered my things. "I should be going." I slung the pack onto my back, then headed for the door.

Dags waved a hand. The door slid upward into a hidden slot. Magic and engineering both, it seemed.

"You're a wizard?"

A black tongue lolled from his mouth as he spat in disgust. "Blargh! Don't offend me so. I'm an abomination. I've my own tricks."

As I made to step through the portal, the scroll in my pocket radiated warmth. I stopped, hand falling to my pocket. My palm tingled where it hovered. What was I doing? I possessed an item of mysterious origins, and here was a creature who might know more about it. If knowing what others didn't was a boon in the way of wizards, I would be remiss not to take the opportunity before me. Further, my list of people to trust was running woefully short. And I liked Dags. Perhaps he wished to stick yet another thorn in Omatuu's side by helping me.

I turned back. "Wait. I—I have something. I've not shared it with anyone. Maybe you could tell me more about it?"

"Oh, secrets!" He rubbed fleshy, leathery palms together. "Acting like a real wizard already, eh?"

I fished into my trouser pocket for the scroll and pulled it out.

"Pfah! A love letter?" Three brisk steps later and Dags was holding the scroll...unrolling it. "But we've only known each other..."

Whatever joke he'd been about to say died in his throat. A second later, he gasped, giving me a start.

Hands shaking, he lowered the scroll, staring at me in awe. His black tongue wormed over thick lips. In all our years of friendship thereafter, I would never again see him so unnerved. "How...how did you get this?"

I kept my lips tightly sealed.

His multicolored eyes flitted from me to the scroll. Shifting the straps of my pack, I waited. Under his breath, he let out a string of inaudible curses, then said, "What do you want for it?"

I shrugged. "Well, first off—"

"Here!" He swept a pile of trinkets across the table toward me, then shot me a furtive look.

I frowned and gaped. Grimjaw chewed a massive lip. "More eh?" Then he started piling things onto the mound on the table. Three casks of troll's blood, far more than I'd brought with me; dozens of boneshards; various bowls chased with alien alloys; the ax with the man trapped inside; and finally, a score of vials that clattered and tumbled and broke, splashing their contents across the floor and undoing his cleaning from the morning in a single sweep of his arms.

"Grimjaw." The pile of valuables continued to grow as he ignored the mess. The whites of his eyes were frantic. I raised my palms in the hopes of inciting calm. "Grimjaw!"

At this, the abomination paused, panting. He wiped sweat from his brow with a trembling hand. "Take it all! Take anything you want. Just...please just let me keep it."

Lips set in a firm, thin line, I stepped forward, hand reaching for the scroll in his grasp. A tear welled in one eye as he watched me take it. To my relief, he gave no fight. If there was one quality defining Dags Grimjaw, it was honesty.

The bloodtrader fell to his knees, hands clasped together. Begging, however, was not beyond him. "Please, El, I'll trade you anything for it."

I looked at the scroll, then back at him. "Tell me what it is first."

He laughed, a maniacal thing as he shook his head in disbelief. "You have the Sun Scroll and you don't even..." Tall ears twitched. He sought calm in a slow exhale. "It is a guide of immeasurable value."

Parchment rustled as I unrolled the scroll.

Trade nothing.

Longingly, I looked at the touchstone from the shores of the Blue Colossus. Morning light played over the iridescent marbling, azure light streaked and rippled within.

I wanted that stone—the secrets it held. Dags saw my admiration and gave a short, meek chuckle. "The touchstone? I'll give ya every damn one I got. I'll—"

"No." Jaw clenched, I shook my head. His reaction to the Sun Scroll validated its importance. "I can't."

The Sun Scroll, as I suddenly knew it, had led me to where I was. The guiding star for my journey. As aggravating as it had been, it had yet to steer me wrong. If I gave it up, I could be lost, and that might make all the difference. "I won't trade it." My voice was dispassionate. "Not for anything."

Dags wilted, sobbing and moaning. When it didn't appear he would stop anytime soon, I made to leave, but a heavy hand snared my trousers. "Wait! Wait! What if...what if I just held onto it for a little while."

"No." I jiggled my pant leg.

"One hour! That's all I ask. In exchange you can take anything you'd like. Just let me hold it for an hour." I looked into his eyes, saw how meaningful it would be for him.

The Sun Scroll said nothing about letting him borrow it.

Dags took the scroll, handling it as if it were made of a million fine threads of twisted glass. Seeing this, I grimaced a little. I had crumpled it, stuffed it into my trousers, sweat on it, and soiled it time and time again with grimy hands.

He rushed outside to the rim of the pond. He placed the Sun Scroll at his feet then sat cross-legged and stared down at it.

Satisfied he didn't mean to steal it, I perused the tables, finding objects of infinite curiosity and allure. Yet every time I decided I might take one, my eyes returned to the touchstone.

Nevertheless, I waited for the hour to be over before claiming the onyx-and-blue marbled stone. I walked out to join Dags by the pond. Tears filled the creases of his cobalt face. The sunlit parchment washed his visage in a soft glow.

I waited a few extra minutes and then cleared my throat. "It's time for me to go."

With a solemn nod, he regained his cloven-hoofed feet. "Thank you." As he placed the Sun Scroll in my hand, he grimaced, true pain etching his features. "I'll forever be in your debt."

I shrugged. "It seems a fair trade."

"You took a touchstone?"

I nodded.

Dags rolled his shoulders back, returning to form somewhat. "A predictable pick for one who has the intellect of a troglodyte." He snorted. "It'll serve you in some way down the road, I'm sure."

"If I make it that far."

Dags stared at me flatly. "You will. You have the Sun Scroll. You will." The seriousness of his expression and the hardness rimming his eyes was less comforting than I believe he intended. He snapped his fingers suddenly. "You have to take some concealment powder, as well."

"Why?"

"Because." A half-smile curled under one cheek. "The Sun Scroll said you must. 'Give the keeper of this scroll concealment powder.' It's bonded to ya, it seems. And whatever the scroll says to do, ya do. I'm no exception, even if I'm not its keeper."

Threads of fluttering ecstasy wound into my hand from the Sun Scroll, a feeling now rendered eerie by the tone of warning in Dags's voice. He made it sound as if to deviate from what the scroll command-ed would lead to some horrible doom, much like the Elder had done.

The back of my throat grew thick and gummy, a feeling I couldn't move no matter how many times I swallowed. The hand holding the scroll started to itch. "You still haven't told me how you know what it is, or where it came from, or what it does."

"I know of every sacred object from here to the Crack beyond Mahjiri." The bloodtrader broke into a fit of harsh laughter. "You really don't know, do you? Oh, El..." His laughter died as he thrust a jeweled finger at the Sun Scroll in my open palm. Weary, desperate eyes held me. "Young fool, you hold the soul of Idrinnia the Everlasting Maiden in your hand!"

Chapter Nineteen

ECHOES MADE SACRED

On my return journey to the Cloudbreakers' camp, I must have looked at the Sun Scroll no fewer than a thousand times.

The soul of Idrinnia—how could that be? The Everlasting Maiden had fallen to the Great Archon two hundred years prior. Who had taken her soul and bound it to a piece of parchment? And how had the Elder come to possess such a thing?

Despite the wonder and excitement rippling through me, a gaping pit opened to consume it all. While Dags Grimjaw's knowledge on the matter was ample, a number of burning questions remained unanswered. Unless I gained an audience with the Great Archon, or crossed paths with the Elder again, I wondered if I'd ever have the full truth about the scroll.

"All I know," Dags had said, "is that Idrinnia's soul resides in this parchment. In death, she has seen the horizons at the beginning and end of time. As the maiden of good and purity in this world, ya mustn't question her intentions. She loves all with a heart unrivaled. Even if she tells you to kill yourself, ya must, for that's what's best for the world."

The last part made my heart skip a beat. I hoped it wouldn't come to that.

"Oh don't worry there." Noticing my discomfort, Dags nudged my side with a fist. "If you disobey the Sun Scroll's command, your doom is sealed all the same."

His words set me on edge. As I traveled, I searched the woods with rapidly increasing wariness. What I carried in my trouser pocket was of immeasurable value, and in the Wildness, that meant immeasurable danger. If Omatuu were to discover the legendary scroll, he would no doubt steal it or kill me without a second thought. I had to assume any other wizard would, as well.

"Tell no one of the Sun Scroll," Dags had said in parting. "Especially not Omatuu. Protect it with your life."

The warning echoed at the back of my mind.

I stopped to listen. Birds gave their final trills to the dusk, but there was no other sound. I checked behind me, then quickened my pace. My imagination took hold, placing a troll or bear in every shadow, waiting to tear me apart at any moment. What might be the fate of Idrinnia's soul, then?

Eager to rid myself of the pressure accompanying such gloomy thoughts, I turned my attention to those more worthy and calming.

To Trin.

After my near-death experience at Khemetri's hands, I'd been suppressing my feelings and any pathways of the mind or heart that might lead me to them. For four months I'd been a Cloudbreaker, and in that time, I'd barely thought of Trin at all. Call it denial, or a survival mechanism. Call it whatever you wish, it didn't change the shame creeping into my bones. Now, as I closed in on the six-month mark since my hasty departure, her loving face comforted my mind's eye with increasing regularity—both boon and curse. Equal parts joy and abject regret burned through me like a poison, clawing up my throat from a place I wished to bury in my quest for the Power.

Our once unbreakable bond had been broken.

But it was for Trin's own good, I thought. If I'd told her why I'd fled Cannalis, she might have followed. And most likely, she would have died. No, lying was better. Betrayal was better. I could not—would not—see her crushed by an ogre or burned to a cinder by a wizard.

I touched the Sun Scroll. *Idrinnia's soul...*

My heart faltered, skipping a beat. If Trin only knew I carried it with me.

Sickening grief seeped into my awareness. I was surrounded by Seekers and wizards who'd kill or betray me, or Trin, for an edge. As much as I hated myself for the choice I'd made, it was for the best.

Even with such logical justifications as these, dark hooks remained, dragging me low. And in this way they would persist for centuries as a subtle and bitter paste coating my mind.

Tears threatening, I stopped to rest a while. Water poured down my parched throat, cold and satisfying. I unrolled the Sun Scroll.

Despite the sun shining on the horizon, the parchment was blank. I blinked at it in surprise; before, it had only needed to be day for words to appear.

Frowning, I held it up to the brightest part of the sky. Still nothing. I stuffed one of the biscuits from Dags in my mouth, and then took another swig of the waterskin. I started forward, marching a hundred yards with the scroll held before me like a compass.

Nothing.

I stared at the sun. "Are *you* broken? Or is Idrinnia's soul?" Neither answered, so I assumed it was my fault. If I continued onward in a straight line, I would cross a brook, then into an open meadow filled with wildflowers, but if I turned to my right or left, I would hit a dense stand of evergreens.

Heading to the right, I made for the forest, curious if something might change once inside its dark understory. In the gloom, I cautiously navigated upthrust root systems and the occasional ruin of a snag. After a hundred yards or so, I consulted the Sun Scroll; it appeared it would continue its silence.

I trekked onward, checking in periodically with Idrinnia.

Dark letters started to appear.

Trust your instincts.

I slowed to a trudge—stopped and surveyed the woods. I looked back at the Sun Scroll.

Trust your instincts.

I licked my lips, sensing I was on the verge of something important.

I walked back to the point where the Sun Scroll's words had finally appeared. Now keen, I took another step in the direction I'd come from. 'Trust your instincts' disappeared. I pivoted and stepped in reverse. The words reappeared.

My heartbeat quickened.

I moved forward and at a slight angle. Again, they were gone. I moved at another angle, slightly different than the first, and they were back.

In a zig-zagging line, I weaved through the darkening forest with the scroll stretched out before me. The sun slid behind the horizon as I made my way out of the forest. I kept the place where I'd first noticed the change in words consistently to my right as I went.

Eventually, I found myself standing in the evergreen forest opposite the point where I'd first entered the wood. I'd traveled in a perfect semi-circle. There was an invisible barrier with some invisible meaning.

I was clueless, so I went through the list of things Dags and the Elder had told me about the Sun Scroll.

It's sacred.

It can only be read when the sun is in the sky.

It only worked outside of Cannalis.

It contained the soul of Idrinnia the Everlasting.

Before I could come to any real conclusion, a high-pitched whistle cut my ruminations short. Half rolling, half crumpling the scroll, I hurriedly shoved it into my trouser pocket and took up my spear.

A clipped laugh eddied over the plain. Night soaked my vision, marred further by puffs of streaming breath. Cursing, I swung my spear left and caught motion there. A pair of gray headbands bobbed toward me.

"That you, Truespear?"

Hellas.

"Yes," I called back. "Here."

The Seeker materialized in the fading light, his cascade of blond hair catching its last rays. Laertha walked alongside him. They came to stand a stone's throw away. "Careful with that thing, troll slayer."

I glanced at my spear and found it still leveled at them. "Sorry. I wasn't expecting anyone out here." I lowered it. "What are you doing this far from camp?"

"Omatuu sent us to find your tracks," said Laertha. "Thought you might have gotten lost."

"Or killed," said Hellas. "Wanted us to retrieve the troll's blood if we could."

The Prime's vote of faith was limited, it appeared. "I wasn't due back until tomorrow."

"Omatuu isn't one to make a plan without a backup plan. We're actually the second group he sent to ensure you were on track." The squat Seeker rubbed his belly. "Besides, he likes to throw us out on patrol on occasion. Easier to run across Seekers from other cabals that way. The man thrives on the information we trade with them. The rise and fall of enemy wizards and all that."

I nodded. "I'll be glad to tell him I survived myself."

Hellas clapped my shoulder as I moved to join them. "We'll escort you back. Give me any reason to get out of this damn boring duty."

As we went, I marked the exact landscape, carving every inch of earth, every tree, every bend of brook and wildflower, into memory. As soon as I could, I would return to this place.

Idrinnia the Everlasting Maiden had a secret she wasn't telling me.

"You're late." Omatuu snatched the pack from my back. Thankfully, he ignored the two new pouches strung around my waist; they held the touchstone and concealment powder, given to me by Dags. The Sun Scroll, meanwhile, was safe and snug in a newly sewn pocket hidden behind my thigh. Silently, I watched Omatuu as he searched the pack for the items he requested. Now that I knew I carried Idrinnia's soul, worry filled me that the wizard Prime would discover it despite my cleverness. That he would kill me and take it.

Attempting to balance out his indignant mood, I made sure my tone was companionable. "I thought today was the deadline."

He ignored me.

"Here." I removed one of the waterskins from around my neck. "Dags said it was too much. A few points of troll's blood leftover and returned."

Omatuu paused, the dark-stained iron bowl in hand. "I've never known Dags Grimjaw to be so generous." His upper lip curled then twitched as he took the blood. "How very mysterious."

I shrugged. Omatuu continued to stare at me. Eager to avoid further conversation about what occurred at the bloodtrader's cottage, I changed the subject. "I've accomplished the task you gave me. In return, I only request that you answer a question."

Omatuu's eyelids fluttered. "In...return? How brazen you are to think—" The skin around his jaw line went taut. "Fine. Proceed."

I stood straighter. I thought of the scroll and how I might unearth the reason behind its odd behavior in the woods. "What does it mean for something to be sacred?"

"It means it holds power but also follows a set of rules or laws." Omatuu returned the iron bowl to the pack, then put the waterskin of troll's blood in after it, his movements purposefully slow. "Satisfied?"

"Almost." I smiled. "What if something sacred and another thing that's sacred interact? Does one of those rules or laws supersede—"

"Both are nullified." Omatuu stepped toward me, his tone suddenly threatening. "My, you are curious today, aren't you El? Dags must have been so very informative."

To my credit, I did not balk. Anyone should have feared Omatuu, but I refused to let him know that I did, even if it would have been in my best interest to do so. I remained outwardly neutral. "If I lack understanding, it could cost me my life. You said that. I am only trying to learn."

Omatuu's cheek twitched. "Careful, now. An abundance of understanding could cost you your life just as easily."

We locked eyes. It was Omatuu who broke away first. "So, you wish to learn at a faster rate. At present, I have more pressing things to attend, but when I return from a short journey we'll...discuss. Your curiosity has piqued my own. Rarely do I wish to get to know one of my Seekers better. I trust that both of us will willingly answer any questions the other might have." His eyes scanned me toes to crown, crawling over the hidden pocket I'd sewn into my trousers. The urge to flee shot through me, but I held fast. "About anything...anything at all."

A shiver settled into my spine.

Tell no one of the Sun Scroll. Especially not Omatuu.

He didn't know what I had, but he knew I had something.

And he was sure to find it when he returned.

Chapter Twenty

PREDATOR AND PREY

An hour before midnight, with the full moon hidden behind a bank of glowing clouds, Omatuu left the Cloudbreaker camp. After passing beyond the wall of gashbrush, he took off at a forty-five-degree angle, walking briskly.

I stayed at a distance, unsure what powers he might have to detect me. Under the moon's light we traveled. His wizard's cap poked at the sky as he strode fearlessly across meadows and over rolling hills. I skulked after him, heart hammering in the shadows of any cover I could find. I played a dangerous game, stalking such a man when he required secrecy.

And secrets were more valuable to wizards than anything Dags Grimjaw possessed.

When Omatuu headed up a hill and then into a thick wood, I worried I'd never be able to track him under the blackout-dark of the canopy. He turned slightly, bearded chin hovering over a shoulder. I ducked behind a stone redoubt, applauding myself for traveling light in favor of staying nimble. My spear and the touchstone were left in my tent at camp.

What seemed an eternity of horrified moments followed. Blood pounded in my ears and my chest ached fiercely, for I expected a fireball or concussive wind or spike of ice to usher me toward death at any second.

Ten heartbeats passed and it didn't come. Courage finally summoned, I peeked out from my hiding place. An intense blaze, no larger in circumference at its base than Omatuu's hand, crackled in the wizard's palm. A brilliant glowing nimbus cast the surrounding grass and tree trunks in yellow light.

Omatuu entered the wood.

I followed, feeling nominally comforted by the fact that the wizard would be night-blind even if he suspected my presence. Now, it was up to me to tread quietly. I reached for the pouch of concealment powder at the front of my belt.

"You could be talking to a friend a foot away and a pinch of this stuff will make it so you don't exist," Dags had said. "Or rub a bit onto something you want hidden and it'll wink out like that—" He snapped his fingers.

I wished I had thought to ask if 'don't exist' covered sight as well as sound. "How long?" I had taken a pinch and gestured at Dags for reassurance.

He nodded at the amount, then crossed his arms. "Believe it or not, I don't know everything. Like a strong ale, it affects everybody different. Experiment with it a bit, ya pitiful wretch!"

If only there had been time to do so. Given how Trin's father drank himself to death, I'd promised her I'd never touch ale or spirits, leaving me with no framework for how the dusty substance might affect me or how long it could last.

The steady light given off by the tiny blaze in Omatuu's hand guided me forward at a hurried pace as I dipped index finger and thumb into the pouch. I hesitated. Dags had said the powder's comedown could leave me exhausted. What if it didn't last long enough?

The risk was worth it. I needed to know Omatuu's secrets if I was to escape the life of a Seeker as quickly as I desired. I brought the powder to my lips; it sapped the moisture from my tongue where it touched. Dryness gave way to a numbing sensation. I took a pull from my waterskin in an attempt to counter the parching effect, but to my unpleasant surprise, wherever the tepid drink ran, it failed to mitigate the numbness.

The feeling spread at an alarming rate.

Horror accompanied the sensation of fast-dulling nerves as it slid into my jaw, and then the rest of my face. I grabbed my cheeks. It was as if the tips of my fingers were coated in candle wax.

I cast about, an animal with its leg in a trap searching for freedom. Dull warmth cascaded through my arms and into my torso, moved in a wave down my spine and severed my physical understanding of the world. The crickets' song became a hollow buzz inside my skull; my own rapid breaths suddenly and overwhelmingly loud.

Ahead, the ruddy silhouette of Omatuu's pointed hat moved deeper into the wood, the hovering flame dwindling to a distant flicker. Vaguely, I realized, I was losing him, even with the fire in his hand. If he were to snuff it out, my ability to track him would disappear.

Even as the numbness entered my thighs, I staggered forward, legs little more than sacks of gruel. Yet, they held me up better than expected as I hustled after my target.

I gulped in a weak attempt to return feeling to my throat. Every footstep was a dampened, internal thud. It was a miracle I didn't fall as I stumbled through the forest. Though my sense of touch was muted, I still felt the give of earth under careless feet.

Omatuu's flame drew nearer as I recovered lost ground. When the concealment powder overcame my body entirely, my toes felt like they were sliding into pools of blood. I started to adjust to the powder's effects a few minutes later. The numbness was uncomfortable, the lack of senses unnerving, but I could manage it if I focused hard enough.

When the trees ahead thinned, letting in moonlight, I noticed my vision had dimmed as if filtered through an attenuated veil. I crept from the trees onto a barren slope with a curtain of stone bordering one side. Omatuu's blurry flame disappeared into a fissure in the rock wall.

I gave quiet chase.

Rounding a bend in the rock, I scraped my knee on a handle of protruding slate. I grit my teeth and stifled a cry of pain. Blood wept from the wound, a slickness between my fingers without discernible temperature.

I looked up. A shadowed face and charcoal beard loomed. My already galloping pulse skipped a beat as I backpedaled, pressing myself against the wall of stone behind. The wind knocked from my lungs and I suspected another gash sprouted at one shoulder.

Omatuu was motionless, hands hanging ready at his sides, the flame snuffed out. I wheezed loudly, uncontrollably, fighting to regain my breath. I didn't need to feel it to know sweat broke across my skin. The fire would return to Omatuu's hand any moment, and this time, he would use it to burn me to ashes.

"So, you've finally decided to show yourself tonight," he said.

Fear held me silent. I was like a mouse caught in the claws of a barn cat.

Darkness peeled back from Omatuu as he stepped forward, eyes catching the moon's radiance. He didn't look at me. Instead, he stared skyward. "You'll make this journey shorter than I intended. For that, you have my eternal thanks." The Prime raised his hands. I winced and turned away.

A heartbeat slipped past.

With a sidelong glance, I noticed Omatuu finishing a bow. I traced the line from his gaze. A bank of clouds parted to reveal the full brilliance of the moon.

Omatuu emitted an elated cry, then proceeded to ignore me on his way through a fissure in the curtain of stone.

I touched my throat with a trembling hand, then inhaled sharply. If ever I saw Dags again, I'd give him endless thanks for the concealment powder. I thanked Idrinnia the Everlasting Maiden, too, for commanding him to give it to me.

The fissure started as a narrow tunnel, widening the farther in I went. Blind confidence budded within me. I walked closer to the wizard than I would have otherwise dared. I chided myself for being careless, recalling that I didn't know how long the powder might last. Any moment, Omatuu might have turned, seen me materialize and smote me on the spot.

Yet, wisdom fled before brazen faith. I said I had to trust myself, even if it was to a fault. That was the daring I had to embody.

I proceeded.

Omatuu came to a stop at the center of a sprawling quarry. Pivoting slowly in a circle, he searched the ground, then booted a hunk of rock disdainfully away before taking a seat on the graveled earth. He crossed his legs and faced the moon.

First, he removed his wide-brimmed hat and set it to one side. Then, he drew forth his pack. He nestled the iron bowl into a layer of pebbles before him, then placed the humungalor's boneshard inside. Rays of iridescent blue light was all I saw of the touchstone—the rest of it blended with the shadows of night—as he brought it to rest in his lap.

Unstopping one of two waterskins, he took a quick drink from one which left a grimace on his face and a dark rim around his mouth. I know now this was troll's blood, used to sustain him as he entered the ritual. Omatuu chased the swill with a series of long draughts from the second waterskin. I assumed it water to wash down the pungent, fishy flavor.

The wizard settled into his seated hips, made rigid his spine, and then closed his eyes. All night long, I watched him. In that entire span of time, he gave not one twitch, nor a single shift.

By midday, the sun beat down harshly and the moon became a ghost at the other end of the sky. Errant puffs of cloud threw shadows over the hours as I watched Omatuu perform his ritual from my perch atop a slab of granite on one side of the enclosed quarry.

He never moved.

I sneaked away to relieve myself, and when I returned, a tingle rippled over every inch of my skin. Color grew brighter, sound sharper, and the pain in my knee and back started to burn. My connection to the world was returning. The concealment powder was wearing off.

Twenty feet away, Omatuu's face swiveled fractionally in my direction. He cocked his head, ear turning up ever so slightly. I went rigid, let my hands steadily drift to the concealment powder at my belt.

Just as I took a pinch between finger and thumb, Omatuu's brow creased. I brought my mouth down to my fingers and sucked down the dry, tasteless talc. Sweat raced down the nape of my neck. Tightness constricted around my chest.

All feeling receded like the tide going out. And now I knew it would be roughly twelve hours before it returned.

As Omatuu continued his ritual, dusk settled over the quarry and slumber over my brow.

I nodded off for a split second, and then shot to my feet. I would not allow the low demands of the body to interfere with my pursuit of the Power. I chewed my lip to beat back exhaustion, pressed a nail into my palm to keep me awake. In this, the concealment powder was a detriment; I'd need to do damage if I was to truly feel it.

So I knelt, letting the gravelly earth press into my wounded knee. That did the trick. I winced as I studied Omatuu, pride filling me. It might be years before I had the skill to replicate the ritual he now performed, but at least I knew the items required.

And that made me one secret richer than before.

It was this line of thinking that brought the Sun Scroll to my hand. The parchment crinkled as I spread it apart. Idrinnia's soul was silent, the page blank. Keeping Omatuu in my peripheral for as long as I could, I moved along the path leading out of the quarry. I had a question that needed answering, but I didn't want to miss whatever was bound to eventually happen with Omatuu's ritual.

Near the narrow entrance to the quarry, words materialized on the Sun Scroll.

The way of the wizard lies at your feet. Seize it.

The concealment powder's effects fully upon me, I missed the familiar warmth offered by the ensorcelled parchment.

I stared out at the Wildness, the final rays of golden sunlight bathing a sea of green, red, and yellow treetops.

Sacred parchment, I corrected.

Whatever Omatuu was doing had to be sacred, too, then. And in the presence of that sacred ritual, the Sun Scroll's power was nullified. Omatuu had said as much. *It holds power but also follows a set of rules...*

I smiled to myself at the thought of how much he'd helped me as I picked my way through the tunnel to the quarry and a seated Omatuu. I considered Idrinnia's words. *The way of the wizard lies at your feet. Seize it.*

I stood over Omatuu. His charcoal beard fell over a half dozen straps holding an array of vials and pouches. Gray robes were wrapped tightly around his lean frame, and one sleeveless arm exposed cords of lean muscle and branched lightning. The tattoo shimmered with whispering energy.

My shadow stretched to the iron bowl situated before the wizard. I traced the path of the dark avenue at my feet to Omatuu as I mulled over Idrinnia's words. Night fell, laying the passing minutes in their grave. A breeze lifted wisps of Omatuu's topknot.

The way of the wizard lies at your feet. Seize it.

The man *was* worth hating.

If Distra knew I carried a dagger rather than a spear into danger, she would have been proud. I drew the blade from the back of my belt, wishing I could feel the press of leather in my palm with greater surety. I took a step toward Omatuu, tongue darting over dry lips. The value of seeing the ritual through to its end was high.

But not nearly as valuable as a topknot from one of the most powerful wizards in the Wildness.

Ambition and a taste for greatness buoyed me forward, closing the distance between us in a pair of resolute steps. It would be easy. Grab with one hand, saw with the other. Once I started, I would not stop sawing until the deed was done.

The faint worry that he might react as soon as he felt me clutch his hair gnawed at my courage. Determined, I pushed the thought from my mind and gave myself over fully to trusting in Idrinnia's words.

The way of the wizard lies at your feet. Seize it.

I reached out—paused. I looked down my nose at the Cloudbreakers' Prime. The man had ridiculed me, threatened me, perhaps even plotted my death—but none of that mattered now. Fate had seated him before me. Fate had gifted me with concealment powder. Fate stuck a knife in my grip.

In that moment, Omatuu could have been as sweet to me as Dags Grimjaw, as convivial as Hellas, or as worthy of my respect as Distra, and still, I would have done what was needed. The words of Idrinnia the Everlasting Maiden herself compelled me; even without the bloodtrader's warning to follow them at any cost, I would have ended Omatuu. And gladly.

The way of the wizard...

Iron filled me, raced through my veins and into my killing hand. To survive the Wildness, I had to think like a predator.

And like the waiting heron, Omatuu was my prey.

Chapter Twenty-One

A Mother's Caress

My hand wavered an inch from the wizard Prime's topknot.

I stared at Omatuu's face for half a heartbeat, and then, his eyes flew open. Dirt pressed upward, filling his lower eyelids before tumbling down his cheeks. Sickened, horrified, I stumbled backward.

Sediment poured from his ears, a cascade of earth that left his beard clotted with debris. A low rumble came and went. Then, a fiercer quaking rattled my teeth. With each passing second, the amount of dirt siphoning from Omatuu redoubled. In short order, earthen detritus turned his eyes into pits of shifting brown, his ears spigots of the same.

I cried out as he opened his mouth. Clods of grass, stone, and mud vomited forth, overflowing his lap. Underfoot, the earth heaved. My arms flung out for balance and I fought to stand. Omatuu flew to his feet, spine arched, chin thrust to the heavens.

The touchstone rose into the air, and as it did, so did Omatuu. Light rippled along its oblong shape. A single cord of azure energy surged into the ground, writhing and crackling beneath the levitating wizard.

Gaping rents opened in the earth, swallowing sheets of gravel and throwing up gouts of dust. The frantic slide of pebbles and clack of boulders cast the world into a deafening roar. Branches of bluish radiance coalesced around Omatuu's torso, tentacles of humming energy.

One such beam shot outward and coiled around a solitary pine; with the same effort I might have torn a weed from a garden bed, it ripped the tree, roots and all, from the ground, and then dragged the pine into one of the widening holes with a crack. More coils of energy lashed out, snaring massive hunks of granite to feed them into the deepening pit below Omatuu.

The ground surged and bubbled. The wizard ascended higher, soon eclipsing the quarry's walls.

But whatever happened next would have to remain a mystery. A pulsating tentacle wound from the touchstone and raced toward me.

I leapt to the side as it arced past within inches of my head and snatched up a clump of vine maple rooted to a curtain of stone.

Fearing I would not survive much longer, I fled.

With some distance gained, the last sound I heard from the quarry was an inhuman roar.

Legs fueled by adrenaline, I ran headlong into the night. I didn't care which direction I went, but luck favored me with the right one. The path I'd taken to follow Omatuu the previous night lay ahead. I sped through the dark bracken like a hunted beast. No part of me was eager to face the source of the roaring, nor Omatuu.

A dozen cuts covered my hands and knees, from half again as many falls. Dense canopy overhead buried the benefits of a bright moon. The shapes of things rushed at me, silvery outlines and heavy shadow, leaving but a second to react at every step.

A cylindrical mass loomed suddenly and before I could stop, I slammed into the trunk of a tree. With a grunt, I spun away and fell, my outstretched palms absorbing a mere fraction of the impact.

Half dazed, I crawled inside a fallen snag. At least I'd had the where-withal to do that, should Omatuu follow my path.

Stunned and exhausted, sleep or something painfully similar came easy.

Upon waking, I was overwhelmingly dejected.

My injuries were merely icing on a cake layered in bitter failures. Nothing feels worse than failure. Not broken bones, nor lashed skin, not even a gashed knee.

My fingertips had nearly brushed Omatuu's topknot.

The way of the wizard lies at your feet. Seize it.

The opportunity was gone. I'd tried and failed. Now, I likely faced many more months as a Seeker. Maybe years. Maybe decades.

Autumnal mist entwined my ankles where I sat on a log. I patted myself down in search of the concealment powder. Despite a soggy tiredness soaking me from toe to crown, the talc had proved well worth the discomfort. Finding a frayed strand where the pouch should be, I groaned. In my desperate egress, I'd lost it.

Another failure added.

Little did it matter. Fate had spurned me.

I'm not ashamed to admit that, sitting there in the forest after my flight from Omatuu's sacred ritual, I sobbed. The power of a wizard had been within a hair's breadth, and then it hadn't.

Suffice to say, I wandered back toward the Cloudbreaker camp with no idea as to my next step. Even the beauty of the Wildness in autumn couldn't break me from my reverie of destitution. Limp arms hung at my sides, indifferent to the scrape of branches or piercing thorns. So consumed was I with loss, I barely reacted.

The path to the Power had been right there!

It wasn't long before the sun was at its zenith as I returned to camp along the path taken by Omatuu two nights earlier. I wasn't sure how long I'd slept after my run-in with the tree. My gut told me it had been less than a day, which meant Omatuu may still be back at the quarry. That's what I hoped. An instance in which he was already settled back at camp, eagerly awaiting my return, came sharply to mind as the alternative.

Our promised chats were sure to follow. I chewed a nail, anxiety trilling at the back of my mind in the absence of a plan.

I assessed my options. I could wander back to the Cloudbreakers and undergo what was sure to be a less-than-kindly inquiry from the Prime. The headband of the Seeker he'd killed stained my thoughts. In fairness, Omatuu had only finished what the other person started. To slaughter me outright might cause desertion en masse.

Was that a risk Omatuu was willing to take for the Sun Scroll?

I didn't want to find out.

Another option was to find a different cabal. That meant wandering the Wildness, injured and with little supplies, in the hopes of stumbling into one. The first time I'd done that, it had taken days for the Cloudbreakers to chance into me.

I could follow the River Wild and return to Cannalis.

I expelled a weary sigh. Every option seemed to end in death. By failing to take Omatuu's topknot, I'd gone against the will of Idrinnia the Everlasting, so maybe my doom was inevitable.

My jaw clenched. It wasn't *my* fault I'd failed.

Angrily, I jerked the Sun Scroll from my hidden pocket. Beams of light split swollen clouds, throwing misshapen blots across the grassy knoll around me. I stared a while at the scroll, letting the absence of words sink in as if there was some meaning I was forgetting. Something important...

To my right was a stand of towering evergreens. The same to my left. Ahead, there was a familiar brook and meadow of wild flowers.

Revelation slammed into me. The meaning of Idrinnia's words dawning, a bolt of excitement coursed through my chest. *The way of the wizard lies at your feet...*

At my feet.

Amid the tumultuous fallout of Omatuu's ritual, I'd nearly forgotten. I looked around, double checking to make sure I was in the same spot as before where Hellas and Laertha had found me on my return from the bloodtrader's outpost.

Sacred ground like Omatuu's ritual where the scroll didn't work, just like it didn't work in Cannalis.

The absence of Idrinnia's words confirmed the truth. Omatuu's ritual, whatever it was for, had been a sacred one. The scroll, too, was sacred. And when two sacred things interacted, they were nullified.

Which meant something sacred was nearby.

I ran, recalling where the Sun Scroll had worked and where it hadn't. Before, when I was ignorant about what was happening, I had traced what seemed the partial circumference of a circle. My lips went dry, and I was happy to feel my tongue wet them; an act I sorely missed while under the spell of the concealment powder.

I rushed about, swinging the scroll side-to-side through the air to watch the words come and go. I started finding fallen tree branches and sticking them in the ground as markers. My heart pounded. My chest swelled. Energy filled me, surging into my exhausted legs and straightening my spine.

Every time Idrinnia's words appeared, they fueled me.

The way of the wizard lies at your feet. Seize it.

They hadn't changed. I'd failed to take Omatuu's topknot, and nevertheless, they were the same as before. I wasn't supposed to take his topknot; I was supposed to return here to complete the circle.

Once I'd gotten three-quarters of the way finished, that was enough. I made for the center at a dead sprint. A short way into the dense wood, in an area I had yet to explore, I reached a small clearing.

I fell to my knees, in awe of its glory.

Like braided hair, five thick trunks wound together and spiraled into the canopy. I'll never forget the way my eyes drank in the sweet sight. Overhead, a halo of open sky ringed a massive nest of interwoven vines, lichen, and fungus. Branches curled around the nest like the hand of a mother caressing her child's cheek.

I touched my own face then, recalling the final touch of my dying mother. If I was ever to forgive myself for leaving her side, that would have been the moment, for I stood upon the doorstep of a better fate.

A wizard's tower.

CHAPTER TWENTY-TWO

DURN

Somewhere within the meager foliage crowning the wizard's tower, an osprey shrieked. A solitary oval opening peeked between a pair of knuckled branches. I searched the grounds beneath the wizard tower, inspecting every inch of the monolithic structure. The window was the sole opening.

The wizard inside was safe as much as they were trapped.

I ran a hand along the surface of the intertwined trunks that formed the tower's massive base. From a distance, I thought it possible to climb the thing, but after I touched it, I knew I was wrong. My palm glided over the slick bark like a stone sliding across a frozen pond. Drawing out my dagger, I worked the blade's tip into a crevice and tried prising it apart—to no avail. I brushed a fingertip over the place I'd scored and found it unblemished.

With both hands, I drew back, then plunged forward with all my weight. This was one of the more idiotic things I'd done. Rather than sink into the magical wood, the blade ricocheted off at a violent speed. I gasped, drawing back my palm to find a long red streak down the side. Blood beaded together along the cut. With no way to pierce the ensorcelled tree or the ability to climb it, I concluded the wizard in the tower to be quite safe.

I sucked at the wound on the edge of my hand as I looked up. Even the trees surrounding the tower leaned back from it such that no one could swing over or climb near.

Leaning out from the oval window, a bald head caught the sunlight. The wizard stared down at me and smiled. "Trying to come up here?"

I shook my head.

"Probably a good idea," he said. "You'd waste a lot of effort to barely get off the ground. Still begs the question of why you're fiddling around down there, trying to unsuccessfully chop down this magical tree with a dagger, when we could be talking secrets and such."

"Chop it down?" I was suddenly aware of just how foolish I must have looked. "I was just inspecting it."

"Well," the man said with a chuckle. "It's a tree. Surprised you've never seen one before. You *are* in a forest."

"I know what a tree is!" I said, then muttered. "By the Power..."

"Then, by reasonable deduction, you should know this hunk of magic looks a bit queer to be a regular tree. That it's a man nesting up here instead of some enormous, bald buzzard." The man paused as if waiting for the words to sink in. "It's a wizard's tower. Please tell me you're a Seeker. I'm having rotten damn luck getting anyone to come by, and, well, you can't see my ribs from there but I'm getting mighty famished."

I frowned. "No other Seekers have found you yet? How long have you been in the tower?"

The man huffed. "I did what the others told me to do, like a good little Shadowgiant. Did what every Seeker knows to do and brought a week's rations. You're sure to be found within that time, Malthece said. And I have my bucket and rope here with me to catch the rainwater, or lower it down when a faithful wanderer brings me food."

I listened patiently though I felt my neck tensing. I glanced behind me. The Cloudbreaker camp was a couple of hours distant. Laertha and Hellas had walked within a quarter mile of the tower less than a week ago and it lay along the path most Seekers took on the way to and from camp. The fact that no others had found the tower yet was nothing short of miraculous.

"So a week comes and goes and I tell myself, 'It'll be any time now. You're one of the lucky ones.'" The man sniffed, then slapped a hand on the rim of the window. "Fuck me if I didn't start remembering the rare tales I'd heard about wizards who never got found. The Wildness is damned big—outright huge. Even crawling with cabals, and a tower being a beacon that shoots into the sky, there are times one could go unseen. So I started imagining what I might look like as a skeleton. But at least—damn I'm getting choked up—at least even if I died, I'd still have gotten this far. You can't believe what it's like, kid..."

I fought to keep my frustration down as I got the sense the man might continue speaking for days if he wasn't interrupted. "One day soon, I'd like to know that very feeling." I forced a softer tone. "I know you're lonely, but please, I think we both know time is of the essence."

"You're not wrong." He cleared his throat. "A bit rude, though."

"Sorry," I said. "But as you can see, I'm young. It's been used against me before to hamper my pursuits. I wouldn't want another Seeker coming by that you preferred."

"Understandable," he said. "My apologies, it's been ten days since I've spoken with anyone. One other did come by, actually. Despite all my complaining just now about ill luck, there was that one. A comely young maiden but not even a Seeker yet. Didn't know a single thing about the way of the wizard. By random chance, she just stumbled upon me. I couldn't rightly bring myself to send her to her death at the Spirit Gardens. Besides, it was only my second day up, so I shooed her off to join a cabal, woefully confident another would come to my rescue—"

"Another *has* come!" I cut in.

"Right," he said. "Enough of the past. Here you are! What cabal claims you?"

"Cloudbreakers." A hint of pride in my voice surprised me.

"Omatuu. Strong Prime. Fought more duels than most, the prick. My hope is someone takes the asshole down one day soon."

Instead of telling him I'd been within a heartbeat of doing so last night, I simply nodded.

The wizard sucked at his teeth. "You know how this works, then?"

Retrieve a month's worth of food while he learns the Hand of Life spell in exchange for the secret to the Spirit Gardens.

"Yes." I meant it to sound more confident, so I added another, stronger, "Yes."

"Good." The bald man stroked a thick beard. "You'll go to Ferrek for supplies. It's about a week's jaunt to the east."

Pursing my lips, I fell silent. Trin was in Cannalis. Doubt almost made me consult the Sun Scroll. If I could fulfill my promises to both Trin and the wizard in the tower in a single trip... I had to do it that way, even if Ferrek was the shorter path to the Power.

Then I remembered that being this close to a wizard's tower meant the scroll would have nothing to say on the matter. I made a fist at my side. *This* was my chance to go to Cannalis. While I may have had to follow Idrinnia's words, that didn't mean I had to read them. This decision would be mine and mine alone.

"No. Not Ferrek." My tone was firm. "Cannalis."

I couldn't make out much of the man's face, but I thought he was smirking when he next spoke. "If you want the secret location of the Spirit Gardens, you'll go to Ferrek."

For a moment, I worried he might withdraw his offer, take his chances and wait for another Seeker. Reason soothed fear, emboldening me. The man had betrayed much in our earliest exchanges, specifically, his fear of starvation.

It had to be Cannalis. "I'm sorry but you'll have to wait a bit longer than you like. I have business in Cannalis."

He spoke in sarcastic tones. "Oh yes, of course! Much business to be done out here." Arms sweeping in wide arcs, he motioned at the Wildness around us. "Many forms of booming industry. Busy, busy, busy!"

His shoulders slumped as he sank into a dramatic sigh. "Listen kid, I've been dreaming of this moment for a decade. Nine of those years were spent as a Seeker with the Shadowgiants, dodging death, shitting a stone's throw from troll nests, and hunting the most dangerous beings in the Great Archon's damned Kelundar. The only thing that kept me alive to make it to where I am, right here and now, was the luck of falling in with a good Prime like Malthece, the Power bless her."

At this, I balked. There were good Primes?

"So let me ask you a very important question. If you take too long to answer, then you don't deserve the secret at all, and I'll have to just take my chances." Boughs creaked as he shifted from foot to foot. "You're a Seeker aren't you?"

"Yes," I said without hesitation. My chest puffed out. "But not for long."

The man whistled low. "I was shooting for a simple yes but that was better. You realize *this* is the goal, right? Very few make it to where you are in this moment. To where I am, even fewer. The longer your road, the greater the danger and the more shit can and *will* go wrong. Why choose to make it longer?"

Hard seconds flashed past. Of course he was right. The wisdom laid down, though annoying in its delivery, indicated why the man had successfully made it into a wizard's tower. He was clever, strategic, inquisitive; I would have done well to listen to him.

But when I considered abandoning my promise to Trin, my stomach churned. I couldn't.

"I understand I'll be exposed to greater difficulties this way. You speak wisely. But I have to trust myself even if the decision causes you to linger in suffering."

"Trust is one of the more fickle things on a wizard's path. You'll find that out soon enough." He blew raspberries. "Cannalis it is. Here—"

A hand flashed outward. A shimmering object descended, glinting as it fell, rotating between light and shadow. "Don't lose it!"

I moved to catch it and fumbled the thing. Stooping to the ground, I saw it was a gold coin. Three more pieces jangled as they struck the soft forest duff.

"For a mule and the food," he said.

After gathering the coins, I shouted appreciation then hesitated before leaving. After our exchange, I felt irrevocably connected to the man in the wizard's tower.

His part of the bargain done for now, he'd retreated back inside. I called up to him. "Ho there!"

He popped back out the window. "Still here and going nowhere fast."

"What's your name?"

He raised his face to the ring of open sky as he considered. "Haven't got my wizard name yet. That's for when I step out of this damn tower in six months, fully trained in the war callings and ready for duels." The dreamy tone melted as his gaze settled back on me. "For now, call me Durn."

"Durn," I said with a smile. "Congratulations. You're a wizard now."

The man became serious. When it was clear he might sob, I left him to his moment, simultaneously jealous of his fortune and happy for him. He seemed kind enough. Of the wizards in the Wildness, Omatuu was my sole source of comparison. Before Durn's comment about being lucky to have had a good wizard Prime—Malthece, he'd called her—I was starting to theorize that either all wizards became bad people or only bad people became wizards.

In either scenario, I preferred to think I would be one of the good ones.

Chapter Twenty-Three

RISE! RISE! KILL!

Lacking the supplies to make the journey to Cannalis, I had no choice but to sneak into the Cloudbreakers' camp at nightfall and steal it. I desperately hoped Omatuu had not returned. If he had, I suspected our meeting, or as I thought of it, my inquisition, would be anything but pleasant.

If everything went as planned, I would slip in and out, and then be gone for a long time. During my time with the Cloudbreakers, other Seekers had disappeared for short stretches of time, and while the official rule among peers was to never question each other upon their return, friends and allies were known to inquire in secret.

That none of those aloof Seekers had been killed or robbed in their sleep gave me at least some small comfort as I arrived outside the tangled wall of camp. I imagined the code of amicable conduct stopped short of Omatuu, however. He was unlikely to forget his curiosity about what I may or may not possess, no matter how much time had elapsed.

But I was getting ahead of myself.

I glanced at the camp's solitary opening in the gashbrush. Firelight from behind the pair of sentries gave them a rippling outline of orange and yellow, and their faces were masks of shadow. I didn't know these two.

Falling into a crouch, I clawed at the earth at the base of an oak tree with a sprawling root system. Hunks of clay filled my palms and hidden rocks chafed my fingertips as I dug. An image of Omatuu hemorrhaging earth from eyes, ears, and mouth made me shudder as I quietly pulled out the Sun Scroll, placed it in the hole, then covered it up.

Tonight, regardless of what happened, Omatuu would not get Idrinnia's soul.

The guards traded barbs and gossip as a couple of hours passed. They also discussed the more frigid night air of the autumn season. Then one stated something about Omatuu in low tones. I craned forward to hear better but failed to pick up the murmured exchange.

It was nearly midnight when the sentries changed, ushering forth a staggering pair I knew well. I thanked the Power the rotation hadn't changed in the days since I'd left, for I relied on it for the night's success.

If Omatuu had beaten me back...

My heart beat painfully against my chest. In and out, that's all I needed to do. Omatuu wouldn't see me. I cursed, wishing I hadn't lost my concealment powder.

I patted my cheeks, forcing alertness as I blew out a series of rapid breaths, and then stepped from hiding onto the path leading into camp. I raised my hands in the air as I walked, just in case Hellas or Laertha thought me a threat. The last thing I wanted was to be slain by a fellow Seeker.

Luckily, they were terribly drunk. Brew thickened their wits so much, in fact, they barely recognized it as odd when I emerged from inky night on the wrong side of the camp walls.

"Truespear!" Beads from the last guzzle of the tankard in Hellas's hand lined his cherry-gold beard. He regarded me with an amused expression. "Where've you been all these days? Come on now. Join us for a drink, or guard duty—or who cares the reason—just join us!"

I forced a smile at the pair as Hellas beckoned me to a stump just inside the gashbrush wall. Breath held, I looked to the hill where Omatuu's fortress sat.

"I'd love to but I'm a bit tired," I said. "Heading to bed now."

Hellas wrapped an arm around my shoulders, head shaking emphatically. "No, no." Despite my protest, he abandoned his guard duty and steered me to a campfire where we sat. "Nonsense," he slurred. "One drink."

Laertha followed, toes dragging through the dirt.

"What about your sentry duty?" I said. "You can't just leave."

"Oy!" Hellas slapped a knee. The sharp sound caused my heart to skip a beat. I shot a look at Omatuu's fortress as my chest pumped like a startled rabbit's. Ignorant of my stress, Hellas rolled forward over his belly and motioned at me with a tankard. "Friendship comes before everything. That includes sentry duty."

"Yeah," said Laertha. "E'erything."

The older woman's lids were heavy, her gaze unfocused. I'd watched Laertha and Hellas compete cup for cup on no less than a dozen occasions, until one either vomited or passed out or crawled to their tent. This, it appeared, was another such night.

"What if there's an attack?" I said.

Hellas's head wobbled in mockery. "I'll knock 'em silly. Remember that? When I punched you? That was a damn silly day wasn't it? I'll just punch whoever comes through that opening and then we'll all be friends again." He shrugged, then took a loud slurp from his tankard. "Or Omatuu will burn 'em, or crush 'em...something like that."

"So." I had yet to let the fortress out of my periphery. A chill rolled through me at the sight of the dead Seeker's headband hanging outside it. "Omatuu's here?"

Laertha nodded, a roundabout thing, like her neck didn't work. "Yesterday."

There was silence but for the gutter of wind pressing the fire low. Embers swirled into the night sky. Hellas took a noisy sip then said something.

I was too busy watching Omatuu's fortress to hear it. Any second, I expected the wooden lattice to stretch open, for the canvas flap to whip aside and reveal the wizard Prime.

Frowning, Hellas nudged me with his tankard. "What you doin' here?"

"Enjoying the fire, same as you." If I played coy, perhaps he'd leave it alone. I forced a yawn as I stood. "I have to get some sleep."

Hellas jerked me back to my seat by my tabard. "I mean—you know what I mean. Because I'm meaning what I'm saying and I want you to say what you mean. So...what you doin' here?"

"You left," Laertha clarified, her voice just above a whisper. Eyes closed. Head swaying. "Same time as Omatuu."

"No," I lied. "I've been in my tent this whole time. I was sick."

Hellas stared at me sidelong, then belched. "Fair enough."

"Still not feeling well, either." I crossed an arm over my belly. "I'd better go—"

"I'm going." Laertha stood bolt upright, eyes flying open. Miraculously, she ran in a straight line to the wall of gashbrush.

"Pfah! Sentry duty calls, it seems." Hellas pointed at me. "You...El...T ruespear—damned troll slayer! You stay here, okay? Don't go running to your bed. You gotta stay and drink. You gotta carry the night, okay?"

I nodded. Wind moaned and whistled through Omatuu's fortress. Ice filled my veins. "For you and Laertha, I'll be right here, drinking till morning."

With a roar, Hellas finished his tankard, then handed it to me. "But first, I must piss. The duty before duty." He wandered off in the opposite direction of Laertha who was now vomiting near the camp entrance.

I shot one last hard stare at Omatuu's fortress, then hurried to one of the large supply tents near its base. The first thing I did was refill my waterskin. I stole another and filled that, too. With a few rolls of bread and joints of jerky in my arms, I made for my tent on the edge of camp, keeping my head down as I went.

Once inside, I moved with haste. Yanking open my pack, I made sure to put the stone from the shores of the Blue Colossus in first. Then, I stuffed the clothes I'd worn prior to becoming a Cloudbreaker in around it, followed by the pilfered foodstuff. A pair of apples lie in one corner of the tent as well, on hand to eat at my leisure; these I also added.

I cinched the pack around my torso, and then slung the waterskins around my neck. Lastly, I grabbed my spear. At the slit of my tent, I paused. Had I heard something? I waited a heart-clamping minute until I was convinced it wasn't Omatuu.

The Sun Scroll's hiding place would be my last stop before Cannalis. Soon, I'd see Trin again. And soon after that I'd be a wizard.

Swelling with pride, I took a deep inhale then stepped out.

A flash lit the world, followed a split second later by an ear-splitting boom. I fell backward, flattening my tent in a tangle of canvas and hempen rope. When I sat up, black-garbed warriors flooded the camp. Hoods were pulled over their heads and sashes covered their noses and mouths. Circles of white paint dotted their faces.

The Order of Odd.

Where Laertha had been retching minutes before, a smoldering, flame-licked husk now lay. I sucked in a sharp breath, vision swimming, belly hot and foul.

If not bigger, quicker. If not quicker, smarter. If not smarter, dead.

I disentangled myself and heaved to my feet. *Flee.* In that, I didn't need the scroll to guide me.

Fire crackled along the gashbrush walls. Shouts of alarm from Cloudbreakers and battle cries from the Order of Odd slapped against the dome of night.

Somewhere, branches snapped. I swiveled around, the shock of it all holding me in place. Along the back wall of camp, the thorny bulwark parted, admitting another flood of Seekers brandishing weapons. A wizard swathed in inky robes, much like Vethati had been, led them from the rear. A mask of pearl covered their face but for two eyeholes. Glittering ropes of light shot from a clawed hand toward Omatuu's fortress.

There was a deafening boom, followed by a gust of force. Ears ringing, I lowered my hands from shielding my face.

Omatuu's fortress had burst into flame.

Order of Odd Seekers swarmed the camp, rushing to meet disoriented Cloudbreakers. I grabbed my spear, prepared to flee.

Raucous laughter stopped me.

His laughter.

From the corner of my eye, I saw Omatuu's fortress open. As if scattering feed for chickens, the Prime swept an open palm and snuffed out the fire. Steam rose from the mound, framing him. Order of Odd Seekers scrabbled up the hill, falling to knees to fire bows, or aiming weapons for a throw.

Omatuu swirled his arms, summoning a vortex of wind to bat away arrows and hurled axes. His jaw hinged to one side and teeth grit, he punched out with a fist.

One of the roots forming his shelter, unfurled, striking a Seeker's head with a sickening crunch. Omatuu beat the air, fist making an upward arc. The tree limb mimicked the motion, raking the mound and kicking up a thick veil of dust in its wake. Most of the Seekers leaped free, rolling to the bottom of the hill in a daze, while a couple too slow to act were crushed.

I'd seen enough. The opening at the front of camp was contested by pockets of fighting. If I wished to win free and make it to the Sun Scroll beyond, I'd have to be fast.

Before I could go, a hand snared my elbow. I spun, spear leveled, ready to kill. Distra's expression was a series of hard, flat lines. She glanced at my pack. "Come. Fight," she grunted. An ax jumped in her grip, anxious and ready.

Over her shoulder, I watched the white-masked wizard drag a clawed hand upward from the waist. Trailing fire splashed into an oncoming Cloudbreaker. The wizard slapped the air, sending a gale of wind toward Omatuu, but he brushed it aside.

The fire and the smoke and the shriek of steel blended together, a singular blur of chaos.

I didn't move.

"Come fight!" Distra urged.

I shook my head, pulled my elbow from her grasp. "I have to go."

She pursed her lips then nodded. "Go. Be strong." Her final command to me as Head Seeker.

I hurried away, spear gripped tight, hoping to avoid the worst of the fighting as I headed for the scroll. Rhythmic thunderclaps dogged my heels. Powerful winds buffeted me from behind. Screams and grunts and clashing steel whipped past my ears. The earth rumbled underfoot, much like it had during Omatuu's ritual.

Just ahead, a trio of Cloudbreakers ganged up to dispatch a Seeker from the Order of Odd near the break in the wall.

Hellas stood beside Laertha's smoking corpse, ax in hand. At his feet lay a motionless man in black, his shoulder no longer connected to the neck as it should be. Dark blood stained the dirt around him. Broad chest pumping like a bellows, Hellas ignored my approach. The battle fever was upon him as he threw himself into another scuffle.

Fighting was everywhere. A dagger sliced a smile beneath a hooded woman's chin. An arrow thudded into a temple painted with lightning. Steel sang where it met and sighed gruesomely when it found flesh. I dodged over the dead, weaved around the living.

At the breach into the Wildness, I shuffled sideways to guard my flank from an enemy Seeker, spear upraised until they realized I was fleeing and no real threat.

Safety and darkness lie beyond. I afforded one final, backward glance. The mound beneath Omatuu's fortress drew my attention quickest.

The wizard Prime hovered in the air, fists pressed to his sides. With a shout of triumph, he jerked them upward. The ground shuddered, causing me to stumble. I should have continued running, but I couldn't pry my eyes away.

A tremor moved in a wave across the mound. The earth cracked—cracked again like a massive, dusty egg. Fragments of dirt and stone erupted skyward.

"Tattaghor!" Omatuu's face was rabid with glee. "Rise! Rise! Kill!"

A massive chunk of the mound surged upward, tree roots straining and popping around it. Shoulders wider across than a wagon plowed up from the earth, shrugging the fortress over sideways. A pair of immense horns slid into the air beside Omatuu where he hovered. Ghostly chains of magic bound the creature's wrists but dissipated by the second.

All motion ceased as the Order of Odd fell silent. The Cloudbreakers, too.

A humungalor had arrived.

The monstrous bull snorted dust from fist-sized nostrils. It surveyed the sea of eyes watching it. Using three of its meaty arms, the creature dragged itself the rest of the way from the earth, while the fourth swung a bronze mace the size of a tree limb at the Order of Odd. One Seeker stuck to the iron head like a swatted mosquito. Another hurtled limply beyond the walls of the Cloudbreakers' camp. Cries of terror lent me greater speed as I fled to the oak tree where the Sun Scroll was buried.

Fingernails caked in dirt, I retrieved the scroll and stood. Tattaghor towered above the gashbrush, half again as tall. A fireball flew at its face, dashed by a concussive wind the moment before impact. Omatuu's laughter chased me into the shadows as a pillar of lightning split from a bank of clouds. That was the last thing I saw as I let the night swallow me.

Chapter Twenty-Four

A Welcoming Prison

In the forests outside the Gate of Cannalis, I stripped any garb marking me as a Cloudbreaker and changed into the clothes I wore in my life before the Wildness. It was a funny thing, and shocking, too, how much more comfortable it felt to wear them again. As someone who saw themselves destined to be a wizard, I expected returning to my old clothes would make my skin crawl with bad memories.

Whatever anger I held for the Brotherhood and the conditions of Cannalis evaporated, leaving me with a gentle sadness around my heart. I missed my mother. I missed Trin. On the cusp of gaining the secret location of the Spirit Gardens, I found it oddly paralyzing to be going back into the past. I wanted to see Trin almost more than anything, yet I feared the person I'd become. How would she react? What might she ask?

When I'd left, I'd been a naive child, known as kind and dutiful among family and friends. Since then I'd plotted and fought and killed. I traded away my rugged innocence in favor of calculating ambition. The Stormseye had pummeled and plied the soft child of their making like dough. How could Trin know me now with this stony pit at the center of my being? No. This would be no joyous reunion.

I buried the thoughts, along with my spear and other belongings, and then waited.

At midday a group of spice traders from Ferrek trundled up the road. I stepped from behind a tree, waving slowly so as not to be shot by the mercenaries guarding it, should they have bows. I offered one of the gold pieces Durn had given me in order to join them on their way through the Gate of Cannalis. Fleeting suspicion from the guards was met with hostility from the lead trader. "What cowards you are to be frightened of some kid offering good gold for help through the gate?"

The discussion ended there.

The traders and I were admitted into the city by a pair of leather-tongues with clubs at the gate. "Pay your respects," they said as they gestured at the Stormseye seal hanging over the threshold. All of us bowed our heads in honor of the Great Archon and we passed without further issue.

After a hundred yards or so, and at nearly the exact spot where I stabbed the lictor's horse, I peeled away from the group to join the masses flowing through the streets.

I paused at an intersection, one hand finding the wall of a building as I caught my breath. I wasn't winded from exertion, I was overwhelmed with nostalgia, worry, and expectation, but even more so, I was over-whelmed by the smell. I'd been in the Wildness for months; open, clean air and nature as far as the eye could see.

In Cannalis, cool grass beset with wildflowers became cobblestone streets strewn with mud and feces. Rotted timbers and the creak of rusted iron hinges replaced supple trees full of birdsong. No longer did the familiar pungent scent of Cloudbreakers sweating through their leathers fill my nostrils. Now, starving cripples and diseased children caked in filth coated my throat.

Altogether, Cannalis reminded me of my mother's deathbed and the inexorable stench of the dying. The city was but a sprawling grave.

I straightened and looked one way, then the other. Should I check on my old home first, or should I go see Trin? Fear pricked my insides, propelling me toward the latter. A part of me didn't want to see finality of any kind regarding my mother. I wanted my memories of sharing our home together crystallized, not shattered.

I moved in the direction of the blacksmith's shop where Trin lived with her family. Familiar streets came and went. Patrols of Stormseye knights passed me, onyx armor gleaming, gold eyes on their breastplates and sword pommels shining brightly. I shrank beneath their gaze, face fixed to the cobbles. And for good reason.

I was a criminal.

Soon, I saw slate gray eyes in the visor slit of every helm. And then, in the face of every citizen. The memory of the lictor was everywhere. Cold sweat covered my back as I made my way, legs shaking whenever I slowed my pace. The scent wasn't the only thing overwhelming about Cannalis. I wondered if there was some spell that made the population inherently more fearful. I paused and leaned against a butcher's shop to gather my wits.

A long time had passed since my assault on the lictor. In planning my return, I wagered that he had forgotten me, but trust was a fickle thing, Durn had said. Coming to Cannalis was a calculated risk. I needed to be smart about it, no matter how slim the chance of my being recognized might be. With this realization, I cursed myself for seeking out Trin first. My priority had to be Durn. I needed to get the mule and food. If I was forced to leave quickly, I needed to make sure I had what was needed. Durn's life depended on it.

Therefore so did mine, for without the secret of the Spirit Gardens, I'd never be a wizard.

Two of my gold pieces, less a silver, went toward the mule, a drastic overpayment. One look at its creaky joints and jutting rib cage told me it had nary a few journeys left in it. The woman who sold it to me cried when my coins touched her palm. A naked child hugged one leg. I left them and found hard eyes watching me from a row of beggars.

Possessing gold in Cannalis could get you killed just as quickly as its absence.

My feet begged me to hurry on. Vulnerability, I remembered, was a beacon fire to predators.

For the hardtack and cheese, I went to a more prosperous area of Cannalis near the city's center. I'd have to travel longer but it was worth it to avoid being robbed. It would smell better, too.

The Great Archon's ziggurat crouched ominously nearby like a black, predatory beetle, waiting for an unsuspecting bug to wander by. The gold eye looked over Cannalis from walls of onyx stone. Lictors, knights, and the occasional Stormlord strode across the wide plazas and multi-storied stairs.

By the time I finished haggling with a merchant situated on the edge of the central plaza, I was left with a silver and two saddlebags full of food. Durn would be pleased.

And I could finally see Trin.

My heart skipped a beat as I drew close to the blacksmith's. Thoughts rifled through my mind like aimless wind, sloshed around like a bowl of water being shaken. With no discernible beginning or end, they flowed chaotically from one to the next. I fought to clear my mind as I rounded a corner to the blacksmith's shop. Holding the mule's lead, I jerked it to a stop.

Stale wind passed through me.

A crouching painter dipped her brush in a bucket of gold, then raised it to coat a ring within a giant eye. For a long time, I stared, disbelieving. The blacksmith's shop was gone. In its stead was a chapel of the Stormseye Brotherhood. Trin and her family...

Gone.

A voice from behind startled me. "Never seen a chapel before?" Whirling, I found a Stormseye knight standing within reach of my shoulder. His sword was drawn. I froze.

With a chuckle, he stuck the tip in the dirt, then laid both hands over the pommel and leaned forward over it like a walking cane. "You look lost. The chapel will be ready in a couple weeks. It's a great place to be found. You sure look like you could use the gathered wisdom-teachings of our Great Archon."

Body numb, I blinked.

"Yeah, I get it. You're lost alright. I've seen that look before, years ago, staring into a puddle at my own reflection. Before the Power chose me to be an acolyte of the Brotherhood, I was beggin' and stealing for food. Worry not, Stormlord Ravkin will give you the guidance you need. He teaches the Great Archon's word better than any." Clearing his throat, the knight sheathed his sword suddenly, then puffed out his chest. "Speaking of, there he is."

The knight shouldered past me.

I turned, watching him go as if time slowed, as if everything were being pushed through water. He marched up the street then knelt before a plump figure robed in saffron. An amulet, wrought in the image of a gold eye the size of my fist, swung from a chain around the Stormlord's fat neck. Gray braids streaked with white clung to the back of his balding pate. A double chin formed under his clean-shaven face as he regarded the knight. He clapped him on the shoulder, then lifted his gaze.

Cold, reptilian eyes sent chills down my spine. Something flickered across the powerful wizard's expression. A slight tug at the corner of his mouth. A curious tilt to his head and a crease in his brow. Recognition?

Fear slapped me around, breaking my gaze from his as I pivoted away. My hands shook at my sides, so hard I nearly lost hold of the mule's lead. I didn't dare glance back to see if I was being followed, or if the Stormlord still watched me. If he somehow knew by magical means that it was me who'd assaulted the lictor, I had to be gone from Cannalis with haste.

The farther I traveled from Ravkin's stare, the calmer my nerves became. Falling in with the thronging crowd, I flowed around a corner leading me away from the Stormseye chapel. The place where Trin once lived.

I chewed the inside of my cheek, eager to be gone despite the ache in my chest demanding that I find Trin.

As the crowd poured me onto the main street leading out of the city for the second time that day, I noticed a mounted Stormseye knight watching the thoroughfare. Gut clenching, I tightened my grip on the mule's lead and stared straight ahead, shuffling behind the teeming wall of humanity at a laborious pace.

Closer to the gate, the crowd thinned to a scattered trickle of wagons and merchants. The Brotherhood relied on the harshness of their stories about the Wildness to keep the populace under an iron thumb. Citizens coming in or going out weren't much concern, to my benefit.

I slipped in at the tail end of a caravan.

A leathertongue held up his club.

"Trader, bound for Ferrek," the drover said. The man's scrutiny flitted over the goods, then landed on me. He seemed to be taking note of my age and tattered clothing. But something behind me drew his gaze.

I craned my head around to see where he looked. Slate gray eyes watched me. Whether what I saw was a reflection of the past or the truth of the present moment, I wasn't sure, for the image dissolved quickly into a mad swirl of unfamiliar faces.

A piercing whistle sounded in my ears and the acolyte waved us through. I hurried onward into the Wildness.

Only once I was clear of the Gate of Cannalis did I let my emotions take hold. At the place in the forest where I buried my Cloudbreaker livery, I wept.

For the second time in my life, I relived the trauma of betraying my best friend and abandoning my mother.

CHAPTER TWENTY-FIVE

AUTUMN'S FEAST

Fleeing through the Gate of Cannalis for the second time that year was both different and the same. While I no longer ran for my life toward the complete unknown, my mother's specter was a cloak of shame clasped tightly at my throat. Trin, too, was gone. Disappeared just like my mother.

Over the intervening months, I had justified my actions a hundred times and more. 'No choice,' I'd told myself as I trained and carried out duties for the Cloudbreakers, all the while shoving down the bitterness. The seal had finally burst through such petty validations. Feelings, long suppressed, arose.

Where could they have gone?

For Trin, the most likely truth clicked into place as I journeyed toward the wizard's tower and Durn. The sudden realization gnawed at my heart. Dead. Kicked out by the blacksmith, or sold to some back alley slaver. And I had left her to it. I kept away from the slim chance that my incident with the lictor's horse had somehow come back to condemn Trin. The other thoughts were bad enough. My mother and Trin were forever lost.

Sacrifice immeasurable. Suffering to break the soul. That was the way of the wizard. That was the path to righteous power. I always knew it would be difficult, for the world wasn't crawling with magic users, but I could never have fathomed the heartache.

The prospect of bringing Durn food in exchange for the Spirit Garden's location was the only thing keeping me from giving up right then.

To lie down in the forest and surrender...I romanticized that kind of death. It seemed a peaceful way to go. That ballast of hope tethered me to life, otherwise, I might have done it. The pull was strong. After my final breath, perhaps I would see my mother and Trin again.

Alas, I kept on, wallowing in my sorrows without them.

Not a day passed when I didn't curse myself, so when I reached the wizard tower and Durn, my sour mood clashed with his own far more elated demeanor.

"By the Power, if I had a bucket big enough, I'd eat that mule," Durn said. "You're a savior and a champion, you know that?"

"Just lower your bucket so we can begin."

Durn hacked, then spat a flimsy gob. It dissipated into foamy fragments before striking the ground, closer to me than I would have liked.

I glared upward.

"Sorry," he said. "Forgot it spreads out so much from this height. Anywho, have any trouble? You got the right food I take it? A month's worth of hard tack and—"

"I got it all," I said. "A leftover silver piece, too."

"Keep it. Money's shit out here anyway. Blood and secrets are the far better currency. By the way, I realized something after you left." Durn waited, clearly inviting me to guess. My mood being what it was, I rejected the opening as he lowered the bucket. "I never got your name! You took off after I gave you mine, but I was too foggy-brained to get yours. I'd love to know who I'm giving the secret to. Just in case we must duel someday."

The last came as a shock. I hadn't considered the possibility. "We could end up as a Prime and Second in the same cabal, too, you know."

"That would certainly be my preference." Durn laughed and the bucket thudded to the turf. I loaded it with a portion of the goods from the mule's packs. "So what is it?"

"El." I puffed up a bit. "Some call me Truespear."

Durn scoffed. "Okay, sure."

I frowned. In silence, we finished loading the last of the supplies into the buckets. For a few long minutes, Durn disappeared inside the wizard's tower.

"Don't short me my secret, now!" I shouted.

Durn popped back out of the window, then dragged the rope through the opening. "I was just getting it." Something plinked into the bucket. "Coming down now."

The bucket jostled and clattered during its descent, the object inside ricocheting about. It came to rest on a patch of sunlit earth. I took a step, leaning forward for a closer look. A piece of bleached, petrified driftwood sat within.

"That's not the secret." Energy swirled in my chest, hot and furious. "You—you've tricked me."

"If you knew what the secret looked like, you wouldn't be asking me for it, would you, you stupid dolt?" Durn stifled an angry growl. "Pick the damn thing up."

I was thankful none were around to witness my embarrassment. Nevertheless, I cast about just to make sure, then warily reached into the bucket.

The hardened wood was smooth as stone, icy to the touch, and far heavier than expected, as if it were made from a material denser than gold. I rotated it in my hands, inspecting it for an inscription. A long moment passed. "Is something supposed to—"

As I glanced up at the tower, the world was torn from sight. I reeled and then I was no more.

All that remained was a distant image in a sea of blankness. A city with a harbor under a starry night sky. Nearby, ships cast in lanternlight bobbed and swayed. Each bore the gold ringed eye of the Brotherhood—Ferrek? A new image splashed through the first like a stone thrown through the reflective surface of a pond. It became a beach strewn with the carcasses of sea creatures.

Detached and floating, my vision sped along the strand toward a crag shaped like Omatuu's conical hat. Light flashed and then receded, thrusting me into darkness.

Dust motes swirled in a fist-sized hole of daylight coming in through a flue at the height of a tapering cavern. My gaze fell to the floor where the luminous pinpoint stopped. A black maw yawned at the center of the cave floor, darker than the night sky, swallowing my attention, beckoning me within, calling my name.

"El," a chorus of voices whispered.

A drumbeat pounded in my ears as I took slow, mincing steps and looked down into the inky depths.

The susurrus of voices rose again, louder, almost as if whoever spoke stood at my heels. "El. Come to us."

The Spirit Gardens.

The rim of the maw flexed as if alive. Cold terror pinioned my awareness.

"Come to us."

The vision ended in a whoosh of sight and sound and senses regained. I was back at the base of the wizard tower, staring up at Durn's grinning face.

"Kind of fun, wasn't it?"

Mouth slack, breath heaving, I shook my head.

"Yes indeed. A fun ride for all," Durn said. "Now, send it back up, just in case I get a second would-be wizard helping me out. I should be good now, but who knows. I don't mean to be a skeleton anytime soon."

Most of his words washed over me with little comprehension. I reeled from the experience of the secret sitting in my palm. I knew exactly where the Spirit Gardens were, just as well as I knew how to open and close my hand. I knew like it was embedded in me...like it was branded into my brain.

I grabbed my pack. Soon, the Spirit Gardens would gift me with the seed for my own wizard's tower. Doubt flickered at the back of my mind as I recalled the stories about Seekers who failed to get a wizard's lock first. They became brash, dangerously daring. In my best estimation, I was already there. Momentum and luck would favor me, I convinced myself. That was the kind of self-trust necessary for me to gain the Power.

"El," Durn called. "Good luck!"

I waved to him, allowing myself to smile for the first time since I had arrived. "And to you, my friend."

On rubbery legs, I stumbled from the tower and surrounding clearing, driven in haste by my visions of Ferrek and the Spirit Gardens beyond.

***

Durn was right. The road to Ferrek was much quicker than the one to Cannalis. At the fervent pace I set, it went even faster, for which my mule soon paid the price.

With less than half a day to my destination, the animal quit walking. A viscous slaver rimmed its mouth as it heaved. When I listened intently with an ear to its chest, I heard a whistling sound, which told me it might be some time before the animal was willing to move again. After an hour of sitting around at midday, I pulled at the lead, hoping the mule might be more interested in moving if I wasn't riding him. But the old pack animal had barely the energy to pull its head away, and instead searched the ground for some fresh grass.

"Fine." I released the lead to let it graze; its stiff legs shuddered as it went. Feeling guilty, I added, "I'm sorry, old fella."

The mule cast me an indifferent, sidelong glance, then resumed its grazing.

Disgruntled with the progress of the day, I sat on a log and opened the Sun Scroll.

Befriend the king.

The king? My hands drifted to my lap, scroll crinkling. King of whom?

In all of Kelundar the closest thing to a king was the Great Archon. If Idrinnia thought such an evil tyrant was open to friendship with me, I had to question whether she'd gone mad during her centuries trapped inside a piece of parchment.

The Great Archon?

No. That couldn't be it.

I wracked my brain for other answers, starting first with the cabals. The wizard Prime of each group was a leader and a ruler of sorts but calling any of them a king or queen was a stretch. Perhaps it was a specific name rather than a title. There were some magi in the Wildness—those solitary wizards who'd gone insane and lived like animals after losing their topknots, just like Vethati—who were known by royal monikers. The Gray Countess. Agnoll, Prince of Bears. The Black Herald...though that one wasn't quite 'royal.' Cua'Qaia the Bat Queen. None of the ones I'd heard stories of were kings.

At a loss, and noticing the day wearing on, I rose to find the mule in the hope of compelling him onward. Before that moment, I thought nothing could be more stubborn in its withholding than Idrinnia's soul.

I was wrong.

Another hour passed before the mule let me lead him back onto the path to Ferrek.

The forest welcomed us into its bosom. We descended into a depression in the earth. Shoulder-high banks of dirt formed berms to either side. Robins raced through the branches of trees lining the path, the tops of which leaned toward the center like the steeple of a chapel. A chipmunk regarded me from its haunches as I passed before leaping to tasks most urgent. A few months until winter, it gathered nuts as if the cold arrived tomorrow. I reveled in the simple yet effective planning of nature; a stupid animal with a foolproof strategy. One could learn wherever they looked, apparently.

One hand firmly pulling the mule's lead, the other gripping my spear, I repeated the scroll's words in my head. Nothing I'd encountered seemed to fit. Worry punched my gut; maybe there was a king still to come?

My heartbeat quickened at the thought of my journey to the Spirit Gardens. My excitement could not be quelled. I'd be there soon. And then I would have a seed for my very own wizard's tower.

I took a moment to kick myself. If I'd taken Omatuu's topknot when I had the chance, everything I needed to be a wizard would be within my grasp. I could have had a Tome of Callings within the year. But my lack of success with Omatuu didn't stop me from aggrandizing the steps I had taken. In my opinion, I'd already transcended the life of a Seeker. With one half of the equation well under way, my birth as a wizard was nigh.

I turned my attention to the Spirit Gardens, for I didn't know the challenges awaiting me, and like the chipmunk, I wanted to be prepared post-haste.

And so it was with this in mind that I nearly died.

"Befriend the king," I said aloud as I wended around an outcrop of rock.

"A king, you say?" said a man's voice a moment before I saw him.

I cried out and jerked my mule to a stop. Not just any man. Him.

The gold eye on the lictor's breastplate stared at me. A wall of black plate mail and visored helms flanked him. The knights of the Stormseye sat motionless atop their warhorses twenty paces ahead, their lances couched, sheathed swords menacing at their hips.

The lictor's helm was tucked under one arm. He had a shock of gray hair to match the slate of his eyes. He watched me, a fox sighting a heedless chipmunk.

"What? No smile for me this time? You were so sure of yourself outside the Gate of Cannalis." Cruelty edged the lictor's tone.

I knew my smirk of defiance at the gate would haunt me. Clearly doomed, I took my spear into both hands. Then, I surprised myself by offering the biggest fake smile I could. If I was to die, I'm proud to say, I was going to do so with style.

"Cute." The lictor's mouth became a flat line, then he dismounted. "Let me introduce myself. I'm Lictor Hazash."

A quick death, right then and there, would have been my preference. Stories abounded about the years of torment a lictor could inflict on their prisoners. Horrors upon horrors, they said.

Yet, Hazash had a kind face. Good looks, truly, were as much a predator's lure as they were a beacon of attraction.

When he smiled, the air of cruelty about him returned. Lictor Hazash cleared his throat. "It's your turn. Give me your name. Now."

"El," I said in a rush. "Wh—what do you want?"

"Oh not much. The everlasting power of a Stormlord for starters. I'll soon have it, too. But first, I've been tasked with tracking down an orphan who is said to possess something the Great Archon wants very badly. A scroll."

By the Power, if I was lucky, I would be killed outright. The Great Archon wanted my scroll. Just for possessing it, I would be tortured for eternity in the pits of the Black Ziggurat.

It was a harrowing prospect. Torn and stabbed and burned over and over. The smile fell from my face as I descended into shock.

"Oh my." Hazash smirked. "You're paling quite rapidly."

The gravity of the situation threw me into darkness, my psyche's last-ditch effort to protect me. A dissociative numbness carried me away as I toppled from the saddle.

Warm earth swung toward me—slammed against my face with a crunch of dead leaves.

Chapter Twenty-Six

THE KING

I woke to the crush of fallen leaves at my mule's feet. They'd slung me across its back but hadn't gone through the trouble of tying me up. The clatter of hooves and armor was a dizzying cascade to the senses. Such a noise would be hard to conceal in the forest; it seemed impossible that a score of knights could sneak up on me. Then I remembered they'd been sent by the Great Archon, wizard Prime of all Kelundar and perhaps the world. Whatever Dags Grimjaw had at his outpost, the Great Archon was sure to have a substantial amount more.

Each jostle of the swaying old mule sent a stab of pain through my skull, credit to my collision with the ground. I worked my stiff jaw, then lifted myself into a seated position in the saddle. Blood rushed out of my hands, leaving an uncomfortable prickling in my fingertips. Yet I was grateful for the feeling. Grateful to still have hands at all. Hazash would wait until we reached the Black Ziggurat before removing body parts.

The blur in my vision dissipated by the second. I squinted at a stoic knight beside me, then swiveled to the other side.

Hazash inspected my spear.

"From the sheen on the edges and the stains in the blade's crevices where you failed to clean, I assume you've managed to use this on something other than..." He sniffed it. "Apples?"

I grimaced.

"No need to answer. The spear has already told me all its secrets. However." He tossed my spear to a knight and then plucked the Sun Scroll from his belt. "This is of immense curiosity."

There aren't words sufficient for what I felt, sitting there chewing the inside of my cheek like some ravenous idiot. I had possessed the soul of Idrinnia the Everlasting, history's greatest hero, and now, I'd let her fall into the clutches of its greatest villain.

Hazash stared at me as if expecting a response, then unrolled the parchment.

"Blank." He showed me. "Riveting."

To me, however, it read the same as before.

Befriend the king.

"You've not tricked me, have you, replacing the real scroll with a false one?" Steel entered his voice. "If you lie to me, I'll make the nightmare of your death last a very long time. Troll's blood will help keep you alive for years under the carver's blade. Maybe even decades."

"No, Lictor Hazash." I shook my head vigorously, needles poking the backs of my eyeballs from the motion. "That is the scroll I've always had."

Faced with eternal torture, a quick end was all I could hope for. Courage poured from me. Truth was all that remained. If he asked a question, I would answer it. Stouter hearts than mine might claim they would do otherwise and I name them liars. Or ignorant fools, unaware of the Brotherhood's mastery in the art of torment.

"And where did you get this scroll?"

"A beggar," I said. "In the streets of Cannalis."

Hazash reached forward with a dagger. I flinched away, too late. With a casual slice, he took a piece of my upper ear. Seconds of rigid shock melted into me. Blood raced down my cheek. I gasped then screamed.

Birds squawked and fled to safer spaces.

Hazash made lazy circles in the air with his dagger as I reeled. "I want you to understand something very clearly. Until the age of ten, I dreamed of being a surgeon. It wasn't until I started listening intently to the mandatory sermons that I let such trivial dreams die to make space for my truth and purpose. Through Lord Ravkin, the Power showed me how ludicrous and selfish my desires were as a child, and it showed me the path I was destined to take. I'm to be a Stormlord. Do you know why?"

Face contorted in pain, I said, "Yes."

But before I could say why, Hazash shifted in the saddle to deliver a stinging slap to the area around my eye. Fire burst at my ear where he struck it, causing me to whimper. "No. You don't. That was a stupid thing to say, El. But it figures. I'm to be a Stormlord because I demonstrate in abundance what you seem to lack in earnest, that is, the ability to listen and obey. Remember that when you answer my next questions. You have so little of your ears left for me to remind you." He snatched up a fistful of my hair and brought the knife close. I froze, almost felt the cold radiating off the steel an inch off my cheek. "I have no doubt the person who gave you the scroll appeared as a beggar, but you know that's not what I was asking."

"He was a wizard!" I yelped. "We called him the Elder. He was bald with ruddy skin and an empty eye socket. Gapped teeth. Hates the Stormseye. Please, that's all I know." Compelled to keep talking so long as the dagger was close, I started to stammer, unsure what else to say.

"Enough." Hazash let go and called a halt as he inspected the outside of the scroll. Sunlight bled through mottled parchment. His eyes narrowed. "I am at a loss as to why my God would want such a thing as this. Must I activate it in some way? Speak quickly!"

"No," I said. "Usually it works under sunlight. I—I have no idea why it isn't working for you."

"Do you mock me?" he sneered. "Lay blame at my feet?"

My eyes fell to the mule's mane. "No. I'm—I'm sorry." In truth, I was as confused as he was. Dags had been able to see it.

"Hold it," he said peremptorily. "Show it to me."

I did as I was bidden. Hazash leaned over in the saddle until the outer edge of his pauldron dug into my shoulder. Palm pressing against my wounded ear, I read.

Say nothing.

Panic rifled through me. Lie to a lictor? Without a plan of my own to avoid torture and death, I had to trust the scroll, even if it felt like Idrinnia was steering me wrong.

"Well?" Hazash slapped aside my hand and grabbed my tattered ear. "What does it say?"

"Nothing," I whined. I hoped my next lie stirred no suspicion. "Sometimes it goes blank without warning. I only check it to—"

"Save your lies for the Great Archon."

My insides turned to liquid. Vomit rose to the back of my throat. My worn Cloudbreakers' tabard clung to my frame as sweat poured from me. Once more, I found myself teetering on the edge of fainting.

The Great Archon of the Stormseye...

It was said he could fracture the consciousness of his enemies and send them into different dimensions. I was frantic to avoid such a fate.

"Please," I begged. "Lictor Hazash...please."

He laughed. "You are right to fear the Great Archon. He is the one true Power."

I started to weep but a shout from the front of the column caused me to choke back further tears.

"What's this?" Hazash spurred his horse forward, a different mount than the one I had stabbed, I noted.

A lone figure challenged their progress in the road. I prayed to the Power for it to be Idrinnia the Everlasting or some other such entity out of legend come to rescue me.

"A single warning is all I shall give you," said Hazash coolly. "Go your way and we shall not peel you toe to scalp like an apple rind."

A woman chuckled into a painted green palm. She was swathed in russet robes and boots of nut brown; a stripe of the same earthen coloring ran beneath her eyes and across the bridge of her nose and lips. A bear fur enclosed her shoulders, its head forming a hood from which her face now watched Hazash. A crown of antlers sat around the ears of the bear hood.

"What brings a lictor of the Stormseye this far into the Wildness?" She curled a finger around her chin in mock ponderation. "Or have you forgotten your sacred wards are impotent this far from your cities?"

"Irrelevant." Hazash pulled an amulet from under his breastplate. At the end of a chain, an amber glow lit his palm. His other hand traveled in a fluid arc before him. A halo of gold extended outward, encircling the knights around the lictor. "You've chosen death, wizard."

He jerked a sword from the sheathe at his hip then leveled it at her. "Knights of the Stormseye!"

Like a line of soldier ants in their onyx carapaces, they spread out, lances couched, gathering reins into steel-encased grips. Leather creaked as their warhorses snorted and stamped. I licked my lips nervously and glanced down. Hazash had left the Sun Scroll in my hands. With everyone's attention focused on the wizard, I slowly slid the scroll back into my trouser pocket.

"Stupidity blinds the brave to their own demise." A ball of flame coalesced around the wizard's fingertips. With a quick step and throw, she sent it hurtling toward the Stormseye knights. I jerked my mule's reins just as the invisible barrier of gold flashed. Fire roared overhead and to the sides, then harmlessly dissipated.

The amulet around Hazash's neck pulsed with amber light. He spoke with perfunctory calm. "Charge."

Warhorses twitched at the withers then surged forward, grunting and flinging dirt into my face. I squinted through the churning madness as one of the knights snatched my mule by the lead and yanked it bleating into a trot. It took everything in me not to pitch backward from the saddle.

"You should have brought a Stormlord." The wizard slashed at the ground with the blade of her dark green hand. Wind cut across the fore of the knights, showering them in a cascade of dust and earthen detritus. Gauntleted fists shielded eyes as their horses reared in confusion, stalling their charge before it really began. The wizard shrugged. "Oh well. Meet Iniogg!"

Something moved in the line of trees to one side of the path. Leaves tumbled from the canopy, as did a shower of lesser branches.

Before I could understand what was happening, one of the knights loosed a terrified scream. Legs taller than a warhorse strode from the forest. The ground shook as a giant crashed through the trees, snapping limbs and bowing apart slender pines. It lumbered toward the knights, nearly twenty feet tall and carrying a knotted club.

Unlike ogres, the giant moved quickly.

"Charge!" Hazash called.

The knights around him balked.

Hazash trotted his horse forward a few steps, his commanding voice somewhat strangled. "I said charge! For the Great Archon, charge!" But the desperation in his tone did nothing to persuade his men.

Cursing, Hazash swung his lance at a knight who was turning to flee. The man lurched from the saddle, unconscious. "The Great Archon will eat your hearts! Bloody fight!"

This, finally, had the desired effect. A knight spurred his mount as the humungalor closed with them. "For the Power!" Others angled their mounts at the new threat.

The giant punted the onrushing knight from the saddle and the man flew like a skipped stone across the forest floor. Ten feet of knotted oak swept through their right flank, dispersing the Brotherhood. Horses wheeled, a frenzy of neighing and panicked shouts.

The wizard laughed, a lilting, melodious thing.

Another knight stabbed at the humungalor, who sidestepped. With a satisfied grunt, the giant back-handed the man, rocketing him into the canopy and leaving a crown of bloody mist around his mount's withers.

I gaped, reveling in the sight of my savior.

Iniogg, the wizard called him, was nothing like Omatuu's bull monster, Tattaghor. He looked like a normal man, albeit a proportionally gigantic one. His limbs were sinewy and sallow, and he was smooth-cheeked but for a thin layer of stubble. With a low growl he swung a massive arm forward, the snag-made-club in his fist whistling death wherever it trailed.

Most of the knights dodged around the humungalor, heading for the wizard. The bravest among them wheeled their mounts, choosing instead to focus on the giant. For a moment, it looked as though the knights encircling Iniogg were set to hamstring him. The wizard also appeared to be in dire straits since magical attacks failed to bypass the amber shield emanating from Hazash's amulet. Just when the knights were upon her, Seekers leapt from concealment in the underbrush to cut them down. Green paint streaked their faces and bear hides rode their shoulders. Those that had hair wore it shorn and worked into a mohawk.

A trap.

The Stormseye Brotherhood were being defeated.

Dizzy from hitting my head, and bloodless from losing part of my ear, I didn't dismount so much as I fell from the mule. I scrambled to my feet, recalling Dags's words about the cabals utilizing the Fey to defeat the Great Archon. Emboldened by the sight of Seekers fighting the Stormseye, I sought my spear amid the swirling carnage. Anger rippled through me.

I searched for Hazash. He'd slapped me, threatened me, mutilated me. I'd seen him order the death of dozens of Cannalis citizens. And there was a chance he'd done something to Trin and her family, too. Rage consumed me, rendering me a vessel of action and reaction. Where the emotion flooded, my intellect drowned.

Horses pounded past. A knight skewered a Seeker through the chest with his lance with a wet rasp. Another drew down on me with his lance, only to be peppered by a trio of arrows up his side, arm, and face. He slumped over his horse, a death rattle echoing from within his helm.

I spotted my spear gleaming in the hands of a dead knight a short distance away. Just beyond, Hazash reared his horse, hooves whisking the air at one Seeker as he thrust his blade through the green bar around another's eye.

I pried my weapon from the stiffened fingers of the dead knight. The haft was still warm.

Hazash whipped around in his saddle to cut down another Seeker. Apparently noticing fewer than a half dozen of his knights remained, he shouted, "Flee! Back to Cannalis with everything you've—"

Booming footsteps caused him to turn as the giant rushed up behind him. The lictor, to his credit, brandished his blade.

But I was not to be denied. I took one long step and hurled my spear. Iniogg's club drew back, started to descend...

And came to a sudden halt. Blood fountained from Hazash's mouth as my spear tore through his throat. Desperate fingers hovered over the wound. His horse rushed sideways, away from Iniogg, kicking up a flurry of dust and dropping its stunned master to the ground.

The rest of the Stormseye knights fled, died, or surrendered. My stomach soured as I passed Hazash's twitching legs. Wide eyes stared up at me, his brow scrunching in confusion around slate-gray eyes.

I would be the last thing they ever saw.

"Did you do something with Trin?" If there was any chance he knew something, I had to ask. "A girl from Cannalis who lived in..."

Glazed eyes watched the sky, his face slack and impossibly distant.

I kicked the dead lictor and turned away cursing.

A shadow fell over me. A giant's shadow.

Iniogg glared down. My interrogation of the dead ended abruptly and I swallowed hard. A green hand alighted on my shoulder.

"Congratulations." The wizard stepped up to my side and regarded me. Unlike Hazash, her smile was warm, genuine. "You managed to kill a lictor of the Stormseye and piss off my giant all in one fateful chuck of your spear."

"I don't understand. The lictor was my enemy, same as yours."

Iniogg scoffed, then reached down past me, plucking the amulet from around Hazash's neck.

I eyed the giant sidelong. "I fought alongside you. Our victory is shared."

The woman made a tsking noise. "No one *shares* glory with Iniogg. There's nothing the king of giants covets more in this world than trophy kills. And, sorry to say, but you stole his."

Iniogg grunted, then strode away.

I stared after him in shock. "King?"

"The king of giants, yes. The very one you just pissed off." She chuckled. "But you'll have plenty of time to discuss these issues with him yourself, for as long as you're my prisoner, he'll be your guard."

"Prisoner?" I said dumbly.

"A difficult day for you, I'm sure. Allow me to introduce myself." Her hands weaved together, a motion both intricate and precise. Vines snapped from the earth, and before I could react, they shot out to snare my wrists. "I'm Malthece," she said. "Welcome to the Shadowgiants."

I thrashed at my bonds a moment, teeth clenched, dimly aware that this had been Durn's cabal before he became a wizard.

Thunderous footsteps approached. A face larger in circumference than a wagon wheel lowered to meet mine. Like a rabbit caught between a fox's jaws, I froze.

"Be calm," Iniogg said menacingly. "Little thief."

It took every scrap of will I had not to wet myself.

Befriend the king. The Sun Scroll's faith in my abilities to do such a thing seemed woefully misplaced.

Chapter Twenty-Seven

RULED BY WRATH

The vines binding my wrists were the sole marker that I was a prisoner of the Shadowgiants. I rode upright, only just able to take the mule's reins. To my surprise, they'd returned my pack to me. My spear, however, they withheld. For that, I could hardly fault them.

The name Truespear fit me more every day.

Bile rose at the back of my throat. Rarely does one predict their regrets in the heat of the moment. I knew I wanted Hazash dead for what he'd done to me, for what he and those like him may have done to Trin and her family.

Yet, the slackness around his eyes at the moment of death haunted me. I thought of little else but the sound of the lictor's dying. One moment he was there, doling out cruelty and grinning with self-importance, and then, he was a lump of useless mass on an unnamed road.

A sudden shiver up my spine caused me to shake. My mule turned its head brusquely, one ear twitching. I patted its neck. After seeing men bludgeoned into a pulp by Iniogg, and narrowly avoiding endless torture myself, I'd adopted a deep sense of gratitude for the animal, and to a slightly lesser extent, life itself.

I was lucky. Omatuu was right.

Luckier still for the dignity Malthece and the Shadowgiants showed me. The Sun Scroll lay securely in my trouser pocket. I knew circumstances might change at any moment, but for now, I was safe, my person mostly unmolested.

The Stormseye knight they captured was given less hospitable treatment. Cortair, they named him. In all ways, he looked a prisoner.

Gagged with bloody rags stripped from his fallen comrades and blindfolded, he'd been slung over a horse like a trussed-up pig. His armor was gone; his weaponry, too, distributed amongst the Shadow-giants cabal. Vines bound tight around his wrists and ankles rubbed abrasions into the man's milky, bare skin. A line of scarlet trickled from a gash on his forehead, soaking his blindfold. Lustrous hair, a golden wheat brown, and a fair complexion made him look young for a knight.

I looked ahead, taking in the rest of the column. The wizard Prime, Malthece, led roughly thirty Seekers to the top of a bluff. From the rear, all I could see of them were bear pelts, mohawks, and hands painted green. Malthece was the only one mounted, her antlered crown rising with savage elegance above her warriors.

As I watched, I felt a tingling sensation between my shoulder blades. The giant's heavy bootsteps had been so rhythmic, I'd almost forgotten he followed behind Cortair and I, the prisoners. Craning my neck, I caught him staring at me.

He gave a derisive snort. "Puny, wretched little thieves you are."

I twisted in the saddle to meet his hostile gaze. "Me?"

"All humans," he spat. "You take what is not yours. Driven by fear, you steal, enslave, possess, hoard."

The giant's ire summoned my own. "Are all humungalor such hypocrites? You're mad because I 'stole' your trophy. Wouldn't you call that a desire for possession?"

Iniogg turned his nose up at me. "It was I who broke their charge. Their leader's life should have been mine."

"Interesting." A brief form of madness made me forget with whom I bandied words. "In my world, there is a difference between wishing for a thing and earning it."

Iniogg leapt ahead of me with an agility so stunning, I thought it reserved only for cats. My mule brayed and backpedaled from the giant as his club swept overhead. "You've *earned* a swift death with your insulting tone!" Darkness played along the edges of my vision as I took in the hulking scion of the Fey, sixteen feet of whipcord muscle and menace. A sound escaped me, halfway between whine and blubber.

"Tell me," he roared. "Would it be right for me to crush you dead?"

In the distance, a firm voice demanded Iniogg to stop.

I stammered, managing only a pitiful, "No."

"Agreed." The humungalor's heavily muscled shoulders relaxed, tension easing from them. Gone was the harmful intent as the club slowly descended. "Your life belongs to Malthece. It was she who saved it and she who will end it if she sees fit. You are her reward, just as the lictor was to be mine. Whether it was wished or earned, matters little. Right is right and mine is mine."

Sweat dappled my scalp and the area beneath my nose. I gulped, my throat feeling like I'd eaten sand for lunch. "Their leader, Hazash, did this." I showed the giant the place where the lictor severed my ear.

He laughed. "You think a tiny flap of missing meat will garner you my sympathies?"

The rest of the column had come to a halt to watch the conflict between myself and the giant unfold. When Malthece came into view, Iniogg's laughter cut short. He grimaced.

My chin jutted at the giant. "Hazash was the first man I've killed. I wouldn't do so lightly nor without reason. His death was mine to deliver. Not yours."

"Iniogg," said Malthece in a reproachful tone. "I have much to do. That means I have meager room for your petty debates."

"Petty!" he said. "This is a matter of principle you—"

Ghostly manacles slithered up from the earth and around Iniogg's wrists. Loops of chain dangled from them, then went taut, bearing him down. The giant growled and bucked against his bonds, fighting hard but barely managing to keep his feet. Spittle flew from his lips and his eyes flashed with preternatural light. A rigid wave moved through him. Writhing muscles shuddered then went limp, all resistance to Malthece's magic gone. "For such an intelligent creature," she said, "you practice stupidity with alarming regularity."

Phantom chains and manacles disappeared back into whatever void they'd issued from. Iniogg sucked in sharply and threw his club up onto one shoulder as if nothing interesting had happened. The indifferent expressions of many of the Shadowgiants told me this was some kind of routine the wizard and her thrall played out from time-to-time, like a parent bringing an obstreperous child to heel. Nothing new.

But for me, it had a distinct impact.

"You make my enslavement ever drearier, Malthece," Iniogg said. "Your lickspittles are boring, shallow-minded, puppets. You have no one but yourself to blame for my rugged discourse with your prisoner."

With a brief smile, Malthece signaled the column to continue and then rode back to the front. Iniogg watched her go.

"You're right." Iniogg looked down at me, speaking in hushed, secretive tones. "The lictor's life *was* yours to take, and take it you did. A glorious throw. In truth, I am merely jealous. My outburst, an illusory ruse."

Iniogg's demeanor shifted, his measured and calculating intellect stunningly evident. I wish I could have seen the baffled look on my face. Mere moments before, I thought he'd intended to kill me, and now, he congratulated me and apologized in the same breath.

The giant let the rest of the column disappear over the lip of the bluff before herding Cortair and I after them. A coastline covered in short, coarse shrubbery stretched from one craggy enclave to another, miles apart.

"If you agreed with me, why did you..." I shook my head. "I—I don't understand."

"Then you've never been a slave before." He waited for me to catch on, but when I didn't, he continued in exasperated tones. "You're sharp as a river stone. I manufacture reasons to test Malthece's hold over me. I wish her to think me ruled by my rage and wrath. Such is the game of a prisoner who seeks freedom."

Given Iniogg's situation at the time, my next words could not have been more offensive.

"You don't serve Malthece willingly, then?"

Cold, biting silence ensued. The giant's steps seemed to land harder as he looked out over the coastline.

"Sorry." I recalled the ghostly chains, the quiet struggle between Iniogg and whatever magic Malthece used to bind him. "I didn't realize."

The humungalor cleared his throat, a deep rumble. "I used to roam a coastline like this one when I was free. Fighting other humungalor who challenged me, or facing sorcerers, monsters, sometimes, even armies of men. Completely isolated and alone but for the spray of salt on the sea winds and the taste of shark meat in my mouth."

"That sounds terrible," I said.

"I speak of it fondly." He shot me a perturbed look. A dreamy quality entered his tone. "I would do anything to go back. Playing guard dog to a cabal—pfah! Rarely do I get to fight other humungalor of note. They're either too weak or too broken-spirited to offer much excitement, which leaves me with these quick and dirty tussles with the Stormseye, or Seekers from a rival cabal. All of it is beneath me."

I frowned. "How can you live alone and call yourself a king?"

"I am *the* king. King of all giants. Among my kind, such a title is earned." He smiled. "Weaker humungalor are forced to band together for survival, but not because they desire it. The fewer we are, the greater our ability to connect to the earth, and the better able we are to draw upon its power. Those who live in communities lose the power of the Fey. We are solitary creatures. To be alone is to be among the strong. Look here."

He bent down and gathered a clump of rocks in his hand. "Each of these is a human. Together, they are strongest." He whipped around and flung the gravel across the earth. "Each of those is a giant. The stronger we are, the more we spread out. The more we dominate a region. Where I am from, I rule a coastline the length of the entire lands of Kelundar. Everything the Great Archon reaches, I rule in equal measure in my own world."

My lips parted in astonishment.

"So you see," he said, "being Malthece's pet is a canker on my soul." He straightened. "So I test the limits of her power whenever I can. A decade, I've done so—will do so until my dying breath."

"As you should," I said. "If I can help in any way, I will."

Iniogg narrowed mossy green eyes flecked with brown. He scoffed, a smile tugging at the corner of his stubbly mouth. He pinched something from the thick leather belt holding up his skirt of stitched-to-gether cowhides. He flicked his hand, tossing something through the air; it caught the sun's fading rays and flashed a brilliant gold. Reaching up with bound hands, I caught the amulet Hazash had worn. I stared at it in awe.

"A prize. For your first kill."

It was far heavier than I expected. I pulled the chain over my head—

Blinding pain seared my chest where it came to rest. The stink of my own burning skin filled my nostrils, choking the back of my throat with the sudden stench. I screamed into darkness. The last thing I saw before I blacked out were tendrils of smoke rising into the air before me...

From me.

Chapter Twenty-Eight

THE AMULET

I woke in a cave, three glowing faces peering down at me in the candlelight. Iniogg's was five times the size of the others.

"What did you do?" Malthece said.

Iniogg's deep voice rumbled throughout the cave. "Gave a trophy to its rightful owner."

I squeezed my eyes shut then opened them wide, attempting to wring clarity back into my vision. "Wha...what?"

"Easy now." A man gripped my shoulder. He shared similarly distinct features with Malthece: a nest of braids bundled together into a top-knot with dark hair cascading around an angular face, and stark green eyes. While the man's gaze was steady, Malthece's wandering eye gave her an uneasy presence.

The man took my hand, using his other to support me in getting to a seated position. "You're not yet healed."

I groaned and looked down at the puckered, angry flesh around the amulet resting between my collar bones. A soft and warm amber glow emanated from it.

Malthece crouched, inspecting the jewel. She turned to Iniogg. "I told you to keep it safe until our return."

The humungalor shrugged.

The other man, whom I rightly assumed to be both Malthece's brother as well as her Second in the Shadowgiants cabal, bent down to run his fingers along the amulet's chain. As soon as his fingers touched it, I recoiled, a hand wrapped protectively around it.

"Apologies." He straightened. "We cannot remove it for you, but perhaps you can." He looked at me expectantly. "Go on."

I hesitated, recalling the pain from before.

"Do it." Malthece stood abruptly, her voice steel. "Now."

I was stubborn but not to the point of idiocy. Two wizards and a giant loomed over me, so compliance came swiftly. The amulet peeled off my skin with the ease of a rotten fruit rind. Scarred depressions marred my flesh.

The amulet dangled from my hand. Malthece's brother looked at her, then reached hesitantly forward. A fingertip contacted the amber halo pooling out of it.

Sound itself seemed to bow inward, a reverberation in the ears, and then the golden jewel erupted with a blast of light, flinging him against the far wall. Malthece managed to throw wind behind her before colliding with the cave like her brother had; instead, she fell forward to her knees with a grunt. Iniogg shielded his eyes.

"Herastos!" Malthece scrambled to her brother's side.

Iniogg watched me warily as I gaped at the amulet swinging from my hand. It rotated toward the candles and then back into shadows. When it twisted back once more, I thought I saw something within, too faint to make out. A pit or smaller stone set within the gem, perhaps?

Malthece's palms hovered over her brother's body. He lay deadly still. She licked her lips, hands weaving over his torso and face, fast in some places and then slow in others; they passed over his head and hesitated. Tendrils of misty white reached down from her palms into his face. Steam rose from a place behind his ear.

Herastos gasped, touched the back of his head, and brought away crimson-wet fingers.

"The wound is sealed." Malthece hauled him to his feet. "The swelling subdued."

"Thank you." Herastos breathed the words, "By the Power, what is that thing?"

Iniogg grunted thoughtfully. "It did not bind itself to the Stormseye lictor, nor lash out at me when I removed it."

With a hand resting gingerly against his head, Herastos grimaced. "Perhaps the lictor's armor acted as a buffer. So, why then didn't it hurt Iniogg?"

"He is a Scion of the Fey," Malthece said. "It could be sensitive solely to those with the Power."

I stretched the amulet's chain between my hands.

"If you're going to put it back on, I'd lie down first," Iniogg cautioned. "In case you pass out again. I barely caught you the first time."

"El will do no such thing." Malthece's mouth was a grim line. "It belongs to the Shadowgiants now."

Rage burned through me. Too long had I been oppressed in Cannalis by the Brotherhood. I fled into the Wildness to escape captivity and servitude. Undergoing the commands and demands of Omatuu as a Cloudbreaker had been hard enough. I was sick of it; everywhere I went, I was being told what I could or couldn't do, should or shouldn't do, will or won't do.

Swallowing hard and expecting the worst, I looped the chain over my head. I winced as it touched my skin, but this time, there was no pain, no sensation at all except for the solidity of the amulet's weight as it slid into place in the exact spot it was before I removed it.

Malthece's brow darkened. She called in a burly female to attempt to take the amulet off me, to no avail. As soon as the woman exerted any real effort, it burned her fingers. With a frustrated sigh, Malthece dismissed her, then fixed me with a mismatched stare. "What do you hope to accomplish here?"

"Why am I a captive?" I snapped. If she was to treat me like a prisoner, I'd treat her like an enemy. That meant giving nothing without a fight.

"I thought the wizard's edict made it so Seekers had..." I waved my hands in the air as I stood. Still dizzy and disoriented, I stumbled to one side.

"Rights?" supplied Herastos.

"Yes." I propped myself against the cave wall. "Even Omatuu gave me sanctuary when he found me in the Wildness."

"The cabals created the edicts to swell the ranks of willing servants *for* wizards more than they were to protect those who are already Seekers." Malthece sounded tired as she explained. "So while a cabal might revolt if one of their wizards violates the edict too many times, rest assured, my Shadowgiants don't give two licks about a single Cloudbreaker."

"So it's customary for you to kidnap Seekers from another cabal?"

"Not really," said Malthece. "At least, we've never done it before."

"Not Seekers," growled Iniogg. "But humungalor, certainly."

She shot the giant a disdainful look, then cleared her throat. "You, El, are the exception. For though we've never held a Seeker captive before, we've also never seen the Stormseye take such a special interest in one, either. So you see..." She grinned broadly, green paint creasing at the corners of her eyes. I marked her age to be somewhere between mid-thirties and early forties. "One good anomaly deserves another." Her tone lost its cheery edge. "We tracked you for some time. Well, more accurately I should say we tracked the Stormseye knights who tracked you. So, we know you've learned the secret location of the Spirit Gardens. That means you feel its call thrumming through every bit of you. And that means every minute you spend here is another you aren't spending out there."

She pointed down the passageway, drawing my eyes to the sunlit cave mouth. Beyond, I saw the surging sea and realized I'd been hearing the pounding of waves against a distant beach the entire time.

"I recall the pain, you see." Malthece sighed. "The whispers pulling me to its bosom...the feeling of bliss once I arrived. I know you want that more than anything right now. If you don't cooperate, the torment in the interval between will be prolonged...indefinitely."

My outrage spilled forth. Looking back, I suspect it was fueled in small part by the drive to reach the Spirit Gardens. "I've done nothing to deserve this treatment."

"Deserve!" Iniogg's laughter boomed, an echo slapped back and forth down what sounded like a honeycomb of passageways. "This is the way of all humans. Malthece is no exception."

"Be silent!" she hissed. When she locked eyes with me again, there was a deep sincerity there. "I'm sorry, El. I really am." Sorrow fell across her face as she considered her next words. "You hate the Stormseye Brotherhood, don't you?"

Herastos shifted from foot to foot, a half-smile on his face.

I touched the amulet on my chest and nodded, eyes narrowed.

"Good." Malthece said. "Then let us unite around that common goal, for I work to bring the Great Archon to his knees. And that requires more information than we've ever had among the cabals. More innovation. More risks. Fewer wizards serving only themselves."

"Fewer like Omatuu."

"Indeed," she said. "He seeks only to increase his own powers. It's him and other Primes like him that keep the lands of Kelundar under the Great Archon's control with their selfish endeavoring. But if you help me, El, there's a chance we could end the Brotherhood's reign."

As much as I dreamed of such a thing, cynicism tipped the wagers against hope inside me. I loosed a laugh at the absurd declaration. "You can't be serious."

"Deadly." Malthece's lazy eye centered on me. She gestured at the amulet. "That could be a weapon in our fight against him. It holds secrets we need to know that are vital to our cause. Since you've already decided to bear the amulet's burden, I ask you to bear the responsibility that comes with it."

I searched their faces, still worrying that all her talk of fighting the Brotherhood might be some mind game or cruel jest, much like Omatuu might do. But nothing in their expression betrayed a hint of what I sought.

I dragged in a slow breath. The insatiable draw of the Spirit Gardens pumped through me, demanding I go there. Yet it was like the discordant clang of a rake on stone compared to the deeper, far more potent urge that drew me in with its beautiful song.

Kill the Great Archon.

Ever since I'd started my journey to be a wizard, the once-tiny seed of that fantasy had grown, fertilized and watered by Dags's admission, and now, by Malthece's mission.

Still, I didn't trust her. I was a captive. How could I?

"Do I have any other choice?" Ideally, I would go free to gain the Power alone, and then endeavor the Stormseye's fall in my own way.

She raised an eyebrow. "Like set you loose so some other greedy wizard or the Stormseye can steal my weapon? No. I think not. But I could have Iniogg crush you."

The giant scoffed. I knew if Malthece desired it, the giant would be compelled to do the deed, regardless of his wishes in the matter.

"But I'm not one for threats," she said. "I'd rather convince you of the merits of our quest. I simply do not trust you yet, given the circumstances of our meeting."

Reaching through my scorched tunic, I touched the scarred flesh on my chest. I remembered the way my mother spoke of Idrinnia's thousand-year reign of peace. I remembered the way she'd been so sick at the end...the shaking movements belying her desperate need for the pain to be gone. I remembered the way the knight had made me leave her, the way he'd kicked me as I crawled from her bedside on all fours like a dog. But more than anything, I remembered the guilt, knowing I'd never see her again and that she'd been alone when she died.

I looked at the ground just as a drop of blood fell from my clenched fist. I held Malthece's treatment of me in low esteem, but under the expectant stares of those before me, I remembered who I truly hated.

"And if I do something that demonstrates trust? Will you treat me as an ally instead of a prisoner in our fight against the Stormseye?"

"You have my word," Malthece said without hesitation.

Tendrils of warmth trickled into my thigh where the Sun Scroll lay hidden. Like Malthece and Herastos, Idrinnia opposed the Great Archon. I couldn't defeat the tyrant alone and I'd promised myself I'd take risks.

I sighed, then dug into my pants for the scroll. It caught the glowing candlelight as I proffered it to Malthece. "Another weapon in the fight against the Great Archon."

Malthece arched an eyebrow. "What is it? A letter? I—"

"Just open it."

She did. A hand rose to trembling lips. Her chest froze until finally, after a span of heartbeats, she exhaled. "It can't be."

Iniogg scratched his chin. "What is it?"

"Now you know why the Great Archon wants me."

Her eyes drank in the parchment. I licked nervous lips. "I've shown you one of my secrets in exchange for your trust. Now give it back, if you please."

"I do not please." With a resolute sniffle, Malthece rolled up the parchment, then slid it into a pouch at her waist. "And I won't. Not yet."

"But you gave your word," I stammered. "You said I'd be like an ally. You can't do this."

"I may do as I please, but above all, I must do what is necessary to accomplish our goal—the one you share, remember? I'll willingly sacrifice all of my honor. Nothing is more sacred to me than our mission."

"Filthy liar!"

"If I am a liar then so are you!" the Prime thundered. "You said you seek the Great Archon's downfall, didn't you? *This* is what it takes."

She started off down the high vaulted cave's passageway. "Herastos!" she declared. "Test the amulet. Then have my things packed."

The Second nodded.

"You can't go against Idrinnia's soul!" My shouts fell on deaf ears. "You'll doom yourself!" My words of warning trailed away as I suddenly realized something painful.

I did not *own* the Sun Scroll.

If it was indeed Idrinnia's soul, then it had its own prerogatives, its own locus for decision making, its own desires. Maybe even its own fears. And if it could help me, it could just as easily betray me. The moment the Elder had placed it in my hand, I made a fatal error—I thought I was special. A foolish way to blind oneself.

And now, I'd given up my greatest asset.

"See," Iniogg said. "Puny, wretched, thieves, one and all."

Fists balled at my sides, I glared at the humungalor, and then at Herastos who stepped close. His tone pleaded for enthusiasm from me that wasn't there. "In time, you'll see her methods are necessary. She's a revolutionary. It may not feel like it now, but what Malthece does, she does for the good of everyone. You included."

Iniogg guffawed. "Only humans could be so wantonly manipulative. 'I hurt you for your own good.' What glorious rot! Should I give a warm shower of piss to every human that feels a chill?"

Herastos ignored this and turned his full attention on me. He spoke in a voice attempting to soothe. "Malthece's brazen, selfless approach will yield us what we need to defeat the Great Archon. I know it seems impossible, but her plans have already yielded us the most powerful humungalor alive." He indicated Iniogg, and then, with the same hand, swirled the air.

I didn't have time to shield myself. Tongues of flame leaped from the candles lining the cave mouth to consume me. I shrieked and stumbled backward. Herastos made a beckoning motion with his hand. My insides grew suddenly chill, my legs and arms immobile as if frozen. Fire splashed up my pant legs, but when my clothes started to smoke, I felt no burns. Instead, steam rose from my protected skin. But it wasn't the amulet that protected me like it had Hazash. It took Herastos drawing water from the cave floor to douse the remnant flames for me to realize that he'd frozen me before the flames struck.

"Are you burned?" he asked.

I gripped my chest with one hand, heart galloping with adrenaline. Sweat slathered my brow. I shook fiercely. "No," I said through gritted teeth. "I don't think so."

"Excellent." He crossed his arms, a hooking finger pressed against his lips. "Ah. It's a primal source."

"What does that mean?"

"A wizard's topknot is a primal source, a conduit for the Power, if you will. Throw one into the Occuli Rift, receive a magical tome in return. The blood of certain creatures who were birthed by the Blue Colossus—trolls, hydras, ogres, etcetera—are also primal sources. Bone fragments from scions of the Fey are another similar source." Herastos winked at Iniogg. "Anything either born of the Fey, or infused with the Power, holds a reservoir of magical energy within it, regardless of whether it's alive or dead. And as such, primal sources can amplify other powers."

Turning back to me, Herastos smiled. "I hate to tell you, but you have some poor wizard's eyeball slung around your neck. Forcibly removed by the Great Archon himself, no doubt."

I looked down and hesitantly brought the amulet to rest in my palm. I angled it toward the guttering candles lining the cave so light passed through it. There was a faint shadow of what appeared to be an olive...

The dark blot within rotated toward me, returning my gaze. The white had been cut away. Of the wizard's eye once there, only iris and onyx pupil remained.

Awe filled Herastos's voice. "The Great Archon spies in the cleverest of ways."

CHAPTER TWENTY-NINE

JUST MEAT

Iniogg, my guard, paced the cave mouth grumbling to himself about injustice.

With arms huddled around my legs, I watched him as the hours and candles melted around me. Without the Sun Scroll, I felt naked and powerless.

For the first time since leaving Cannalis, my resolve to become a wizard faltered. I'd been burned, punched, tortured, and bound. On four occasions I'd nearly been killed—by ogres, a wizard, a troll, and a lictor. All the strife and struggle and suffering, only to end up a prisoner. And stripped of the most important object Kelundar had ever known.

And then there was the Great Archon's Eye.

With a bitter taste at the roof of my mouth, I looked down. The mutilated orb within shifted, sending a shiver through my shoulders. My ear throbbed with pain despite Herastos's healing efforts, and made my words come out as a pitiful squeak. "I'll throw it away at the first chance."

Iniogg continued pacing, fists pumping at his sides as he muttered angrily.

"Iniogg!" The echo pinged down the cave passageway. I jangled the amulet around my neck. "I'm going to throw this thing into the sea."

The giant pivoted around to face me. "You'll do no such thing."

"I could." The meekness in my tone reflected how much I believed my own words.

"For two reasons, you won't." The humungalor waved a rolling-pin finger in the air. "The first: because when you have no sword, and then your enemy gives you theirs, you don't simply throw it away. You use it. You wear a weapon around your neck even if you don't yet know how to wield it. And the second reason." He dipped his hips, and with chin raised, he roared in frustration, "You must always do what Malthece says!"

The depth of hatred in his tone left a hollow place in my gut. I drew in tighter around my knees.

As he glared up the passage leading deeper into the mountain, Iniogg pounded the arched ceiling. Somewhere, rock broke free and clattered to the ground. A man shouted back in mockery from somewhere inside the vast honeycomb, then laughed. It seemed Iniogg's wrathful tantrums were common enough to be dismissed lightly.

"So you see," Iniogg said. "I must guard you for the very same reason you must keep the Great Archon's prying eye—a wizard's threats. And a hope for their hasty downfall."

The giant spat.

I wondered how Iniogg would have liked being a thrall to Omatuu. The two had similarities enough, but if the king of giants hated Malthece, he'd surely have hated the imperious nature of the Cloud-breakers' Prime. Like Omatuu, I doubted Iniogg suffered anyone who thought themselves superior to him.

"You're very proud, aren't you?"

"If you were me," he said, "you would be, too. You know not the legend who babysits you. This existence is disgraceful."

A long moment passed. The Sun Scroll was gone, but its instruction still echoed through me.

Befriend the king.

Idrinnia's final words were the only thing keeping me hopeful. "Have you always hated us?"

"Wizards?"

I smiled. "Humans. I'm no wizard yet."

"And you likely won't be," said the humungalor. "Out of all humans, wizards are a twisted combination of empty morality and gifted intellect. Sadly, you seem to be neither."

Head cocked, I fixed him with a reproachful look.

"Such thin skin," he said. "I thought after the lictor sharpened his knife on your ear, you'd be a bit tougher."

We shared a brief laugh.

Iniogg continued. "No, I haven't always hated humans."

The giant seemed to soften, taut neck and shoulder muscles relaxing. His ever-tight jaw went slack, his eyes distant. "Malthece dragged me from another world, you know. In many ways, it is similar to this one. Only in a single, but very important way, is it different...this isn't my home." He ran a palm the size of a spade along the cavern wall. "Here, I'm not connected to the earth. Where I come from, humungalor, as you call us, can access gifts and abilities that are out of reach for us here.

"For that reason, among others, we were hunted by humans and pushed to the edges of the world. Until a king of men came along who was different than the rest. A learned man and a courageous visionary, though a downright righteous fool at times. He possessed many flaws, and I suppose working to change the dynamic between giant and humankind was one of them, but it was the type of flaw one should hope for in a friend."

The last surprised me. "Friend?"

Narrowed eyes swiveled toward me, judging harshly. "Yes. My friend. He was the best of your kind. An actual revolutionary with staunch principles, unlike Malthece. In the way of most wizards, she blinds herself to her own desires. Instead of using her passion for good like my friend did, she is swept away by its whims."

The way Iniogg hung on certain words told me of a long-standing pain. And I felt it, too, more than I could believe was possible. I nearly wept. It wasn't until later that I realized a giant's emotions are quite influential, for humungalor are massive creatures with immense energetic output.

A part of me pulled back from asking Iniogg the question I wanted to ask. But curiosity has ever been my weakness as much as it is my strength. "Is your friend dead?"

The giant shook his head. "I do not know. I've been gone." He ground his teeth. "Many years."

"I'm sorry, Iniogg." I thought of my mother, about the story of Idrinnia I never got to tell her. "I know what it's like to lose someone."

In the ruddy wash of candlelight, Iniogg watched me from the corner of an eye. Wind whistled into the cave passage, carrying the scent of decomposing sea life mingled with the stale odor of wet stone. Waves boomed in one direction, while laughter pecked at the sacredness of our grieving vigil from the other. For a few long moments, Iniogg and I shared a meaningful silence that words would only dilute.

Malthece's cheery tone shattered it. "What's this?"

I twisted around. I'd not even heard her approach. The bear pelt was gone, as was the antlered crown. A leather corset was cinched around her torso, revealing a half dozen tattooed vines twisting along the exposed flesh of her shoulders, upper chest, and neck. A bar of green was fixed around her eyes.

She shivered and brought a brown cloak up around her shoulders. "My thrall has many stories, most of them laced with wisdom. You'd do well to listen, El."

I hadn't expected an endorsement so much as a reprimand. I looked to Iniogg who refused eye contact.

"As I'm sure you're well aware, he's a bit temperamental." Malthece flashed a smile. "Though I've not heard of a humungalor who isn't. It's why we must enthrall them."

"You mean enslave them," I said.

Of all the terrible things I'd done, all the malicious acts I would do, there was something about Iniogg's imprisonment that stuck in my heart.

Malthece threw me a puzzled look. "Do you think I balk at keeping one creature in shackles in order to free an entire nation from theirs? Tell it true, is that a worthy comparison?"

I hesitated. "No. I suppose not." I stood, brushing rubble from my tunic and trousers. "What about me? You're going to release me after I help you, right?"

Malthece crossed her arms. "Of course. Again, I apologize for keeping you prisoner, but the work I'm doing is more important than your freedom. More important than my desires, as well."

"The prisoner I guard is guaranteed freedom before me. What a joke you are, Malthece. You're as much a revolutionary as the Great Archon. Pfah!" Iniogg gave a contemptuous snort. "Do not hold your breath, El. It could be years before she's done with you. If only my own years of servility had an expiration."

The wizard pursed her lips.

Iniogg did not relent. "How *are* you different than the Stormseye? Do they not indenture others to meet their own ends? For some greater purpose their inferiors cannot comprehend, isn't it? Tell it true, Malthece, or let your close-lipped brooding be evidence of your thrice-damned hypocrisy!"

"Be silent!" Malthece's eyes flashed with ruinous energy. A luminous wave washed over Iniogg, racking him with pain and turning him a shade paler. Ghostly chains coalesced around his wrists, jerking him to the unyielding stone floor. Muscle and sinew jumped as he strained for control of his body. Jewels of sweat gathered at the crown of his bald pate, shimmering in the candle flame, his grunts bouncing down the passageway.

Such power to bring a giant king to his knees. Caught up in the moment, I thought for the briefest second that the woman might have what it took to topple the Black Ziggurat. The vote of confidence, however, was quickly replaced by a sour churning in my gut at seeing Iniogg so subdued. Even if it was for a righteous cause.

"He brings it on himself, you see. If I could, I would release him. Alas, he is too powerful. Since I've had Iniogg at my side, no wizard has challenged me to a duel, for they know he'll kill whatever humungalor they put before him." Malthece put a hand on my shoulder. "Being a wizard, as you've discovered, is neither simple nor fun." She glanced at Iniogg and the chains disappeared. Released from her magical grasp, he flopped onto his back amid tremors of pain. "We must make hard decisions. Sometimes, those that subvert our ethics."

I looked from the display, nodding.

She came around where I could not avoid her gaze, adopting a fake smile as her wandering eye shifted out of focus. "Come, we have more to discuss." She threw her next word over a shoulder. "Iniogg!"

Still dazed and groaning, the giant was pulled gingerly to his feet by diaphanous shackles of light. At the limits of his tether, he followed.

We strode past rows of glittering candles and upthrust stalagmites along the cave floor. As we went, the sound of chatter grew, as did the number of intersecting passageways. Eventually, we emerged into an immense chamber, four times the height of Iniogg.

Numerous tables covered with food were set up in a haphazard manner around the chamber. Roughened hands cracked the limbs of crabs or dug into piles of seaweed. Greedy mouths slurped at steaming shells until tiny gelatinous critters shot down their gullets.

At the end of one table, Cortair sat wearing fresh bandages. Herastos sat beside the Stormseye knight. It appeared they were in deep discussion as if they were erstwhile comrades. If the look on the former knight's face could be trusted, he was actually enjoying himself.

Malthece put an arm around my shoulder, then whispered, "He's a Shadowgiant now. You see, the Great Archon bleeds power every day. Slow but sure, he loses influence. If we're smart, we can deal him a blow that disrupts the balance of power in Kelundar. Everyone has a role to play in this and that includes you. Together, we can rid the world of his vile touch."

I watched Cortair with hard eyes. To that point in my life, I'd never thought of a Stormseye knight as a human, much less capable of change. They did terrible things for ever more terrible masters. Every single one of them deserved death, yet this one was freer than I. Suddenly, I understood how Iniogg felt.

If Malthece's intention was to sway me to trust by showing me Cortair's shift in allegiance, I swung firmly back in the other direction.

"Am I supposed to be impressed that you converted a Stormseye knight?" I jerked my shoulder out from under her grasp. "I'm not. You keep me prisoner while you let him go free, all because he's doing what you wanted. You're no inspiring leader. You're a manipulative tyrant. And a thief. You took my scroll. Give it back and maybe I'll believe you are what you say you are."

The wizard Prime smiled wanly, hands coming to clasp behind her back as she sighed. "Alas, I cannot do that."

"It'll doom you, you know." Too angry to meet her gaze, I stared at the floor. "Dags Grimjaw said the Sun Scroll will kill whoever fails to listen to it."

Malthece spoke in mocking tones. "I know you so worry for my wellbeing, El, but for now, you'll have to trust that I know what I'm doing. The Sun Scroll will not hurt me and there's only one way to deal with that thing around your neck. Any primal source like the one you carry cannot simply be destroyed. The energy within it has to be transferred."

My chin rose. Our eyes locked. "What if I don't want to? What if I throw it into the sea?"

Malthece chuckled, unconcerned with my threat. "In the chance that you throw the Archon's Eye into the sea, well, I already have the Sun Scroll, so you'll be of no more use to me. Furthermore, anyone who impedes my mission to destroy the Great Archon will be seen as an enemy and dealt with accordingly."

After living under Omatuu's harsh yolk for as many months as I had, her threatening words bore little of her intended impact. Stoic, I waited.

"Let me tell you how it is going to go, young one." Malthece plucked an apple from a nearby table, took a bite and chewed. Her skewed gaze danced across my face. "What you wear around your neck is too important to simply throw away—too many unsavory wizards out there who would use it maliciously. It is also far too dangerous to keep. What we're left with is the unknown." Her voice fell low. "I know your patience to abide unanswered questions is about as thin as my own. Therefore, we must leave immediately."

"To where?"

She took another bite of apple and spoke around a mealy mouthful. "The Occuli Rift. Other wizards think it simply another step that comes and goes on the road to Power, when in fact, it is an incredible tool if used correctly. I once thought its sole purpose was for trading a topknot for a Tome of Callings, but I've since learned it contains in its mysterious depths a far more expansive library of knowledge."

"The Occuli Rift," I muttered under my breath. I let the name sink into me. My compulsion to reach the Spirit Gardens was immense, a drumbeat in my soul ever urging me to go there, but the Occuli Rift was where the Power was born. In the wake of our new destination, the anger I felt at not being able to journey to the Spirit Gardens cooled, like a salve applied to a burn. One wasn't a wizard until they went up in a tower. But to possess a Tome of Callings from the Occuli Rift? That was the dream all wizards coveted.

The Power resting in their hands.

My throat was tight as I asked, "What will we do there?"

"What I always do," she said. "Experiment. Seek new discoveries. Trade secrets with the source of the Power."

My brow furrowed in confusion.

Malthece went to take another bite of apple, but paused. "I forget, you're still so new—surprising, given the chaos and intrigue dogging your heels." She placed the apple on a table and took a fateful step toward me. The Great Archon's amulet tinged when she flicked it. "We go to throw this thing into the Rift."

Worry hooked at my stomach. The chain around my neck felt heavy and hot, as though it burned the skin around it. I grimaced. "What if more Stormseye knights come looking for it?"

Malthece gestured at Iniogg with an upturned palm. The giant stood behind me, glowering at the surrounding Seekers hard at feasting. "That's why we're bringing him. In addition to being your guard, of course."

Panic entered my voice. My next words were sure to rankle Iniogg. "What if the Great Archon has his own humungalor? One that's—uh—stronger?"

The giant hacked, then spat. A few Seekers closest to where it fell jeered at him to watch out.

"For whatever reason," Malthece said, "the Great Archon doesn't utilize the strength of humungalor. Though it hardly matters. I'm confident he's more keeping an eye on his own than spying on the cabals. I could lay out a detailed plan for his downfall right now but he would never dedicate the strength necessary to undermine it because he doesn't need to. The cabals are a scattered and leaderless rabble. I wouldn't be the first to suggest his demise. He fears us about as much as Iniogg fears a cat."

"Revolting creatures," the giant said. "Their urine especially offends me."

Malthece dismissed him. "Get something to eat and then prepare for our journey." Iniogg strode to one side of the sprawling chamber where a pile of salted shark meat waited. He sat cross-legged, and then took up a slab of pink flesh.

Malthece continued. "The truth is this, El. What you wear around your neck is far more of a boon to us than it is of any vital concern to the Great Archon. What we may gain from it once we throw it in, however, is a mystery you and I will soon resolve."

She stepped back, voice raising so everyone in the chamber might hear. "Herastos and Synofra are in charge while I'm gone. Myself, the prisoner, and Iniogg leave on the morrow."

I was reminded of Durn and how he'd come from the Shadowgiants. I wondered if he'd someday be forced to fight the wizards of his former cabal. "You have a Second *and* a Third?"

Malthece laughed. "The smartest wizards do. Only Omatuu's ego is wanton enough to justify being the sole wizard of a cabal. What he thinks of as a way to protect his secrets merely leaves him as a target. Such behavior bogs one down. Likely, this is why he hasn't found the Night Bridge yet."

"What about you?" I asked. "Why haven't you found it?"

"Who says I haven't?" She gave a wistful smile. "I stay in the Wildness by choice. My goal is the downfall of the Stormseye. You've been under Omatuu's thumb too long, El. Some travel the way of the wizard for the good of all, not just themselves. I do hope you'll be my ally one day."

She nodded once, then started to walk away. "It's best you get some food, too. We have a long way to go." Malthece left me surrounded by unfamiliar faces.

Surveying the room, I hesitated to claim a spot at a table. More than a few sets of eyes watched me. Bile filled my mouth as my sights settled on Cortair and Herastos making friendly.

Jaw set, I whisked past a table, unceremoniously snatching a wooden fork from a Seeker's hand on my way across the chamber. The woman I stole it from cursed, but I didn't look back. I marched to the pile of shark meat.

Grease-slathered lips froze mid bite as Iniogg watched me take a seat at his side. "What are you doing?" the king of giants said.

I ignored his question as I set aside my assumptions about the taste of shark and sank my teeth in.

Chapter Thirty

THE PRINCIPLE OF ABSOLUTES

By day, we traversed the white-sand beaches of the coasts of Kelundar, and by night, we sought refuge in its caves.

A few times over the intervening weeks, Malthece, who seemed to know the way as intimately as I knew the way to the Spirit Gardens, brought us to a cleft in the cliffs at dusk, and then proceeded to summon the earth into a tangle overhead for shelter. Iniogg never slept near us. He chose to lie outside at the mouth of the entrance, exposed to the elements.

I suspected it reminded him of home.

Much of our journey happened in silence but for a few conversations scattered here and there. Malthece claimed to need time to ruminate on the Archon's Eye and the Sun Scroll's words. The woman was difficult to read, convivial and cheery one moment, then brooding or crestfallen the next. As we went, the latter pervaded more of her moods, igniting an awkwardness that hung like tar in the air.

By comparison, Iniogg simply ignored us, speaking only when required.

He, too, ruminated. Most times when I looked at him, he was preoccupied taking in the sea. There was a contentment to his expression when I caught sight of it, a softening of the hard lines along his kite shield cheeks which gave me all the understanding I needed.

For some reason, regardless of some of the cruel things he'd said, it helped me realize he wasn't so vicious a creature as I first thought. It wasn't that his silence was born out of hate for me so much as it was a way to honor what he loved and missed most. He communed with the salty, sweeping rains, the thunder of waves as they sighed across the beach, and the sand-strewn earth churning underfoot.

I imagined it a blissful reprieve for him to be so distanced from the flurry of activity in the Shadowgiants' cabal. So I gave him the gift of tranquility by suppressing my questions, hopeful the king-become-slave was finding peace.

At times, the beach tapered, forcing us up onto goat trails amid the cliffs, or into Iniogg's arms to be carried like babes across deep, turbulent shoals.

Once, a sleeper wave swept toward us, but Malthece's hands worked smoothly, wrists winding over elbows in a hurried, rhythmic dance to split the wall of water and siphon it off to either side.

Having only seen Omatuu and Khemetri's magic from a distance, the sight of Malthece weaving the Power stole my breath. My heart pounded, yearning to know the thrill of commanding nature. That night, it was all I could think of as I repeated what I thought to be the motion from my back. Sleep eluded me as I lie there, repeatedly waving my hands in the air overhead.

Malthece slept a short distance away, behind a row of stalactites. I watched her inert form a moment, then sat up and left the cave.

As soon as I was outside, a strong wind jerked my tunic to one side and crawled through my clothes. I crossed my arms in a weak attempt to gather some warmth as I looked at the moon.

"Why don't you try to run?" came Iniogg's rumbling voice. That close to the ocean, it sounded like the distant boom of waves striking rock.

I knew he crouched somewhere in the shadows behind me without needing to look. "You'd stop me, wouldn't you?"

Wind howled between the rocks. "Yes. I am compelled to do so."

"You sound defeated."

He huffed. "Merely recognizing the sad complexity of humans. When we are enslaved by a thing long enough, we are destined to become its greatest student."

"We?" I turned around.

Iniogg sat against one side of the cave mouth with his legs gathered against his chest, kneecaps shining in the moonlight like bovine skulls. "My disdain for your kind does not blind me to the commonalities we share. Both species masticate on problems, though we deal with them much more simply."

Malthece had been right; when Iniogg's cynicism and wrath were set aside, he conveyed great wisdom. Truly, a philosopher king. I thought long and hard about his words, for he seemed keen to have my answer. Despite the growing discomfort of the wind's chill, I felt a tickle of pride suffuse my chest. Iniogg, I realized, was helping me.

Like a friend. Like Idrinnia commanded me to be.

"My mother was dying. I left to become a wizard rather than stay and find out what happened to her." My voice reflected the hollowness I felt inside. "A friend I loved... I abandoned her, too."

Iniogg watched me impassively. "And now it consumes you?"

I turned back to the moon. "Yes."

"The pains of the heart hold us all hostage in some way. If you let them, they can also be your teacher. To lose a thing is to gain another. That is the nature of life. A seal dies to feed a shark, a shark dies to feed a giant, a giant dies to feed the iron bowls of wizards. So..." Iniogg's tone was soft and inviting. "What does your mother's death feed in you?"

I scooped up a stone and hurled it toward the ocean. It fell far short. "Ambition," I said. "A desire to call fate my own. I—" Hot tears raced down my cheeks. I wiped them off with the back of a hand. "I am *meant* to be a wizard."

I heard Iniogg rise, a great unfolding of cloth and shifting sand, and then he came to stand beside me. "Although there are many sub-races within the humungalor kind, all of us follow the Principle of Absolutes. When faced with a challenge, we seek to destroy it with every fiber of our being, or we allow it to be what it is unconditionally. We do not trifle with conditions of control as humans do. Black and white. Never gray."

Waves crashed along the shore. I cast a look at the cave mouth. Within, Malthece slept. "You're saying I need to adopt the Principle of Absolutes in regard to my mother's death."

"Yes." Iniogg's voice was somber. "Your actions around it most of all. What you did was either necessary, and therefore good. Or it was foolish, and therefore bad. It cannot be both. You must choose which, or every decision from here on will be marred by your questioning. Whatever aspirations you have will be wasted in indecision. If you are to be a wizard, hard choices come fast. Opportunities sail past almost as soon as they appear. You must adopt the Principle of Absolutes for everything and everyone if you are to succeed."

Chewing my lower lip, I stared out over the glimmering waves. Moonlight bathed Iniogg's craggy features as I turned to him. "So, your Principle has it told you I'm a friend?"

The corner of his mouth twitched. He gave a single nod.

I smiled. "And what of Malthece? Is she—"

"Malthece is no different from the Stormseye. She'll do good deeds for now, but give her time and she, too, will rule those she deems inferior with a certainty and impunity birthed in those blinded by their righteousness." Iniogg rubbed his face, a coarse shushing filling the air. "Be careful around her. She's dangerous and powerful. If you do as she says, she may let you go after all this is done."

The giant glanced at his wrists, expression souring. "Or perhaps not." He returned to his place at the cave mouth.

I passed him as I entered, though his back was turned to me. I picked my way through the dark cave, guided by a fire Malthece started each night before she went to sleep. And each night, it continued to burn without the need for fuel.

For a long while, I watched Malthece's flame, hovering in the air beside her. Curiosity seized me, beckoned me to creep toward her in a wide arc and circumvent the floating fire.

When I came within a half dozen feet, a thick tendril of the smoldering blaze coiled like a snake in the air to bar my way. It hissed and crackled.

I retreated, found a place between pools formed by a persistent drip, and curled into a fetal position before falling into a troubled sleep.

Chapter Thirty-One

YOUR SENTENCE IS DEATH

I t was like some great beast had taken a bite from the coastline and let the ocean fill the torn-out void. Our path along the beach disappeared suddenly, leaving us ankle-deep in raging sea. We were forced inland up onto grassy knolls. Once clear of the sharp injunction, Malthece led us back onto the strand.

Wind probed the holes in my clothing, causing a shiver. Conditions in the Wildness had wrested the thin layer of fat from my body, earned from a rat's diet in Cannalis, and replaced it with more muscle than I'd ever had. I was growing, getting stronger, and yet I'd never felt more vulnerable. My discussion with Iniogg the night before brought my worst fears and insecurities to the surface. Was I villain or hero? Was my quest impulsive and childish, or was it a necessary sacrifice in the name of some deeper responsibility?

Whatever the answer, the question had left my flesh raw with emotion, my mind full and muddled as if stuffed with soiled rags. I may as well have been naked.

As we descended, I barely registered the abject desolation stretching across the jetty before me.

"The Cape of Ruin," Iniogg said. "An aptly named place."

My gaze swept the strand sloping into the Seething Sea. Ships of every shape and size, mostly unmarked, but for the occasional swirling gold eye, scattered the shore. Gutted hulls lie beside their sundered bowels; a thousand planks of rotting wood dispersed over bone white sand and bobbing surf. Crates were burst open to reveal clouds of flies over swollen, graying food or gold that twinkled under the sun's light.

The sight wove a chaotic tapestry.

When I saw Malthece heading between banks of mounded sand and knee-high grass toward the cape, I felt a flutter of nervousness in my belly and then followed. Iniogg was a long step behind.

"This is where all Seekers come in their journey to the Occuli Rift," said Malthece. "And on occasion, where a wizard Prime comes to discover the secrets of the Great Archon."

We crossed the sand until we were in the thick of the wreckage. Tattered sails pulled by gusting winds caused their broken masts to creak, their rigging to clatter. It felt haunted there, and I quailed to think how many had died along the coastline over the years. For every ship I saw, I knew a half dozen more gathered barnacles beneath the surf, each one acting as a grave marker for scores more lost souls.

The Seething Sea was treacherous, yet even the worst of storms could not account for the number of decimated ships I saw. "How did this happen?"

Arms crossed and tapping her lips with a finger, Malthece responded with half her attention as she searched the beach. "There are those who think the Occuli Rift is inaccessible in the fall and spring because of storms. But that is only partly true. The storms are difficult, to be certain, having claimed more than a few would-be wizards. But it is the migrations of the Equia'raxa that should be most feared." Fists balled at her sides, she cast about. "Where is that damn boat!"

Brow creasing, I watched her go. She peered between sundered, seaweed-strewn ships as she went. Iniogg displaced a mound of sand that covered my foot as he stepped up beside me.

"The Equia'raxa are Fey. They guard the waters of life, just as hu-mungalor protect the earth. Centaurs, bloodmares, unicorns, and moonstags, to name a few. If we're lucky we'll—"

The giant's face jerked toward the surf. The club resting on his shoulder drifted to his side. I followed his gaze but saw nothing. Iniogg sniffed, a grimace rolling from one side of his mouth to the other beneath narrowed eyes. "Scratch that. If I'm lucky, they'll kill Malthece for me."

My heartbeat quickened. I'd never been afraid of horses of any kind, but the way the giant froze was unsettling.

"Iniogg!" Malthece's shrill cry shot a spasm of fear from my crown to my knees.

Ghostly light flashed around the humungalor's wrists. He growled, and then sprinted off, club at the ready. "Stay close!" he shouted to me in parting.

Eyeing a cresting wave as I went, I thought I saw something like a patch of sunlight on the water but it quickly disappeared. A wave of horror entered me, sheer panic to a depth I'd never known. Even then, naive as I was, I knew the emotions flooding me were not my own. They were unnatural—something done *to* me. But by who?

I tripped and something sharp cut my hand. Sand kicked up to sting at one eye. The pounding waves drowned out my yelp of pain. Blinking away tears, I came to my hands and knees. Iniogg and Malthece were a short distance up the beach. Both in defensive postures. Both facing the sea.

As I rose, a glimmer of steel caught my attention. It was a short, bloodstained blade shaped like a crescent moon. The handle was made of polished pearl. I grabbed it in case I, too, needed to fight whatever approached, though I doubted I'd be much help. I regretted not listening to Distra about training with a dagger more as I slipped it safely into my belt then pulled my tunic over it.

I rounded the charred-out hull of a ship as I heard Malthece saying, "We have no quarrel with you. We respect the Equia'raxa and seek only to cross your waters—preferably without conflict."

A smooth voice, like the whispering ripples on a lake's surface, responded. "Wizards always bring trouble. It is their nature."

"I assure you." A ghostly sword of green flame sprouted from one of Malthece's hands, while sand rose from the beach to pool and swirl beneath the other. "My respect only extends so far. If you mean to provoke me, you'll have more than trouble."

When they came into view, I stopped a dozen paces behind Iniogg. Seven Equia'raxa spread out in a V-formation behind their leader. The rearmost were submerged to the withers in the water. The leader stood alone on the beach.

He was the largest horse I'd ever seen, half again as big as the warhorses of the Brotherhood, and at eye-level with Iniogg's belly. The stallion's mane was sea-foam green, his hide a murky gray and cobalt blue. Strands of seaweed were tangled in his hair, and his eyes were as black as a shark's during a blood frenzy. A hollowness opened in the pit of my gut, swallowing my breath at the sight of those abyssal eyes.

Instead of hooves, the Equia'raxa had three fat toes and a bulbous dewclaw, each sporting a razor-sharp talon. The leader took a step forward. Circular suction grips like those of an octopus tentacle lined the underside of his descending foot.

Flicking his mane, the Equia'raxa leader lowered his head, then stamped. The horn jutting from his skull was a twisting lance of opalescent shell, deadly sharp at the end and longer than my spear.

"The unicorns of the Seething Sea have spilled the putrid blood of a hundred wizards and skewered their duplicitous tongues in their whining skulls," the leader growled. "I, Tyranox, the exalted champion of King Hathophane, have eaten the twisted hearts of no fewer than ten."

"Seekers, you mean." To her credit, Malthece was not cowed. She laughed, a mad thing, one eye wandering out of focus. "I'm a wizard Prime, reckless stallion. More than capable of making a gelding of you.

The blood and metal of the Power courses through my veins. You'll have no easy meal here."

The unicorn vanguard flashed forward in unison, advancing a step, horns dipping, ready to charge. The waters around them stilled and became a glassy nimbus. Waves of supernatural fear, panic, and horror forced me to my knees with a gasp.

Malthece muttered something—a protective ward perhaps. For a moment, Iniogg's haunches trembled. He cursed and growled, then shifted his weight to subdue the tremors.

Tyranox laughed meanly. "The magic of the Fey may not affect you, wizard, but it cuts through the core of your servants."

I caught my breath and struggled to my feet.

Malthece shifted uneasily, but it was Iniogg who spoke. "What do you want?"

"We want back what was taken." Tyranox's opalescent lance swayed toward the giant. "The horn of our king, Hathophane, stolen by a wizard. Until its return, these waters will run red with the blood of every human who dares cross our path." He stamped the sand, his voice shattered glass in my ears. "How can you serve them? You are Fey! A disgrace!"

"I, too, am a king of the Fey. Now, bound to slavery." Iniogg motioned his head toward Malthece. "None wishes this one dead more than I."

If Malthece felt betrayed by her thrall, she did not show it. Her control over the giant was absolute.

"Then let us kill her together," said Tyranox. "I shall gift you the pleasure of her first screams."

"I cannot." Iniogg spat. "I'm bound to do her bidding."

"This is pointless," hissed Malthece. "I didn't steal your king's horn. I merely seek peaceful passage as hundreds before me have done."

"The mendacity of a wizard knows no bounds! You seek to siphon more power from the Fey, like the rest of your kind." Tyranox trotted in a quick circle in the sand, shoulder muscles jolting as he roused his troops by clacking his horn against theirs.

Malthece twisted her head to each shoulder, neck cracking, then took a breath. "For the last time, King Hathophane's missing horn is neither a fault nor a concern of mine. In fact, it seems the blame lies with you. What kind of exalted champion—lo, what kind of king—allows their horn to be stolen? Lunacy! My only business here is to kill the worst wizard of them all, the Great Archon. Now let us pass in peace."

"No." Tyranox snorted. "It was a wizard's trickery that took it, so I'll not suffer chances of the same. As exalted champion of King Hathophane, I, Tyranox, find you guilty of the actions of all your kind. Your sentence is death!"

Iniogg's club creaked in his grip. "We do not have to do this."

"Honor compels us!" Tyranox's abyssal eyes settled on me. "Or have you lived among these vermin-hearted humans so long you've forgotten what that is?"

The unicorns advanced.

Before I knew what I was doing, I pushed past the alien terror begging me to flee and rushed forward. "Wait!" Arms held in surrender, I fell to my knees between the Equia'raxa, Iniogg, and Malthece. "Please, wait!"

Tyranox reared before me. When his taloned forefeet struck the ground, he thundered forward, his horn a pinpoint in my view as it hurtled toward the space between my eyes.

"No!" shouted Iniogg.

My heart caught in my throat. Reflexively, my eyes closed. After a long moment, the rush of blood ringing in my ears subsided. Was I dead? A heavy shudder of breath told me I wasn't.

I opened my eyes. Onyx orbs regarded me from either side of a spiral of pink and white horn. "You would sacrifice yourself?" Jets of steam huffed from Tyranox's nostrils. "Why?"

"What are you doing?" Malthece whispered angrily. "Get out of the way."

I exhaled slowly. "I want to restore honor to wizards."

Tyranox glanced sidelong at his brethren as he laughed. I, too, laughed, though in relief, for his horn no longer pointed at my face. "Impossible. Do you also wish to capture the sun's flame? Or still the ocean's waves?"

"No," I said, shaking uncontrollably. "But I will kill the Great Archon, the greatest wizard of all."

The towering unicorn bent low, sniffing at me. Tyranox seemed to decide something, and like the tide receding, the unnatural magic instilling terror and panic in me was gone. The icy prickles in my belly disappeared. My emotions were my own once more. Still, I trembled, but it was more manageable than before.

With the Fey magic no longer compelling me, a hint of steel resolved in my voice. "I promise, I will find your king's horn. When I become a wizard, I'll be able to go where you can't, meet people you never would have. If you kill me, you're losing an ally who can help you."

Tyranox was unconvinced. "One measly human, little bigger than a crab and little smarter than a starfish. You expect me to trust you when I could have the pleasure of seeing your guts strewn about my lance?"

"I do." Emboldened, I pointed at the other unicorns. "Because my death is not worth the lives of your kin. You'll definitely kill me, but Malthece and Iniogg are powerful. At best, a few of you will survive." I gulped back a lump in my throat as the unicorn's black eyes narrowed. "If a wizard stole your king's horn, you won't get it back without allies."

Tyranox's head raised suddenly as he huffed and wheeled about. Then he dropped low again to meet my eyes, low voice still bristling with rage. "What do you propose then? I sought blood today. Whether it be, yours, mine, or theirs, matters little. The waters of the whole world will turn scarlet before the Equia'raxa allow a wrong this grievous to go unpunished."

"Then let me make it right!" My words tumbled forth rapidly. "I will return King Hathophane's horn within two years. If I don't, I'll—I'll return to the Cape of Ruin to await whatever punishment you see fit."

Iniogg's voice boomed. "I vouch for the child." I whirled to find him watching me with a flat, assessing stare that bordered on proud. "El, the Truespear, is courageous and has a pure heart. You would do well to have such a promising young wizard as an ally."

"What good are the promises of wizards?" Tyranox's tone was critical, yet I sensed him looking for a reason to believe in me now. "How could this child be any different?"

"If you must know," said Malthece, "the child possessed the Sun Scroll before I took it. I plan to give it back on our return." The sand orbiting her fell to the ground as she produced the scroll. As soon as it caught the sunlight, the unicorns stepped backward as one in seeming reverence.

"Impossible!" Tyranox said.

"You know it's her," I said. "And Malthece has promised to give it back after we go to the Occuli Rift. If I don't return from our journey, you can always attack her then."

At this, the wizard said something harsh I couldn't decipher. Inwardly I smiled, for I had assured myself a safeguard. If she was lying, she would pay for it.

Tyranox bucked, then turned to confer with his soldiers. A minute passed before he approached me once more. He was relaxed, though still bitter as the sea wind. "You showed courage throwing yourself in the path of my horn. And you show wisdom seeking to avoid bloodshed. While I preferred to see the contest played out, it is lucky for you that I act on behalf of my king and not myself. Hathophane's horn is my highest priority." He glanced at Malthece and considered something before returning his attention to me. "You deserve respect for possessing the Sun Scroll, for Idrinnia the Everlasting would not choose her bearer wantonly. And you must have some shred of honor, for you gamble a great deal to do right for strangers. However..."

Tyranox knelt on his massive forelegs in the sand and lowered his head, horn-tip mere inches from my heart. "If you wish to leave this beach alive, you will prick your finger and be bound by blood to your task."

I shot a sidelong glance at Iniogg. The giant shrugged. This was my choice; he and Malthece were confident they would win the struggle. I, on the other hand, had no doubt I would be the first killed.

Teeth clenched, I pressed a fingertip against the unicorn's horn. A gentle shock rifled through my hand, up my arm, and then into my heart, causing it to skip a beat.

"It is done." Tyranox rose. "Two years, El Truespear." He followed the rest of the Equia'raxa back into the sea, waves swallowing them.

A bone-bleached prow thrust up from the water in their wake. It slid up and out of the surf and landed on the water with a loud slap.

"Those bastards," said Malthece. She turned to El, a coy smile on her lips. "I wonder how many other Seekers will be compelled to search for the unicorn king's horn under threats of violence?"

"None so willingly as El," said Iniogg. "I must say, Tyranox's methods inspire."

So, I would not be the only one bound to the task by blood. Even if I survived my attempt to become a wizard, I'd be competing with others to find Hathophane's horn first. And if I didn't within two years...

I would surely die.

Chapter Thirty-Two

Into the Void

The White Ship, an unbreakable vessel used by all wizards to cross the Seething Sea, could hold no more than a handful of people. Runes were carved into its sides as were smears of something dark that made my blood run cold.

Forced to swim alongside us, the sweep of Iniogg's arms caused the ship to buck and sway. Malthece made me row with a single set of oars, a most grueling chore. The damp of ocean spray chilled me, and yet, I burned on the inside from exertion.

At the bow, Malthece traced the length of her body with her hands. Sweat beaded her brow as steam rose from her shoulders, keeping herself warm but not me. In that moment, I was wildly jealous of the simple but awesome use of her power.

I heaved at the oars and looked out over the sea. A curtain of haze hung in the distance. "Rain is coming, I think."

"It is," shouted Iniogg between breaths. I glanced back, saw his boulder-sized head bobbing after us.

Once, I thought I spotted a unicorn horn jutting from choppy waters not far off but as soon as my eyes sought to grasp the image, it vanished. I pursed my lips. "The more I think about it, the more I know the threat of violence from Tyranox a feint. If they'd wanted us dead, they would have let us out onto the water first."

Malthece shook her head. "They're strong, but I am stronger. Besides, the White Ship would protect us. Its job is to safely get any Seeker or wizard to the Occuli Rift."

"What about the storms?" I said.

"They are prohibitive. When one is wrapped inside a fifty-foot-high wave, there's little the Power can do to save you." Malthece smiled wanly at her lap. "The White Ship protects from the other creatures lurking in these waters. The road to wizardry is hard enough, so, we put into place what we can to ensure at least some safety for our kind. Use the White Ship and travel when the Equia'raxa are not migrating in the summer season. You should know these things if you're to be a wizard."

I watched my hands, white-knuckled where they gripped the oars. "Oh? Could be tough to do when I'm held prisoner." The image of the Spirit Gardens tugged at my soul. I would do anything to get there as soon as I could.

"Like I promised, when we are done here, I'll release you. You seek the downfall of the Stormseye Brotherhood the same as me. And the Sun Scroll—"

"The one you won't give back," I snapped. My upper teeth dragged over my lower lip as I strained to propel us through the choppy waters.

The Prime gave a mirthless grin. "The very same. We'll need it against the Great Archon." Her eyes drifted to the amulet around my neck.

The White Ship creaked.

"Everyone has their story. Do you truly wish to become a wizard and bring down the Great Archon?"

I hated the Stormseye for all they'd done. The Great Archon, too. He stole my family from me with his knight's blades and his rotting city's disease and famine. But becoming a wizard...that was a beast of my own desire. More than anything, I wished to possess a fate that was mine and mine alone. If the Great Archon didn't exist, I believe I still would have yearned to be a wizard.

But I wasn't interested in sharing these complexities with Malthece, so I gave the simplest form of my answer—the only one she cared to hear, anyway. "Yes. He is a blight on the land I mean to see eradicated."

Minutes trickled by. Malthece fell into a silent brooding for a while, then said, "It's curious that they wanted you. Hazash could have just killed you and taken the scroll."

I had to agree but said nothing. Whatever the wizard was thinking, I would give her nothing to use against me or prolong my estrangement from the Sun Scroll.

My arms ached by the time night swallowed us. We found a crag jutting from the ocean like a canine's tooth. It wasn't the Occuli Rift by any means, but it was a place to rest all the same. I steered us into a narrow inlet that was sheltered from the sea. The rock we crawled over was worn and clearly used by countless others over the centuries, making the path to the top easy to decipher.

It was there that the stars glittered brightest.

Exhausted from a day of swimming, Iniogg went straight to sleep. A guardian flame jumped into the air from Malthece's cupped-together palms; she set it beside her and then went to sleep. I watched the tongues of fire a while as it floated there, coiling lazily, unaffected by the wind. By the Power alone it was birthed, and only by the Power would it wink from existence.

As I fell asleep, I wondered what the Power truly was. Control, I decided. My eyelids grew heavy. Absolute control.

Control over beginnings...

Over endings...

And over everything in between.

From sunrise until midday, the Occuli Rift drew closer. The Seething Sea lived up to its name, thrashing around the base of the titanic blossom of stone as if angry it couldn't gain entry. The walls of the Rift were two hundred feet high at least, great swaths of volcanic sea floor arching up and slightly outward. We circled the perimeter, careful to avoid the waves dashing us against its base.

Where the waters were calmest, a quiet inlet beckoned. Anticipation climbed within me, lending a burst of strength to my rowing. Finally, at midday, we landed.

Iniogg was the first out of the water, dripping wet and sucking air like some plow animal. A loud scrape resonated from the hull as we slid onto a rocky incline. Malthece stepped indifferently into the surf, submerged to the waist. I hopped out after, intending to drag the White Ship ashore, but Iniogg reached past me. He picked it up and carried it a short distance up the slope and then let it clatter to the ground.

Dull reports from the crash of waves echoed after us as we wordlessly ascended. Just before we crested the lip of the immense bowl, we stopped to eat, drink, and catch our breath. The Seething Sea stretched in every direction. From the direction we'd come, the lands of Kelundar were but dark panes of earth laid flat and wreathed in fog.

"It's smaller than I thought," I said.

Malthece chewed a hunk of hard bread. "Look there." She pointed to a shimmer of heat, a thin line three times as far and in the opposite direction of Kelundar. "The Golden Lands. Mahjiri."

My head swiveled, studying both stretches. The Golden Lands had a longer coastline. "It always seemed like the Great Archon owned the entire world."

"That's what he'd have you believe," Malthece said. "You see it now though, don't you?"

"Yes." The word was dense with hate. "I see." *Possibilities. Endless possibilities.*

We resumed, gaining the summit shortly thereafter. The wind was surprisingly strong along the crest; twice, I nearly lost my footing as I was buffeted by chaotic bursts.

We descended, picking our way through twisting ravines. I used the jagged rocks to either side to hoist myself and then swing my legs through the narrowest gaps as we wended downward. Iniogg had to move slow, for the terrain did not favor the giant's broad, bare feet. He was forced to step on upthrusts of rock, and it wasn't long before I noticed bloody cuts and tattered flesh hanging from the soles of his feet.

"Do we need him?" I asked Malthece. "He could return and guard the boat."

"He stays with me," she said flatly.

With an angry sigh, I leaned over and stared down into the massive crater that was the Occuli Rift. A thick layer of mist covered the basin, a density of meandering whiteness. A yawning black pit sat at its center. Vapor rolled slowly over it, the topmost layer forming a thin, effervescent dome while the rest was dragged into the abyss. Prismatic light emanated from the gaping puncture in the earth, causing the mist to pulsate with glowing, shifting hues of color.

My palms started to sweat. I stared at Malthece's back, little more than a bear pelt and antlered crown. My pulse quickened.

We reached the bottom, then headed straight for the pit. The expanse of the basin was far greater at ground level than it looked from above. Roughly half the size of the entire city of Cannalis, it took us the better part of an hour to approach the Rift, that throbbing eye at the center of the crater.

I glanced back at Iniogg, pleased to see that the jagged footing along the rim no longer hurt him. The ground was smooth and level now, a shining surface like smoke trapped in glass.

His narrowed eyes flicked down to my waist where my curved knife rested. One of the broken files of rock must have snagged my shirt and uncovered it. Trailing Malthece, I glanced furtively in her direction and then adjusted my tunic, pulling it over my belt.

The Rift itself was bigger than I imagined. If I threw a rock across the chasm's breadth, I'd need luck for it to hit the other side.

We drew closer. Sweat trickled down the back of my neck and dampened my clothes. Humming filled my ears and subtle vibrations tickled the soles of my feet. I took in the infinite pool of iridescent light pouring into the world. The Power. Deep in my bones, I ached for it.

Malthece stopped at the edge of the swirling Rift, as did I, a dozen paces behind. My fingers twitched nervously as I eyed Iniogg in my periphery. The giant's expression was stoic. He shook his head.

In somber tones, Malthece said, "I still remember when I first came here. A decade has passed since that day. Even then, I was twice your age, El." Her voice cracked. "When I was young, my father used to tell me stories about Idrinnia the Everlasting Maiden. For that, I'll always love him. But he also used to say that Seekers were freedom fighters, and for that, well, I can't bring myself to forgive him. What a lie that was!" At the sudden uptick of emotion, I went rigid, afraid I'd been caught. "Seekers only look out for themselves. That's the way it's always been. It took me seven years to claim a wizard's topknot. My Prime took one in a duel and gave it to me. Before that, I'd already stained my hands with the life of a few Seekers from rival cabals. In those days, I rarely stopped to consider why fate brought them before me only to die. Behind the face of everyone I killed, there was a story I never wanted to know. Still don't.

"But that was the way of it. The way of all wizards. All births are bloody—mine was no different. Seekers fighting Seekers, scraping for power like a nest of rats."

My knees shook. Nevertheless, I took a resolute step forward as Malthece continued. "For a long time, I blamed the Seekers—the rats. Blame is a powerful weapon. I used it to justify killing them. To justify killing wizards, too, once I became one myself. But the reality of taking a life, even in a consensual duel, is something that never leaves you. Despite my best justifications, the shame was always there, waiting."

Iniogg moved so that I could see him off to one side, his steps silent. He was careful to remain out of Malthece's line of sight. Again, he shook his head at me. A warning. A plea.

I felt the hardness of my face set in a grim mask. My heartbeat pounded, yearning for something greater. I ignored the giant and drew within ten paces of her.

Malthece sighed loudly. "But fault doesn't lie at the feet of the rats. Fault belongs to those who trapped them and gave them only enough to feed a few. The Stormseye Brotherhood. The Great Archon. Once I realized this, I sought revenge. I could wipe away the guilt of so many dead with one final kill."

The crescent-bladed knife whispered free of my belt. To my left, Iniogg flashed his teeth in a snarl. The tip of his club drifted upward, readying...

Malthece pulled the Sun Scroll from a pocket in the folds of her robes. "Only now, since reading this, I think Idrinnia may be as much to blame as the Great Archon. Do you know what it's like, El?"

I froze, now only three steps from the wizard Prime's back.

Malthece's face lifted from the glowing Rift to take in the slate sky. "Do you know what a betrayal it is to have your father show you the path to walk, to have him lovingly lead you into the very hands of your hero..." Bitterness entered her tone. "Only to have her turn her back on you?"

Before I had time to hide the knife in my hand, Malthece whipped around. She ignored it and thrust the Sun Scroll at my face instead. Caught off guard, I backpedaled a step, heart hammering. I'd lost the element of surprise.

And she was still too far.

"It says to let you kill me!" she raged. "Idrinnia the Everlasting Maiden, the savior of the people. My...telling me to..." She choked back sobs. "Telling me to die."

I faltered in my resolve. The knife trembled in my hand. I gripped it harder, hoping to subdue my fear. The truth of my mistake became clear and swallowed all courage. Malthece had known my intentions all along.

And now, I was trapped. If I moved, I would die. Like a rat.

I glanced at Iniogg. Sadness etched in the lines of his face. A look of farewell. He knew what came next as well as I did.

Tears welled in Malthece's eyes. "But I refuse to listen to her. No one, not even Idrinnia herself will stop me from killing the Great Archon! I still have a choice." Her face was suddenly placid. "My fate is my own."

Her words burned through me, stoking to life an unquenchable pull for the Power. For control.

My memory of what came next unfolded in slow motion.

The hand holding the Sun Scroll fell to Malthece's side while the other swept inward as if playing an invisible flute. Then, her palm thrust outward. Flame boiled to life in her hand.

To my left there came a bestial roar, followed by the thunder of footsteps. A column of shadow fell over Malthece, narrowing as ten feet of knotted oak descended. Her face contorted in outrage as she diverted her fiery hand toward the shadow's source.

A flash of light accompanied the slap of concussive force. The club snapped in two. A sharp ringing filled my ears as I watched Iniogg slam to the earth in ethereal chains. His broken club tumbled from limp fingers and then rolled over the lip of the Occuli Rift.

My friend, the king of giants, had afforded me a heartbeat of opportunity, a sweet breath of possibility. There was only one choice for me and I made it with absolute certainty.

I lunged, knife outstretched.

With Iniogg subdued, Malthece pivoted to face me. I had no time to shield myself from the blast as a jet of flame blotted out all sight. A golden lens, stretching from head to toe, split the fiery onslaught like a ship's prow breaking waves. Smoke trailed me as I burst through the attack. Malthece's eyes went wide as the space between us dwindled to nothing and my knife sank into her chest.

She gasped.

I stared into her eyes as she gulped for air.

She shook in my arms, dark stains spreading across her robes. When she tried to speak, ropes of blood spat onto her face and I looked away, numbness creeping through my limbs. I recalled the Principle of Absolutes that Iniogg taught me. "You would have ended up like the Stormseye. This was necessary."

The words were hollow and did little to comfort me. As I watched the light leave Malthece's eyes, the words we'd shared reverberated in my soul. *My fate is my own.*

I jerked the knife from her chest.

With a perfunctory sawing motion, I took her topknot, then pried the Sun Scroll from her stiffening hands. The blood on it disappeared as soon it touched my fingertips. When I stuffed it into my trouser pocket, I felt the familiar tingling warmth along my thigh. I was whole once more.

A knife clutched in one hand and a wizard's knot in the other, I rose to face Iniogg. His face and knees were scored with dozens of shallow cuts, and an egg-sized purple mass along one eyebrow.

The king of giants inclined his head.

"You're free." My tone fell short of celebratory.

He scrutinized me. "The Power demands a steep price from you."

"You said yourself, she would have ended up just like the Great Archon." I stared at her corpse, convincing myself and wishing it had been Omatuu. "It was necessary."

Iniogg approached the Rift and leaned out over it.

"Sorry you lost your club," I said.

"A paltry sacrifice for my freedom." He stepped back, half-smiling. "I am forever in your debt, El."

"Don't be. As much as I wanted to see you free, I did this for myself."

Iniogg stared at the Archon's Eye on my chest. "It saved you."

I glanced down at the golden jewel. "That it did." Though I couldn't fathom why it chose to do so in that moment and not when Herastos attacked me in the cave.

"What will you do now?"

I looked furtively toward the prismatic light flowing from the Rift. I felt a swelling sense of pride, an electric current pulsing through me as I came to stand on the lip. I held Malthece's topknot aloft, then let it fall into the void. It drifted forever downward, an impossible distance until I saw it no more.

Seconds of nothing dragged, and I started to wonder if anything would happen.

Then, from deep in the abyss, a soundless flash of blinding light forced me to shield my eyes. When I opened them, a thick tome hung in the air before me. I reached out, felt it drawn to my hand as though compelled by unseen forces. Warm leather greeted my palm. The sickness I should feel at realizing it to be Malthece's flesh never came. I was in awe. My knife clattered to the glassy ground.

My Tome of Callings was smooth and warm against my palm.

Energy jumped into my fingertips and crackled at the edges of my vision. I opened the ponderous book and read the first page aloud:

"Heed these words, wizard, for the extent of my knowledge shall define the potential of your power. Signed...Malthece."

"You'll be a wizard now," Iniogg said.

I nodded and snapped the tome closed. "And you? What next for the king of giants?"

Iniogg scratched the coarse stubble on his chin. "Do you ask with the intention of finding out where I've gone so you might summon me once more? That would be a most villainous thing."

I laughed. "And have you conspire against me as you did Malthece? I think not. When the time comes, I will enthrall a less moody creature." Seeing the crestfallen expression on Iniogg's face, I quickly added, "Or none at all. Enslavement is an unsavory practice."

"Good," said Iniogg. "Then I must take my leave. You can call on me for aid if ever the need arises."

"How?"

"You'll figure it out. You're going to be the wizard, not me." He smiled. "Instead of a slave, you'll have an ally."

"I'll have a friend."

He cocked his head then shrugged. "So it is." With that, he hurried from the crater that was the Occuli Rift. I watched him go, and as I did, I recounted our conversations knowing I would forever cherish them. The idea to kill Malthece, I suspected, was more than a little influenced by the humungalor's words of wisdom. He was an exceedingly clever creature, and I thanked the Power he would be no enemy of mine.

I pivoted back to the abyss and reached for the amulet burned into my flesh. With a sharp intake of breath, I yanked it free. Malthece meant to cast it into the Rift to glean whatever secret it might possess. In this, I would not deviate from her plan.

The Archon's Eye clung to my palm as I turned it over in my hand. Once it was perpendicular to the abyss, it finally fell.

A gout of amber flame erupted. Heat poured over me as the blast knocked me onto my backside. Instead of the manifestation of an object like the Tome of Callings, a thousand auric flakes fluttered and gyrated through the air. I caught one between my fingers and saw a brief flash. The flakes drifted lazily around my face.

I inhaled.

The Occuli Rift disappeared. My consciousness was transported back to the streets of Cannalis. A warhorse swayed under me. I looked at my hand, encased in a black-enameled gauntlet and marked by a swirling gold eye. I twisted in the saddle. A row of Stormseye knights spread out behind me, flanking a wagon with a handful of corpses sprawled across its bed. Their faces were familiar...

The dead watched the sky, pale flesh parted at the neck where their throats had been cut. My heart sank as it registered who they were.

Trin's mother. Her brothers. All dead.

Trin, however, was nowhere to be found.

Light flashed, taking me elsewhere—away from Cannalis.

Trin?

Trees towered around her. She was sweating, her clothing soiled, her eyes alert and prowling the encircling woods. She brushed a strand of blond hair tangled with leaves from her face.

She whirled around as if hearing something and looked straight at me.

Before I could shout her name, the vision ended, and I was thrust back into my body on the lip of the Occuli Rift. I collapsed to my knees. "Trin!" I panted. *She's alive.* "Where are you?"

I asked the question a hundred times, a thousand and more as I made my way from the Occuli Rift, the Tome of Callings held tightly to my breast.

But the answer was always the same...a secret only she knew.

ACKNOWLEDGEMENTS

There are few moments in life I relish more than writing acknowl-edgments for a publication. It's not only a rare opportunity for me to immortalize the truth in my heart at a defining moment of my life, but a time capsule for those I mention. At any point, they can look in the back of this book and proudly know that they have the ability to bring a little magic into the world.

Now, let's start giving credit where it's due.

Without the god-like patience of my wife, I probably would have never started this series. A couple of months into our courtship, she listened to me bring this book to life one evening in a manic-creative deluge that lasted four straight hours—that isn't an exaggeration, either. That was the penultimate demonstration of love, support, and patience. Anyone with someone like this in their life should be eternally grateful. If she had been too bored, too tired, or too impatient *Way of the Wizard* might have never existed. This is but a drop in an ocean of amazing qualities she possesses. I could write an entire book on her saintly merits. I'm certain, she'd happily listen to that one too.

To my children, you give impetus to my every day, and while I've always been a writer at heart, nothing has driven me to be successful more than the desire to teach you that purpose and passion can move mountains. Actions should reflect importance, care should reflect love, and parents should demonstrate their values to those who look to them for guidance. Thank you both for being so excited about my creations even when I'm not.

To my editor, Rachel Marchesi, you gave so much time to this piece. Your insights, your attention to detail, and your dedication to accuracy made all the difference in my perception of whether or not this was worth publishing. I'm confident your skills can make anything shine.

Nino Is, your ability to translate vision into reality is a gift from another dimension. Myself and so many others, bow down to your artistic glory. And J Caleb Design, I couldn't be happier that I found you. You've been one of the best surprises on my publishing journey. You two are incredible.

To my family and friends who helped me see that my purpose in life is to entertain with my words, thank you for seeing the truth. Thank you for urging me to take this courageous leap over and over again.

To my beta readers, ARC readers, and all the future readers who have or will take a chance on my work: I will never give up on trying to please you. I'll always work to hone my craft. I'll always stay productive. I'll always strive to deliver the highest quality story I can. This is my sincere promise to you.

In a world where joy is fleeting, novelty is scarce, and worry gnaws at the soul, I hope dear reader, that this book lets you forget that reality doesn't have to be so real after all.

It is and always will be exactly what you make of it.

ABOUT THE AUTHOR

Michael Michel lives in Oregon with the love of his life and their two children. When he isn't writing, editing, or doing publishing work, he can be found exercising, coaching leaders in the corporate world, and dancing his butt off. His favorite shows are Dark, The Wire, and Scavenger's Reign.

REVIEWS: If you enjoyed this book and feel it should be spread far and wide, please leave a review on Goodreads, Amazon, Reddit, your socials, or wherever else you feel called to share. I would greatly appreciate it!

SOCIAL MEDIA:
Goodreads - https://www.goodreads.com/book/show/63945821-the-price-of-power

Instagram - @michaelmichelauthor

Website – https://michaelmichelauthor.com/

Twitter - @Michael__Michel (two dashes in the center there)